REVENGE HAS NEVER BEEN SEXIER

A WOMAN

SCORNED

A NOVEL BY: ERICKA WILLIAMS

A WOMAN SCORNED

By Ericka Williams

Life Changing Books in conjunction with Power Play Media
Published by Life Changing Books
P.O. Box 423 Brandywine, MD 20613

Library of Congress Cataloging-in-Publication Data;

www.lifechangingbooks.net
13 Digit: 978-1934230718
10 Digit: 1934230715

Acknowledgements

First and foremost I must thank my Lord and Savior, Jesus Christ, for his protection, grace, and mercy. As always my mother, father, sister, and brother...you love and support me all the way, even though sometimes it's tough love. To my minister and best friend, Victorian Brown, your Bible Study has seen me through. All of my friends who have been there from day one, I cherish and love you and need you. My right hand man and woman, Lamartz Brown and Rhonda Tombiling. Were it not for you two, where would I be? My family who has always shown me much love. My children, Tori Sharan and Saniya Rain, I do it for you two. To all of the readers, and people I don't know who encourage me when I meet you at signings and events, you are greatly appreciated. To my LCB family, we are in this struggle together. Tressa, thanks for always putting up with me and having my back.

Love,
Ericka

Dedication

This book is dedicated to all women who have been emotionally, mentally, or physically abused at any time in their life. You can make it. Don't resort to negativity because two wrongs don't make a right. Rise above and conquer, while loving yourself, at the same time.

Chapter 1

She stood in her kitchen wearing a sexy, terry cloth, one-piece jumper watching T.V., and preparing brunch for Dante, her loving husband. Brielle Prescott waited impatiently for him to finish showering so they could eat and go pick out baby furniture for the new nursery.

Brielle, six months pregnant with their first child, seemed ecstatic to be having a baby girl, not to mention Dante's baby girl. The fact that she had miscarried twice didn't steal her joy, but did fill her with mixed emotions. She was excited, yet a little optimistic about carrying a child to full term. They'd done all the right things to prepare, like purchasing their plush, four hundred thousand dollar home in Fort Lee, New Jersey. A suburb of New York City.

Money was no object, and life seemed good on the surface, but each of them held a deep, dark secret. Brielle had succeeded as a successful interior designer and Dante, an executive at a Fortune 500 company, making $300,000 a year as an engineer. They made the perfect couple, Dante, tall, handsome, and resembled the hue of a Hershey's Chocolate bar. Brielle complimented him well with her deep caramel complexion and sultry brown eyes. People often told her she resembled the actress Lauren London, just slightly thinner and shapelier.

Dante and Brielle were both in their early thirties, he thirty-five, and she thirty-one. They managed to become financially secure quickly, which was a change from both of their upbringings. Dante had grown up in Harlem and Brielle in, Paterson, New Jersey, both from families who were considered poor. Their common-

alities attracted them instantly considering they were products of
love-starved homes. To top things off both had experienced the
early, untimely deaths of their mother's. To those who could be
fooled, they seemed to be a match made in heaven.

As Brielle cut the green peppers to dump into the egg mix
for the omelet, she reminisced about her six year relationship with
Dante. They'd had their ups and downs as a couple, but vowed to
remain together.

Brielle smiled as she recalled the day that she and Dante
met at Garden State Plaza, a local mall. She was twenty-five at the
time and just escaping from a three year going nowhere relationship, with a loser named Paul, who she met during her last year at
Rutgers. Brielle had decided not to jump into another relationship,
but instead focused on building her career. She had been in four serious relationships all before her twenty-fourth birthday, and all
were emotionally damaging.

A slight smile escaped from the corner of Brielle's bottom
lip as she remembered walking past the Foot Locker and setting
her eyes on the most beautiful, milk chocolate man she'd seen in
years. At 6'3, and roughly 250 pounds of toned muscle, he reminded her of Tyrese, the singer, but even more handsome. She especially liked the fact that he towered over her petite frame.

She remembered struggling to maintain her composure and
pretending not to even see him passing by. As she passed, their
eyes met, but Brielle quickly shrugged off the instant attraction. In
a matter of minutes, she'd convinced herself he was no good until
he gently grabbed the crevice of her arm, forcing her to face him,
acknowledging his demanding presence.

It didn't take long for Dante to whip out his mack game. He
was good at wooing the ladies and Brielle was no exception. Minutes passed as they made small talk, with him holding onto her arm
for dear life. Brielle spat out reasons why she didn't want to go out
with him, while he responded with reasons why she appeared to be
just another scorned woman in need of a good man.

Brielle loved the sound of his voice. It was soothing, and so
were his exact words. The fact that he knew she'd been scorned by
a man, hell four men, allowed her to let her guard down. Before

long, they were headed to the food court, not knowing they would talk for hours, and eventually become one.

Brielle suddenly forced her hand into the scorching skillet as if she were frying her hand instead of the omelet. At that moment, everything changed. She realized her hopeful flashback had now taken her to the cold reality. It wasn't the first day she'd met Dante. This was four years later and she was now in the comfort of her own home frying her hand and about to do something even crazier.

For the average person, both the heat and the pain would've caused them to pull back from the torture. But not Brielle. She wasn't herself. Tears began to stream down her face as she thought back to how that day at the mall Dante carefully chiseled away the stone around her heart. They became exclusive immediately and she eventually married him two years later. She knew nothing about him other than that he was from Harlem, had graduated from Morehouse and was an engineer. It all sounded damn good and she immediately fell right in.

Her right hand remained flat, face down in the hot pan, as she turned up the fire, refusing to alter the disappointment shown on her face. The pan became increasingly hotter as the skin on her palm began to turn white and dry. She could hear heavy footsteps trotting her way, yet refused to snap from her few good memories.

Quickly, Brielle switched her thoughts to a frightening time after they'd been married, when Dante did what he always said he wouldn't do. It was two weeks after a beautiful trip they'd taken to celebrate their second wedding anniversary. They were at a party given by one of Dante's co-workers. When they got there, Dante proudly introduced her to just about everyone at the party. They were drinking, playing cards, playing board games, watching movies, and listening and dancing to music. There were about seventy-five people at the party, but one person seemed to stand out after about an hour of being there. One woman seemed to follow Dante and Brielle everywhere they moved. When Brielle couldn't dismiss it as a coincidence any longer she asked Dante about the woman.

"Who is that?" she remembered asking. Her nod was clearly in the direction of the woman, yet Dante played as if he was clueless.

"Who?" he said, with his famous, *yes, I'm a liar look*.

"That woman right there, with the yellow dress on. What's her name?" she asked again, staring into his dark eyes while he wouldn't look back into hers.

"Why?" he asked arrogantly and without care.

"Why? Because every time I turn around she's in my fucking face. Who is she? Better yet, why didn't you introduce us? She has managed to whisper in your ear at least three times, thinking that I didn't notice while I was talking to other people. What's up Dante?" Brielle crossed her arms.

"Look, I don't know what you're talking about."

Brielle instantly knew something wasn't right. She approached the woman as Dante stood back stunned. "Hello Miss, I'm Brielle, Dante's wife. I haven't had the pleasure of meeting you, but couldn't dismiss the fact that you've had some deep conversations with my husband. Is everything okay?"

The woman was instantly and visibly angered. "Everything is fine. Don't you think so, Mrs. Prescott? The party is very nice. I mean…the party I paid for is very nice."

"Actually, no I don't. Unfortunately I'm beginning to think that you may be fucking my husband. And if I were not a lady, you could be getting fucked up right here at this party."

The woman leaned in close to Brielle's ear and whispered, "Try me, bitch! If you feel that you have to fight over your husband, then do it. I'd be mad if I had to do that, too." She laughed hysterically, making Brielle angrier.

Before Brielle could decide whether to grab the woman's neck or maintain her composure, Dante jetted over and grabbed her, yanking her from the room. He inconspicuously pulled her into a downstairs bathroom. No sooner than he closed the door, he pushed her in the shower stall and had his hands tightly clasped around her neck. Brielle gasped for air as he told her she was out of line.

"Bitch, this is my livelihood! This is my job! That hoe got power and I'm trying to stay on her good side. She's my boss, bitch!"

Brielle was stunned, shocked, and petrified. Her eyes were almost out of the socket glaring at the love of her life, whose eyes had reddened and resembled a monster. He released the grip and she slid like a rag doll down to the floor of the shower stall.

"I should turn the fucking water on your ass, but I don't want anyone to see that you made a fool of yourself."

Brielle quietly sobbed as she got up, stepped out of the stall with tears streaming from her eyes. As she looked in the mirror, she cleaned the running mascara off of her pudgy cheeks and fixed her clothes and hair. He walked to the door, opened it, and put his arm out for her to pass in front of him as if nothing happened. They returned to the party where Brielle had to endure seeing the smirking woman look at her while continuing to whisper in Dante's ear. Of course he continued to smile and grin.

Brielle briskly pushed that horrible memory from her mind, and jerked her hand away from the pan as she felt the flutter of her baby inside her stomach. She couldn't dwell on something that happened two years earlier. The new house was supposed to be their new start and Dante had promised that he would make things much better. His promotion at work allowed them to buy their house in Fort Lee; of course the promotion came compliments of his boss.

Startled, Brielle jumped as she heard her husband's voice. Quickly, she rushed over to the sink to submerge her scolding hand in water, hoping to get some relief. The pain had started to set in drastically as Dante fiddled around in the refrigerator. As soon as he moved in Brielle's direction, she grabbed a dish towel nearby and wrapped it around her hand hoping to hide the evidence.

"Honey, what's wrong?" he asked caringly.

"Oh, I just burned my hand by accident. It just stings a little, I'm sure it'll be fine. Here, eat your omelet," she said, pushing the small plate in his direction.

Dante smiled, reached across the granite counter top, and dove his fork into Brielle's special creation. His head remained downward as he moaned and sang praises about her cooking. Meanwhile, Brielle frowned behind his back and listened to the voices.

"Let it go Brielle. Things are better now...so you think. Maybe he'll straighten up so you guys can be a real family."

She rubbed her protruding belly and forced a smile.

"Babe, I know you trying to look sexy for me in all with your butt cheeks hanging from that one-piece, but you not gonna eat?" Dante asked, lifting his head up from the plate.

She attempted to remove the weird look from her face as he moved in her direction. "I'm just not hungry," she uttered, moving her injured hand closer to her back.

Dante moved seductively into her space. "Why you looking so good while cooking? This aught to be a law! Umph," he said, laying on the compliments extra thick. "Terry cloth booty shorts...umph," he said, sliding his large hands across her ass. "A one piece at that. Damn, I never knew maternity clothes could get me going so fast," he ended, kissing her several times, delicately on the neck.

Regardless of Dante's numerous infidelities, Brielle was still very much attracted to him. So it didn't surprise her that the massaging of her ass was turning her on. Most of the time she just couldn't get enough of him, his charm, or charisma. Dante knew it and used it to his advantage. Soon, he switched gears and began to rub her belly gently, while he outlined her mouth with his wet tongue.

"I love you," he told her sexily, "and I loved that omelet, too. What was in it?" he joked.

She blushed and told him that she made just what he'd ordered; an omelet with peppers, onions, turkey sausage, and lots of love. "I already mixed another batch just in case you want another one."

"That's my baby. What are you gonna do when I love our daughter more than you?" he asked grinning.

"I guess I'll have to have a son, to love more than you." She rolled her eyes and put her head down as Dante played around with the full curls in her shoulder-length wavy weave.

"You better not ever love anybody more than me. I need your love to be the way it is for me."

She rubbed the flawless, dark skin on his face in soft, sweet circles, while making her way toward his low-cut, fresh haircut with her only available hand. She wished he behaved affectionately on a regular considering how good the moment felt to her. All of a sudden, Dante grabbed Brielle's chin and looked in her eyes intently.

"You dyed your hair black?"

"Yep."

"You better be glad it looks sexy, cause I didn't approve that before you did it." He grinned. "You know I'm king, and I get what I want."

He slapped her on the ass.

"Whatever. Let me get dressed so we can go. Because you know you only have a little bit of patience when it comes to shopping with me." She took a forkful of her delicious omelet, glad that she'd snapped from her demented state.

"Yeah, but this is for Summer Rain Prescott, she can get that."

Brielle loved to hear the sound of her unborn daughter's name. It made her feel gooey inside, and also made her believe that her marriage was on its way to recovery. While she rushed upstairs to change, Dante decided he would be the perfect husband, and clean the kitchen.

Soon after, Dante hollered upstairs letting Brielle know he would be outside waiting. Before long, she had made it to the front door when a UPS delivery man walked up and handed Brielle a package which she signed for, and threw on the couch. She rushed outside to meet Dante who was pulling their 2007 Black Chevy Tahoe out of their driveway. Brielle opened the door and carefully stepped up and got in. At that moment Dante seemed concerned.

"You must've really hurt your hand if you got an Ace bandage on."

"I told you it's nothing," Brielle said happily watching her husband back out of the driveway and cruise down the street like the happy couple. Neither of them noticed the woman parked down the street watching them closely.

It didn't take long for them to reach the mall. Unlike most times, they had a harmonious and pleasant afternoon, with no altercations or arguments. Dante, of course was very impatient and controlling, but Brielle did everything in her power not to cause him to become agitated. Several hours flew by before they found the crib that Brielle wanted with matching furniture. Like the perfect gentleman, he let her pick all the accessories, from the lamps to wall adornments.

After a full day of shopping, they decided to dine at Olive Garden hoping to have a great time there as well.

"Dante, how do you think things are going to change between us once I have Summer?" she asked enthusiastically, bouncing in her seat.

"I think we'll be closer. Why?"

"Because it seems like couples break up after they have kids nowadays. Kids use to keep people together, now they tear them apart." She shook her head.

"Well, you're gonna be busy so you won't have the time to get on my nerves like you normally do."

He laughed, but she didn't. Brielle tried to decide whether to continue the conversation or not, hoping to end the day the way it started. There was no need to give him an excuse to get mad and go out after dinner. Dante ordered his second drink of cognac, while she patted her foot to control her temper.

"Why is it that I always get on your nerves? What the hell is it that I do so wrong, when all I try to do are the right things?" She whined and took a bite of her Chicken Alfredo with extra mushrooms. For seconds, she chewed slowly and looked at his puppy dog eyes.

"You're a woman. You pester and nag. That's what women do. If you would know how to just sit there and say nothing you would be better off. And so would I!" He laughed again.

"Dante, I don't even nag you anymore. You do what the hell you want to do. What do I nag you about?" She started chewing her food hard, smacking her lips and moving her head.

"Everything," he said, downing his second drink and signaling the waiter over to order another one.

"No, I don't Dante!"

"You asked me, I'm telling you. A man don't want to hear

that shit." He checked his cell phone for messages, then placed it back into the side clip.

"What shit?"

"The shit you're doing right now. Why are you asking about how you nag? That's nagging. Shut the hell up and eat!" He took his cell phone out and looked at it again.

"Okay," she said, and lowered her head. She picked up her food with her fork and put it in her mouth. He looked at her watering eyes.

"Baby, I am not trying to hurt your feelings. Just be happy, for a change, stop searching for answers that you won't find." He took her chin in his hand and kissed her lips.

"I'm trying to avoid problems by understanding what I do wrong." She wiped her tears with the backside of her hand and picked up a fork-full of food.

"There are just some things that you will never understand. Like men. You will never understand what being a man is all about." He quickly turned to watch the back of a woman who walked by their table without Brielle noticing.

"Well, that's why I'm asking asshole!"

Without warning, Dante reached across the table and blessed Brielle with a strong back hand slap, then repented within seconds. "Listen, I don't feel like explaining right now. Just know when to be quiet. When to stay in your damn lane."

Brielle simply held her face in disbelief hoping the stinging would stop. Dante had never hit her in public before; always in private where he could still portray the good guy image. At that moment, Brielle picked up her glass, drank her pineapple juice, and put it back down before glancing around the restaurant. When she saw other couples talking and laughing with each other it made her even more depressed.

"Baby, I love you. Okay?" he said, from behind the new glass that he was slowly raising to his mouth. "I'm sorry I hit you. Forgive me. okay?"

"Okay," she responded uneasily.

"Let's change the subject. You like the furniture?"

"Yes, I love it baby." She reached over to touch his hand.

"It's what you wanted?" He asked calmly.

"Yes, and I'm so glad you came with me and we picked it out together." Brielle rocked back and forth smiling.

"See, you should be happy. You have a man who loves you and who gave you a daughter." He finished off another drink before looking down at the bandage. "Ah, you better get that hand checked out," he said, with a worried look on his face. "If you gotta wrap it all up you might need something more than some cream on that shit."

"I will," she said, nonchalantly.

They finished eating and headed home in silence. Brielle had decided she'd treat her man to a night of hot sex. Thoughts of what she would do to him danced around in her head until fifteen minutes later when he pulled the truck into the driveway and told her he would be back later.

"Where are you going at ten o'clock at night?" Brielle asked in a disappointed tone.

"I'm just going to Julius' house to watch the game."

She looked at him in disbelief.

"I won't be out late, okay?" He poked his lips slightly, begging for approval. "I promise," he added.

Brielle didn't answer. "You better get used to staying in the house, you're about to have a baby, Dante."

Dante turned his head before she could even get his last name out and revved on the engine.

"Dante, we're about to have a baby!" she shouted.

He remained silent until Brielle got completely out of the truck. Although he knew she was angry, he pulled off like a madman as soon as she stuck the key in the front door. Brielle simply shook her head. She didn't want to think anything bad, and especially about another affair. He'd had four in the past and promised to never do it again, so she put her suspicions out of her mind and went inside to relax.

Brielle waltzed inside the house and kicked her shoes off in the middle of the foyer. She was exhausted and too tired to think about what Dante had up his sleeve. She didn't even feel like questioning her future with him, or whether he was going to start cheating again. After all, she was about to become his baby momma.

She laughed at herself and walked upstairs to change into a black, sexy, crotch-less, one piece. It was Dante's favorite, so she wanted to look as sexy as possible when he returned home. She thought about lounging across the couch ass-naked so that when he walked in the door, the marathon could begin; but within a matter of minutes, she decided to stick to the black one-piece which gave her belly the support it needed.

Before long, she'd waddled downstairs to the kitchen, made some Red Zinger tea and sat in the living room with her feet kicked up on two cushions. She turned on the TV and rested her head on the hard edge of their plush couch. Brielle felt something hard under her and hopped up realizing it was the unopened package that had been delivered by UPS earlier. She picked up the brown envelope and began to tear it open at the seams. She expected something small she'd ordered for the baby, but instead the content was shocking. It was what she dreaded most. Dante. His deceit exposed. *How could he?* she thought in a state of shock.

The package revealed what appeared to be pictures. As she began to pull the nude photos out frantically, she started to recognize Dante's dick, all ten inches; and an all too familiar face, Monique Troy. Monique was the affair that had her ready to leave Dante three years ago, when she lost her second child. The scandalous photos sent her completely over the edge. The voices were back.

"Oh, hell no!" she shouted as she rose from the couch. "Go find that motherfucker now!"

༄ Chapter 2 ༄

There were about fifteen pictures at a number of different locations. They kissed in some. Smiled in others. Fucked in most.

Brielle screamed, "You fucking bastard!" She sobbed uncontrollably and her hands shook as she looked at one picture after another. For starters, she was upset that she'd decided against going out to look for Dante.

Inside, it felt like her world was about to end. Brielle had really made herself believe that Monique was history, especially since Monique had stopped the harassing phone calls that she used to make to Brielle's home when Dante first dumped her.

One of the pictures showed Dante and Monique in a car, going into an unfamiliar high-rise building, which Brielle assumed was Monique's house, and at a park having a picnic. The pictures at the park showed them kissing, embracing, and being very affectionate toward each other. Brielle was in shock. In one photo, Dante was chasing Monique and managed to grab her from the back. They were laughing and having a great time. Another one had him feeding Monique ice cream; something that he always did for Brielle as well.

She looked at Monique's face on the photo, intently. She was just about as tall as Dante. She was almost an Amazon compared to Brielle's small frame. She wasn't ugly though, Monique appeared to be mixed with both Spanish and black. With bone straight hair, she was well proportioned, to be so tall. However, even with all that beauty, Brielle just couldn't understand what he saw in her.

Brielle cried and cried until she lapsed into an unresponsive stare that lasted about a half hour. She just sat there staring at the photographs on her lap. Her mind then reverted back to a day when she was ten years old and was out with her father. They were supposed to be going to the movies, but instead he pulled up to someone's house. Her father was a tall, distinguished-looking man, who at that time was always compared by his friends to Nat King Cole.

"Daddy, whose house is this?" she remembered asking timidly.

Her father smiled. "Oh, just one of Daddy's friends. We won't be long."

When they approached the door, a woman was standing in the doorway with a cigarette in her hand and a bathrobe on. While she was smiling from ear to ear, Brielle wore a frown.

"Brielle, say hello to Dorothy," her father instructed. Brielle instantly didn't like what she felt on the inside, nor did she like the woman. She didn't respond. "I said say hello, you don't go into someone's house and not speak."

"I want to go home, Daddy." She crossed her arms and stopped dead in her tracks.

"No you don't. You want to go to the movies and we're going, I promise baby, okay?" Her father kissed her cheek.

"Hey, pretty little girl. I won't bite you. Come on in." Brielle remembered the woman laughing infectiously.

Brielle was told to sit on the couch and watch TV while her father and Dorothy were in a back room. After a few minutes, she heard the woman making noises that were strange and similar to the noises that she would hear coming out of her parents' room, every now and then, when her father decided to spend a night at home. She knew that whatever it was that was going on in that room wasn't right. She knew that her father didn't belong in that room with a woman who wasn't her mother. And she knew they were doing something that little girls weren't supposed to see.

The phone rang and it made Brielle realize she'd been recalling her younger days. She got up and rushed to the phone hoping it was Dante. By the time she answered there was a dial tone. Instantly, she dialed Dante's cell number, but it went straight to voice mail. She hung up without leaving a message and called back about ten times with the same result. At that point, she threw the cordless house phone against the wall and screamed out with rage.

Brielle hollered. She began yelling out strange names and hysterically raved all through the house. She walked into the bedroom, snatched a framed picture of her and Dante from the dresser and threw it across the room, shattering the glass. It felt good to her, which started a move to destroy everything she could. After about two hours of trashing the place, and having an emotional breakdown, she began to feel piercing pains shooting through her back and stomach.

She stopped abruptly and stared into space. "Not again," she chanted. Brielle knew she was about to lose yet another child, a third one due to the stress of being with a selfish and unfaithful man. As she was about to call an ambulance, she heard Dante come through the door. She wobbled her way back downstairs while sobbing and wailing all at the same time.

Brielle was grabbed her stomach and bent over in pain as soon as she made it to the bottom of the staircase. Dante screamed at her, "What the fuck is wrong, what the hell is going on?" he asked, wanting to know why she looked so crazy and was so distraught.

She directed him toward the living room advising him to look at the photos, while holding her stomach tightly trying to stop the painful contractions that had begun.

"Go look on the couch you fucking bastard! You're still fucking her? Still! Two years later!"

"What the fuck are you talking about, bitch? I ain't fucking nobody!"

"Go look! Look at the woman who is making me lose Summer right now!" She pointed in the direction of the photographs.

Instantly, Dante rushed into the living room as Brielle stumbled into the kitchen. "What should I do?" she whispered to herself. She looked around the kitchen and her eyes fixed on the wooden knife holder on the island by the sink.

"Kill him," a voice said.

She grabbed a four-inch steak knife and hid it behind her back. Brielle stood there looking as if she were ready for sex in her lace one-piece, but instead she was ready for revenge. When Dante appeared in the doorway of the kitchen, Brielle's hand began to tremble along with the knife.

"Slash this motherfucker, bitch!" the voice urged. She didn't want him to see the knife for she knew he would turn it on her. Brielle leaned her elbow on the island and sat down on the stool, so he wouldn't notice her hand being hidden. She knew Dante wanted to give another bogus explanation.

"Baby, I can explain. It's not what you think." He had that familiar crooked smile on his face, the lying one. He scratched his head nervously.

"No, what I thought is that you wouldn't see Monique again. I really believed you this time." Her facial expression became more and more demented by the second. "You know about all my bad relationships. You know about my fucked up childhood. You know what I've been through. So why?" she asked in a louder, sharpened tone.

"Brielle, you just don't understand. Why can't you just accept me for me? Why can't you love me unconditionally? What are you concerned about another female for? I love you. Don't worry about another woman."

Dante raised both hands in the air and held them there, shrugging his shoulders, as if he had made a simple statement. Meanwhile, Brielle twisted the knife behind her back several times, holding onto the black handle.

"Oh yeah? Just let you have us both, huh? After you promised and promised that you wouldn't hurt me again. Now you just want me to accept it? Make it easy for you?"

Brielle's eyes widened as she spoke, and an evil look spread across her face.

"Come here, let me hold you," Dante muttered. He held his arms open to receive his wife.

Brielle had a pitiful look on her face as she walked with her head down toward him. Suddenly, her sorrowful look turned to rage. She approached him as if to accept his apology. Then it happened. The moment she hoped wouldn't happen. The knife. She plunged it deep into his chest piercing his heart. Dante gasped! Instantly, he gripped her arm tightly, trying to hold on just before he began to slump down. Then Brielle lunged again. She removed the knife and stabbed him again. Then again. And again.

"Accept this! I loved you enough. I loved you enough not to ever want another man again. With all of your faults, I loved you. I thought it was me and you!"

Brielle began banging the wall and scowling at his dying face all at the same time. Dante couldn't talk. He could only stare. He looked at her demonic face for what seemed like an eternity.

Brielle finally made her next move. She kicked his arm to release his grip from her. "Fuck you. You hurt me for the last time. I was nothing but good to you and all you ever brought me was pain! Rot in hell muthafucka!"

Dante stared at her with a frightened look on his face.

"Brielle, I'm dying," he said weakly then looked up at her with fear in his eyes.

He started gasping for air and then just seconds later, Dante's eyes closed. Brielle felt numb. She didn't feel remorse but only panic for her unborn child.

"Please Lord, let me keep my baby. He doesn't deserve to live but she does! Please Lord! He killed my spirit, let Summer bring me back to life!"

Stumbling toward the phone, she continued to pray out loud. She called 911 and hysterically told them to send two ambulances.

"I need an ambulance! I'm at 255 Brewington Lane. My husband tried to kill me! I stabbed him! Help me!"

She paused while listening to the operator.

"I don't know if he's dead...I'm scared to touch him! Please hurry! I'm losing my baby, please!"

She hung up the phone and stood over Dante's motionless body. She wanted to take the knife out and stab him one more time making sure he was dead. Instead, she took the knife out and cut three, long marks into her own skin, just below her shoulder bone to show self defense. Almost like a pro, Brielle knew she'd have to answer to the police so she took Dante's hand in hers and used his fingernails to scrape her neck. Finding her skin under his fingernails would surely show that she was trying to fight back.

Brielle screamed at him, "Why? Why couldn't you just love me the way that I loved you? Why? Why couldn't we have the family that we said we both dreamed of?"

She looked in his face and felt one more instance of love for him. She kissed his lips one last time just before she lay her head upon his chest. Shortly after, her maternal reflexes kicked in. She rubbed her belly affectionately just as a gush of blood flooded her panties. Suddenly, a horrendous pain shot through her body. Brielle struggled to move away from Dante's body as the contractions increased, yet she couldn't. Her temperature seemed to rise as she knowingly felt what was next. Within seconds she'd passed out a few foot-steps from Dante's lifeless body.

Chapter 3

The moment Brielle opened her eyes, she knew trouble surrounded her. While she lay in her hospital bed a fat nurse stood nearby with a sorrowful look in her eyes. Quickly, Brielle's glare re-focused toward her flattened stomach followed by a questionable look. It didn't take long for the nurse to confirm, Brielle had indeed lost the baby. It was all Dante's fault. It was always her choice in men that became the problem. She couldn't help but to wonder why she always chose men with issues. Some were emotionally abusive, some physical, some professional liars and some just plain ole dogs.

Of course she thought Dante would be different. After all, he was all she had. Brielle's mother had died when she was sixteen after many years of mental and physical abuse by Brielle's father. Her mother officially died from a brain tumor, but Brielle always knew that her mother died from a broken heart, courtesy of dear old dad.

Without having the time to grieve, two unknown visitors waltzed into the room unexpectedly. Before Brielle could tell them to leave, the female spoke.

"Mrs. Prescott, my name is Detective Shields." The black woman extended her hand and Brielle shook it hesitantly.

"And I'm Detective Roberts," the white male said, clearing his throat. "Can you give us a moment?" he asked the nurse.

"Oh, great," Brielle said sarcastically as she watched the nurse disappear. "And I just lost my third child. Do you need to speak to me now?" She wiped her tear-filled eyes with a tissue and blew her nose.

"Yes, we do," Detective Shields answered in her light

voice.

"We need to know how your husband became deceased."

"I killed him, in self defense. And I told that to the officers who responded to my home."

Brielle sat up higher in her bed.

"Yes, we understand that," the white detective replied, "but we need the details."

"Details? Ahhhh… how about he tried to choke the shit out of me." She thought for a moment and decided that she'd be better off being cooperative and not hostile. "I'm sorry, I've gone through a lot. My husband has been abusive in the past. He came home drunk and agitated. He started choking me in the kitchen and I grabbed a knife in self-defense." She took the remote and changed to the news.

"The first officers on the scene said you had an injury near your shoulder. Did Mr. Prescott manage to cut you?"

Brielle touched her self inflicted wound. "Yes, he cut me when we were struggling for the knife. He tried to take it from me, but I wouldn't let go. I knew he would kill me if I let go."

"What was it that agitated him?" Shields asked.

"I don't know. He was annoyed when he came in." She looked intently at the female detective.

"How did you know he was annoyed?" Roberts asked.

"By his tone of voice." Brielle put the remote down.

Detective Roberts checked his phone and excused himself. Brielle didn't buy it. She knew Shields would use that time to try to play good cop. So, she decided to play along. Question after question, she nodded politely. Even when it seemed like the woman was blaming her. As she was speaking to Detective Shields, Roberts came back in the room. Brielle glanced his way but kept telling her story.

"While we were struggling, I kicked him in his crotch area so he could loosen his grip. That's how I was able to put the knife right into his heart," she said with remorse. "You have no idea how scared I was. He would've killed me. I could see it in his eyes."

Brielle recanted the whole day while breaking down several times in between. The fact that she kept talking about her unborn, deceased daughter puzzled them. It was almost as if she didn't want to accept the fact that she was gone.

"My daughter was gonna be a dancer like me. I took dance lessons as a little girl, you know. Summer would've been a professional dancer."

They both looked at her as if they were unsure if she was a little psychotic. Brielle continued to talk irrationally, but spoke calmly when she spoke of Dante. This made them feel that she was mentally competent. She said she signed for the package, saw the photos when Dante dropped her off, and waited for him to come home to explain.

"Did he get mad when he saw the pictures or was he already mad when he came home?"

"I don't know. I guess drunk and mad. I told him I wanted a divorce," Brielle replied.

"Mrs. Prescott, is there any reason why you would want to kill your husband?" Shields asked. "I mean with him being abusive, is it possible that you may have just gotten fed up when you saw the photographs?" She leaned in toward Brielle.

"Detective, we've had many physical fights. They are all on file at the station. But things had been much better over the last few years. I was about to have a child with my husband, whom I love dearly. I wanted to share this experience with him. I was upset when I saw the photos and yes, I was fed up. That's why I asked him for a divorce. But killing him was not a part of the plan," she said convincingly.

"Oh, I'm sure," Roberts said, lifting his head for a quick second.

"All I could think of while he was choking me was that he was finally going to kill me," Brielle said in between sobs.

The officers looked on for a few moments. "So, you were not irate when you saw the photographs, Mrs. Prescott?" Roberts asked, doubtingly.

"Of course. But when he started choking me, I was just trying to get away. The knife was the only thing there for me to save myself. I was feeling contractions and I was more worried about my baby." She paused. "I lost my husband and my baby in the same hour," she commented, staring into space. She hoped that they would feel sympathy for her.

"We're sorry about your loss, Mrs. Prescott. We will, however, probably have to have some more communication with you." Shields paused, showing a slight bit of concern. "It's our job, so please understand. We may have to do an investigation at your home," she added, following Roberts out the door. "We'll have to locate Monique Troy also. Get some rest," she ended.

As soon as they left, Brielle started dreaming about the day she first learned of Monique. She had emptied Dante's pants pockets so she could do their laundry. His cell phone was still in his pants, and it signaled that a new text message had been received. She opened it and read the message.

I enjoyed our night last night, I hate that it had to end.

She saw the name and number that the text came from and wrote it down. She walked into their bedroom and threw his phone directly at his head. He'd had other affairs before; mostly one night stands. But this was something different, she felt it. She couldn't prove it, but she knew in her heart that this was serious. He woke up, checked the phone and immediately jumped in her face. "What the fuck are you looking in my phone for?"

"Who is Monique?" Her hands were on her hips.

"A fucking friend. I can't have friends? There you go starting another problem with us."

"Sure Dante, sure," she remembered saying just as her nurse walked backed into the room.

"Mrs. Prescott, the hospital psychiatrist wants to talk to you later this evening."

"Forget about it," Brielle snapped. "There's nothing wrong with me. It was him. He brought that shit on himself!"

The nurse stopped in her tracks and stared at Brielle. Her erratic behavior troubled her. "It's up to you dear…"

"Get out!" Brielle pointed to the door.

As soon as the door shut, she ranted to her mother, "Mommy, why couldn't you have treated me better. This is all your fault!" she cried. "What I've become is because of you! Why why, why, did you do those things to me?"

❧Chapter 4❧

Three days later, Brielle was released from the hospital feeling like she had no life to return to. For a mid-April afternoon, the sun shone brightly, yet the mood remained dull. When she entered her home, an eerie feeling came over her. It was as if Dante's evil spirit was still present. Her mother's sister, Janelle had flown in from Atlanta and had been at Brielle's since the murder. Her cousin, Janay, had also flown in with her aunt to stay with her for a week or two.

"Welcome home, baby," her aunt belted, as she hugged Brielle tightly.

The first thing Brielle did was to stop and stare at her cousin's crimson red hair color. Janay was known to change her hair color as often as she changed her thongs, but the new look was over-the-top. Brielle had to admit, the short bob-looking haircut that was half-shaven just above her ear down to her neck line signaled- hot. Just like Janay's sex appeal.

"What's up cuz?" Janay said dryly.

Aunt Janelle quickly grabbed Brielle by the shoulders, "Hurry and get dressed, the funeral starts at noon."

Brielle's mouth hung open. "Today? Damn, he just died."

"Yes, today. I told you last night at the hospital," her aunt reminded her. "It seems as if his family has made the arrangements, and it's today. So, let's go."

Dante had a big family, but she'd never been close to any of them. Brielle seemed to be in shock and mad all at the same time. She was the wife and they had decided to plan the funeral. Then her thoughts shifted. She couldn't accept the fact that she'd really killed Dante. She missed him one moment, and despised him the next. Yet, it didn't take long for her to realize the best thing about his death was that she would soon be receiving five hundred thousand dollars from his life insurance policy.

At that moment, she realized it was best if she showed up at the funeral. She didn't want to cause any additional suspicion. She looked at her aunt Janelle and cousin Janay and saw the worry in their eyes. She wanted to assure them that she was okay. "I'm fine Aunt Nelly. Don't worry about me."

Her aunt smiled bleakly.

"I guess you bought me this to wear, huh?" Brielle held up the black, wrap dress with brand new tags. As she started to undress right in front of the living room window, she smiled and looked at her aunt intently.

"You look very pretty this morning, especially in that form fitting dress. And I love how long your dreads have gotten. The gray looks good. You're not going to dye them are you?"

"No, I look like your grandmother, don't I?" She looked at her daughter and niece for a reply. They both nodded their heads in agreement. "Yup, I look like my mother, God bless the dead." Janelle smiled.

"Yeah, you better push back from the table, Momma," Janay commented. "You're starting to have her weight, too. You know at sixty it'll be much harder to lose the donut weight." She laughed.

"Like my mother," Janelle reiterated with a smile.

"Shut up, Janay," Brielle said, abruptly while slipping on her shoes. "What are you a size eleven now?" Brielle picked. She stopped and grabbed some potato chips from a bag that sat on the coffee table. "You still got a nice shape, but you better start watching what you eat."

"For your information Miss Barbie Doll, I'm a size nine, not eleven. But you know… you've always been jealous of my banging body, and big tits. You want me to share some of this D cup?"

She grabbed one of her breasts through her shirt and stuck her tongue out at Brielle and laughed. The ladies were glad to see that Brielle could find humor in Janay's jokes.

Her aunt walked up behind her, and fixed the belt of her dress from behind. "I'm glad you're able to be cheerful about something. Now, lets go."

Brielle turned around and hugged her aunt tightly, rubbing her hands across her two-tone dreads. "I'm going to be okay," she told her just before they walked out the door.

When they arrived at the church, Brielle instantly felt nervous. She received many stares and heard numerous whispers as she walked nervously down the church aisle to the front row. As she approached the first pew, she noticed that there was no room for her to sit. With speed she turned, looked at Dante's oldest sister, then his brother. No one offered a solution. She ended up sitting on the side opposite the family in the third row with major attitude.

The church was packed, so of course Brielle expected Monique to show up. Once things started moving, people were going up to view the body and they were able to make comments about Dante. One of his good friends, Julius walked up and gave this bogus speech about how great Dante was to him. Once he left the podium, he stopped, and looked Brielle dead in the eyes. He broke down like a hysterical woman and stormed outside to get some air.

Brielle kept her composure. The next person up was his old boss. The lady who Brielle had the problem with at the party. She spoke dramatically, "I've worked with Dante for four years. He was always cooperative. He always did what I asked or required of him. He was a wonderful person, and I was immediately impressed with him from the moment I became his supervisor. I had to travel all the way from Texas just to pay my respects because you don't always get people who are willing to go the extra mile for you when they work under you. I hope he can rest in peace."

Immediately the congregation showed their sympathy with the long, "Awwwwwwww." Miss Boss lady also stopped and looked at Brielle disgustedly.

Brielle sat there for minutes, forcing herself to bear the bullshit. She felt very uncomfortable at first and then down right disgusted as she listened to all of the praises that Dante received from family and friends. Her aunt Janelle could see the rising steam inside of Brielle and grabbed her injured hand, holding it tightly.

Brielle snatched her hand away abruptly and headed toward the casket. Janelle and Janay quickly jumped up and stayed close behind. Just as she was about to look into the casket, Dante's sister, Rhonda got up and blocked her view.

"What do you want to see him for? Were it not for you, he wouldn't be laying there."

Brielle kept her composure and brushed past Rhonda without responding. She got up close to Dante and bent over into his casket.

She leaned in and whispered in his ear, "I hate you motherfucker! Rot in hell." She kissed his cheek for the onlookers to see and with her head held high, began to walk back to her pew.

His sister said even louder, "The nerve of you to come here. You should be in jail right now!"

Brielle turned around and looked at his sister with a slight smirk. She then quickly made her way to the mic before Janelle or Janay could stop her. She took a deep breath and spoke with emotion.

"Were it not for that man," she turned to the casket and pointed to Dante, "I would have three lovely children right now. I heard Julius talk about how Dante would drop everything for him when he was alive. Of course he would, because Julius and Dante would cover for each other when they were cheating on me and Alecia."

The congregation gasped and Julius' wife turned to him with an evil scowl.

"And Miss Boss Lady from Texas had an affair with my husband," she spat loudly. "I think she helped buy my house." Brielle paused and breathed heavily. "Dante was good alright, he knew how to manipulate. This man did nothing but treat me like dirt, made me lose three children, and almost killed me! You can say what you want about me, but that man right there was nothing but a monster to me," Brielle mumbled, as she began to cry.

She wanted to scream, "Fuck all of you! You all can die as far as I'm concerned." Instead, she took one last look at the casket, walked past the pew that she was sitting in and continued down the aisle.

Janelle and Janay followed within seconds, with Janay hoping she wouldn't have to fight in church, which would indeed mess up her perfect hair. Brielle walked right out of the church before the pastor could even give the eulogy. She decided that it wouldn't do her any good to stay there. Her life with Dante was over. Her life with men was over.

Hours later, Janelle watched her niece stare at what was left of their most recent family portrait. She knew that her niece had always carried deep issues within her soul. She sat down next to Brielle and embraced her gently.

"Brielle, honey, I'm not going to lie and say that I know what you're going through. I can only say that I'm here if you need me." She stopped to catch her breath. "I can say that I know what it feels like to be betrayed by the man you love. The psychologist at the hospital said that you would be experiencing very drastic mood swings and that in a couple of days you should either return to see him, or someone else in his field."

"No way," Brielle snapped. "I tried that years ago."

Aunt Janelle, who was Brielle's favorite aunt and the one who took her in when she ran away from her father, a year after her mother died, attempted to choose the gentlest words to convince her niece.

"Honey, I think that it's necessary, for your own emotional health, sweetheart."

"A shrink? I don't need a crazy doctor. I'm sane now that my nemesis is in hell. I know that's where he is, because he put me through hell on this earth."

"Brielle, it's not about Dante anymore, it's about you. I want you to be well."

"I said I'm fine," Brielle replied, pulling herself away. "I loved him and tried to make him happy for years, and all he did was hurt me over and over and over!"

"Listen, you're like my own child. I took you in when you were sixteen. And I'm going to make sure you get better. Dante just didn't appreciate what he had, but you have the rest of your life ahead of you. The past is gone."

Her aunt was not ready to discuss the problems of Brielle's past which she believed Brielle had put into her subconscious mind. She knew that they would one day be brought to the surface. Janelle was concerned with helping her niece move forward, but she knew Brielle had deep rooted issues with her mother and father, and it had influenced the type of men she was continuously drawn to. She always fell in love with men who didn't treat her well, because that was what she saw growing up in her home.

"What's wrong with me?" Brielle asked.

"Nothing baby, you're just a woman who needs love, like we all do." They hugged. A few minutes later, they joined Janay in the kitchen where she was cooking Brielle's favorite, short ribs.

As Brielle entered, she caught a flashback of herself plunging the knife into Dante's chest. She shuddered but didn't say anything. She tried to ease the tension in the room.

"Girl, I hope you make those ribs right because I have another knife that I can use on you." She started laughing hysterically while Janay and Janelle looked at her uneasily. Janay changed the subject.

"Momma, how does it feel to finally be retired?" She stirred the pot of vegetables.

"Girl, you just don't know. It feels too good. Now all I need is a sugar daddy to take me on trips." They laughed.

"Well, if he acts up on you, I'll send him to his maker," Brielle interjected.

Janay could no longer ignore the crazy comments. "Listen Brielle, I know you're going through a lot and I know that you're just trying to make light of a heavy situation. But, I don't think you should joke about killing people. You could've been charged with murder. Hell, the investigation is not even over. You never know what the detectives are up to," she added. "I don't think you meant to kill Dante, so you shouldn't be joking about it."

"You're right, Janay. I'm sorry. I didn't want you and Auntie Nelly worried about me, so I made some jokes. I didn't mean it literally." Brielle poured some iced tea and sat at the kitchen table next to her aunt.

"Well, I hope not," Janay replied, just before preparing the macaroni and cheese. "It makes you wonder what really happened to our cousin, Tony," she said under her breath.

"Janay, leave it alone," Janelle said sternly, and shot her daughter a firm look. "Look Brielle, maybe you should come back to Atlanta with us for a couple of weeks. Atlanta will be a nice place to rest. Being in this house is probably not healthy for you right now."

Brielle shrugged her shoulders. "I'm waiting for my insurance check," she said nonchalantly.

"In that case, they can forward it to my address. Just call them. I really think you should," Janay responded. "Plus you can stay with me, not Momma," she added before looking around. "Besides, Dante died in this kitchen, so this place is creepy. Why are we eating in here anyway?"

Brielle ignored Janay's comment and ended with, "I'll think about it."

They ate mostly in silence, with a few words, here and there. After dinner, Janay and Janelle decided to go to visit some nearby relatives.

"I'm going to see some of our family in Paterson. You wanna come?" Janelle asked.

"No, Aunt Nelly, I'm gonna stay here. Tell everybody I said hello." Brielle started looking through an Essence magazine, never giving them eye contact as they were leaving. It was clear that she'd suddenly switched moods out of the blue.

Brielle sat at the same counter for over an hour reading relationship articles and comparing each to her past. Soon, an unwelcoming guest rang the doorbell. She skeptically headed toward the front of the house wondering who would want to pay her a visit on the day of Dante's funeral. She was shocked to see Monique Troy waiting outside her front door. She opened slowly while examining Monique's full frame and pudgy belly. She was visibly about five months pregnant. Brielle didn't want to make a scene this soon, so she complacently stepped aside, extended her arm, and allowed Monique to walk in.

Monique still had on her black dress which confirmed she'd gone to the funeral. She was tall just like the pictures portrayed, but her face was even more stunning. Not to mention, her long, bone-straight hair that touched the upper part of her butt cheeks. It seemed to be her best attribute and allowed her fair skin to be noticed more clearly.

Monique was the last person that Brielle wanted to see, especially seeing that she was pregnant. Monique walked in and followed Brielle to the kitchen. Brielle smiled as she again had a mental picture of Dante with the knife in his chest, falling to the ground.

"Yup, you deserved it you no good son of a bitch," a voice inside Brielle's head blurted.

"Okay, so what do I owe the pleasure?" Brielle asked sarcastically, while taking a seat on a stool, which happened to be near the cooking utensils, including the large steak knives.

The wooden holder had all but one knife, the one that was downtown at police headquarters. Although Brielle wanted to take one to Monique's throat, she wanted answers. She wanted the answers that Dante would never give.

Monique hesitated, took a seat on the other side of the island, and then spoke. "Brielle, I know that I'm the last person who you want to be talking to right now, but…"

Brielle quickly became impatient. "Is that Dante's baby?"

Monique suddenly became frightened after seeing the evil expression on Brielle's face, and postponed answering the question.

"Please Brielle, just let me speak," she said, taking a deep breath. "I feel that you deserve to know the whole truth and I'm here to give it to you."

"So, hurry up bitch!"

Monique's eyes tripled.

"Is that necessary?"

"Speak now or forever hold your peace." Brielle sat with her arms folded.

"Well, three years ago when you found out about me and Dante, I broke it off with him. He came to tell me that you had found out about us and that you lost the baby." Monique paused to check Brielle's reaction. "He said that we needed to cool it for a while, but that he wasn't going to ever stop seeing me."

Brielle suddenly felt a lump in her throat.

"I told him that it was over because he had led me to believe that he was going to leave you. He had no intention of leaving you or me. He wanted us both. I moved to Chicago and tried to move on with my life. A few months later, I contacted him…things weren't going so well for me out there and I needed someone familiar." She paused again as she watched Brielle pull the little bit of nails she had left from her nail bed. "Dante came out to visit and we revived our relationship," she continued hesitantly as Brielle drilled an imaginary hole in her face with her burning eyes.

"It was selfish of me, I know." She took another pause. "But as the months went on, I decided that I couldn't deal with the situation again. It was too painful for me knowing that he was with you every night. So, I tried to break it off again. At that point, he became violent and said that he would kill me before letting me go."

Brielle knew Monique was telling the truth. Dante was abusive both mentally and physically. It was a part of his upbringing. It was all he knew.

"Monique, I really don't know if I want to hear any more of this. What I know is enough, my husband was in love with you and…"

Monique cut her off. "Brielle, he loved himself more than you or me, because he wanted everything at our expense."

Brielle cut her off again. "Monique, why are you here?" She looked in Monique's eyes and tried to ignore her protruding belly.

"I hired a private investigator to take pictures of me and Dante when I first became pregnant to send to you so that you would leave him. I wanted him to myself. But then I came in town and saw you at the mall one day and saw that you were pregnant too and I felt bad. Dante never told me you were expecting. When I saw that you were pregnant, I decided to break it off with him, yet again. I wasn't going to keep the baby at first. I only sent the pictures because I knew that you deserved to know the truth."

Monique sounded sincere in her concern but Brielle disregarded it.

"Okay, Monique, thank you for coming to tell me. I'll just tell you that I'm no better off knowing what I know now, especially seeing that you're having Dante's baby while I lost mine. I feel even worse. So, with that said, you can get the fuck out now!"

"I'm sorry Brielle, but Dante was a very manipulative and conniving man." Monique's voice cracked. "I wasted years of my life on his broken promises. I'm a victim too, not just you. Is there any way that we can put what he did to us to the side for this baby's sake?"

She looked down and rubbed her stomach. Then it happened. Brielle's hand began to shake. Then it rose. Rose in an attempt to grab the knife.

"I'm going to need financial help. This is the only part of Dante that is left."

Brielle stood up and rested her hands unhurriedly on the island, in front of the knife holder. She spoke very softly as if there were people around who she didn't want to hear her comment.

"Bitch, are you trying to ask me for my husband's pension and social security to help you pay for your bastard child? Are you that heartless? Are you asking me to cut that baby out of your stomach right now? You know that's happened before in real life," she added.

Monique's forehead crinkled as she took her purse and placed it in front of her stomach. She stood up and began walking toward the foyer.

"Brielle, I just thought that maybe you wanted to be a part of this child's life, since you lost three other children."

"No, what you thought is that you could come in here and rub this child in my face while taking my money. I was his wife; you were his whore, so therefore I get his social security, his pension, and his life insurance. And you get nothing!"

"I could take this to court Brielle," Monique threatened, half way to the front door.

"I could take your life, Bitch! Get the fuck out before I decide to do it."

Monique was safely across the threshold and on the porch when she made her last statement.

"Maybe Dante's death wasn't an accident at all."

"And maybe yours won't be either, so be very careful." Brielle laughed, in a haunting manner while closing the door.

Moments later, she returned to the kitchen and sat back down on the stool. Her mind and heart were racing. She wished Dante could walk into the house so she could kill him all over again. Suddenly, Brielle grabbed a knife that was just as big as the one she took him out with and started toying with it. She started digging into a nearby cutting board that was on the countertop. She dug, and dug, deeper and deeper. Her mind kept replaying the part where Monique said he refused to let her go.

"Why Dante?" Brielle screamed. "Why did you have to love her?" She started poking her hand with the knife until blood filled her palm. Out of the blue, Brielle blacked out. Her mind took her to another painful time in her life.

After Brielle and her father left the woman's house that day, they were in the car driving when she asked, "Does Mommy know that lady?"

"Girl, stay out of grown folk's business. You think you grown?" Her father looked over at her disgustedly.

"No. But I know Mommy wouldn't like that lady."

In an instant, her father took one hand off the wheel and smacked Brielle in the face. "And she won't know about that lady, you hear? Your mother don't know how to make your daddy happy. And if you ever tell her, I'm leaving to go live with that lady." He turned the radio up and kept driving. He never took her to the movies that day and it was a day that she would never forget.

Janay and Janelle returned hours later only to see Brielle on the kitchen floor. She was laid out, clutching a knife and poking herself with it.

"Brielle!" They screamed and ran to her side, trying to pick her up. The thought was that she had attempted to commit suicide. After shaking her uncontrollably, Brielle finally came to, but didn't remember hurting herself with the knife. She only remembered the flashbacks of her father's infidelities.

After making the decision not to call the ambulance, they lifted Brielle up and put her in a warm bath. Her wounds were mostly treatable from home. She had minor cuts on her cheeks, arms, and stomach, but they also noticed a lot of old bruises on her.

"Brielle, why did you stay with an abusive man?" Aunt Janelle questioned, with tears in her eyes.

"Because I loved him. And he was the only man who ever really loved me."

Janelle grabbed her niece lovingly and convinced her to leave with her for a few weeks. "Atlanta will be good for you baby, trust me," she told her, while Janay stood by with a frown on her face.

☙Chapter 5☙

After some heavy convincing, Brielle was happy to get away from New Jersey. The spring weather had sprung, and she was ready for a new beginning. She hoped that the latter part of 2008 had good things in store for her. Atlanta had a lot of cultural and social events and she knew Janay would coerce her into going to as many as possible. Unbeknownst to her, Janay had plans for Brielle.

Janay and Brielle were close on the surface, but there was some old resentment that was hard to hide. Janay felt that her mother had given too much attention to Brielle when she moved in with them years ago. Even though, she only lived with them for her senior year of high school, Brielle didn't have the best memories either. She felt as if Janay treated her like Cinderella. When she was around her friends she would always try to shine on Brielle and make her feel like an unwanted foster cousin, a charity case that Janay had been forced to take in. Janay was still jealous-hearted even though they were older, but had gotten slightly better in Brielle's eyes; yet the rivalry never ended.

Brielle got settled in at Janay's and within the first week they attended a Greek networking party at a luxurious club in downtown Atlanta. Happily single, Janay worked as a publicist for a Public Relations firm that handled a lot of athletes and celebrities. She knew a lot of people, both famous and affluent.

Janay introduced Brielle to plenty of people at the party. One in particular was, Jason a wealthy doctor; one who showed interest in Brielle immediately, especially in her shapely, petite frame. Even though they talked for a while and exchanged numbers, Brielle wasn't sure if she was even ready to date. As Jason got up and left their table, Brielle turned around and noticed another handsome man watching her. He gestured, pointing to the empty seat next to her to requesting approval to come over. She nodded, letting him know that he could come and sit next to her.

He was dark, and handsome; just the way she liked her men, with the exception of his average height. Brielle watched him closely as he pimped over and sat down.

"Good evening gorgeous, may I have a dance with you?"

Brielle smiled. "My goodness. Can we talk first? I may not want you close to me after I hear what you have to say?"

He smiled and pulled himself up closer to the table and rested his chin on his fists. "Sure. What do you wanna talk about first?"

"Well, for starters why do you want to dance with me?"

"That small waist that looks like it needs my arm wrapped around it makes me want to dance with you. Not to mention, the pretty brown face to go along with those curvaceous hips."

Brielle laughed. "Wow, you can see all of that while I'm sitting down?" She rested her chin on her hand and gave him a doubtful look.

"No, I've been watching you since you got here." He shook his finger at her and said, "Aha. Now what else?"

"How about your name?"

"Peyton," he answered.

"So, what took you so long to come over, Peyton?"

She sized him up. His nails were extra clean and he had on Gucci loafers. Shoes told a lot about a man in Brielle's eyes. Either he had a woman who was keeping his hygiene up or he was a naturally clean man. The latter was the preferred instance.

He laughed, "Let's go." Standing up, he gently took her hand and led her to the dance floor.

So Beautiful by Musiq Soulchild played softly as he swung her around and grabbed her waist, pulling her close to him. "I wanted to see how many men you would be conversing with before I made my move," he whispered in her ear. They did the slow two-step in a revolving circle.

"Well, you see there weren't too many," she said in his ear.

"That's because you must be new around here, because I know that you can't go anywhere without a flock following you." He raised his eyebrows at her.

Brielle spent the rest of the dance talking to Peyton, who worked at the phone company and who'd grown up in Atlanta, but now lived in a suburb about forty-five minutes away. When she found out he was single with no children, she could only say to herself, "Hhmm. Never married without any children at thirty-three, something must be wrong with him."

Peyton was very amusing. He had her laughing half the night. The next time they got up to dance, they danced even closer and were even more comfortable in each other's arms. The chemistry was there, and it was instant. She felt something, but wasn't sure what the feeling was.

Brielle had no intention of sleeping with him on the first night, and hoped that he didn't try. She wasn't frisky like her cousin Janay, but knew that she felt extremely attracted to him. As he spun her and dipped her to R. Kelley's, *Step in the Name of Love,* she realized what it was. She felt as if Peyton was already her man.

It reminded her of the times when she and Dante used to go out together. She felt at ease because it was a good feeling to have; a man, a protector, a lover who hung out with you as your best friend.

"Until you find out that your best friend betrayed you for someone else," a voice inside her said.

"What's wrong sweetness?" Peyton asked, feeling Brielle change her disposition.

"Oh, I was caught up in your rapture, that's all. I had to break free and come back to reality. I have to go to the bathroom. Can you go sit back down and wait for me?"

"Sure," he replied skeptically.

Seconds later, Brielle found herself rushing into the bathroom, and into the stall to weep. Not even bothering to close the stall door, she could hear women outside talking, laughing, and having a good time. She opened her purse and took out the sonogram picture of Summer's embryo. She looked at it for minutes, then pulled it close to her heart. "Summer, I miss you and I miss your dad."

She sat there for about fifteen minutes until she heard Janay's voice in the bathroom. She abruptly wiped her tears, straightened her dress, and walked out of the stall.

Janay was running her fingers through the short, piece of reddish hair in the front of her head that she'd spiked for the night when she saw Brielle in the mirror. She turned around and puckered her thin lips after noticing that she'd been crying. Without delay, Janay grabbed her arm roughly noticing the sonogram photo in her hand.

She snatched it, looked at the photo, then back at Brielle. "Girl, what's wrong with you?" she scolded. "You ready to go?"

When Brielle nodded, Janay led her out of the bathroom holding her arm like a toddler. Ironically, Peyton was standing outside of the bathroom when they came out.

Brielle turned to Peyton. "Good night, it was nice meeting you." She then continued walking.

Quickly, he followed behind. "Wait. I'm not sure what I did wrong. Are you at least going to call me?"

"Yes, I will," she said as Janay tried to pull her past his body.

Luckily, Peyton had given her both his home and his cell numbers earlier. He put his hands on her chin and brought her lips to his and kissed her softly before Janay could yank her away again. Janay turned around and saw the kiss, causing her eyes to open widely. Peyton grinned and simply walked away.

"Damn, girl, you don't waste no time, do you?" Janay inquired.

"Girl, shut up."

By the time they got back to Janay's condo at 3:00 a.m., they were both starving. Janay cooked breakfast while they talked.

"Girl, every time I turned around at he club you had another man in your face. I don't understand how you're still single," Brielle stated.

Janay shook her head. "Please, I meet so many men, but I

swear they're all the same. They're all out for one thing and one thing only."

Brielle agreed and took a bite of her food. Before taking another bite she was stopped by the ringing of her cell phone. "Who the hell would call me this late," she said noticing it was a blocked number.

She answered, and held her mouth open when the voice said, "Bitch, you're going to jail for killing your husband."

The line went dead and so did Brielle's appetite.

☙ Chapter 6 ☙

Brielle woke up the next morning excited about going shopping. She didn't remember much about getting around in Atlanta since she'd only lived there for a year over ten years ago, so she was excited. Janay still had a week left on vacation from work so she agreed to chauffer her cousin around the city.

Brielle wanted to indulge in her greatest therapy, shopping. She bought an expensive pair of Jimmy Choo black leather, Gladiator sandals; shoes that she'd planned on wearing on her first date with Peyton. She also bought a black Valentino bag and a pair of True Religion studded jeans. Janay was always known to be the one to splurge while Brielle was normally more practical about what she spent her money on.

"Girl, why you splurging? You didn't get the life insurance check, yet, did you?"

"No, but I'm spending money from me and Dante's savings account until everything is cleared with his life insurance. Besides, have you been checking the mailbox everyday like I asked?"

Janay just shook her head and smiled. "Girl, you need meds."

"No, I need that check to go along with his retirement accounts, the pension checks, and anything else I got coming my way."

Although Dante was a dirty dog, Brielle was glad that he was a successful dirty dog and not a loser in the financial category. Her plan was to finally enjoy herself and spend every dime. They continued to shop and eat and act like rich housewives when Brielle got an idea as they were walking past a travel agency.

"Hey, Janay, let's go away for a couple of days." Brielle stood in front of the door gaping at the poster of St. Lucia plastered on the wall.

"Shit, I'm down. Where you wanna go?" Janay motioned for them to have a seat next to a fountain. They put their bags down and grabbed a seat.

"I always wanted to go to Aruba. Let's go. And I'll pay for the flight and hotel. You just have to bring your own spending money."

"Let's do it," Janay said, kissing her cousin on the cheek. "That's really nice of you. Shit, you made me so excited, now I gotta pee."

Brielle laughed. "I'll go check it out while you're in the bathroom."

When Janay got up, Brielle made her way into the travel agency with a huge smile. She hadn't been this happy in a while. No sooner than Janay returned, Brielle had already booked the trip and had their itinerary. It was official. They would leave Friday and arrive back Monday night, Memorial Day.

As Friday morning arrived, Brielle and Janay were flying out to Aruba, while Monique walked into the Fort Lee Police Department. She strutted in with her stomach hanging over her brown Juicy sweat-suit and her oversized shades covering a large portion of her face. Her hair looked to be wet as if it had just been washed and parted down the middle. It was clear the visit was planned abruptly.

When she approached the bulletproof protective window, she waited for the officer to turn on the mic for her to speak. The officer looked up from his newspaper and pushed the button, revealing his sour expression.

"What can I do for you?" he asked sharply.

"I'd like to speak to the head homicide detective."

He looked her up and down before speaking. "Have a seat.

An officer from Homicide will come out shortly."

"It's urgent," Monique returned.

"Has the homicide occurred already?" the officer asked sarcastically.

"Yes, sir."

"Okay, so we've got time. They'll be out in a few minutes, so have a seat."

Monique decided against responding. Instead, she took a seat, and started fumbling through her purse. She found her planner that she'd written some notes in. Monique started to read it to make sure she was sure of everything that she wanted to say.

Before she knew it, an attractive officer appeared. He had a caramel complexion, stood about 5'11 and built extra stocky. He sported a very low hair-cut, and dressed in jeans and a Sean John T-shirt as if he were a street dude.

Maybe after her daughter Rain was born, Monique figured she'd try for a date with him; especially since there was no sign of a ring. When Monique extended her hand, and he stuck his out in return, she double checked, then hit him with a flirtatious smile.

"I'm Officer Darren Lewis," he began, "please follow me into my office."

He turned and led her through a metal door and into a small office at the far end of the hall. Right away, Monique noticed numerous pictures of Detective Lewis and a young woman. It may have been a girlfriend, but not a wife, she thought, as she scanned his ring finger again.

"May I have your name? And please have a seat."

"Monique Troy," she said after sitting.

"And what brings you here today, Miss is it, or Mrs.?" *Uh-oh, he's checking me out*, she thought, then answered, "Miss Troy. My unborn child's father..." She paused hesitantly. "He was killed by his wife," she revealed abruptly. "And I think it was murder."

"Uhhhh, okay, I guess if she killed him and you know that for sure, then that should qualify as murder," he said with a weird look on his face.

"Well...I mean, she said it was self-defense but I think it was murder."

Darren nodded. "Okay, so now we're getting somewhere. And this happened here in Fort Lee, right?"

He hopped up and grabbed a note pad while Monique nodded enthusiastically, checking his backside.

"Yes, his name was Dante Prescott. He lived on Brewington Lane."

Lewis nodded again. "Oh, yes, I'm familiar with the case; his wife lost her baby, too, right?" He turned down the radio that was playing on his desk.

"Yes. I don't think it was an accidental death." Monique took a tissue out of her purse without the sight of any tears being present.

"And Miss Troy, what makes you say that?"

"For one, because she threatened me, too."

His eyebrows lifted upward.

"And secondly, she told me. She told me she killed him and it wasn't a mistake." She nodded with exaggeration.

"Okay, Miss Troy, let me just be clear." He cleared his throat. "If you have your beliefs, we can most certainly look into any evidence that may prove that you're right, however, if you mislead us in anyway, it will jeopardize your credibility in court. Do you understand what I'm saying?" He spoke intently.

"Yes." She looked away while answering.

"If what you're saying is true, then you don't have to make any false statements."

Monique reacted with a disturbed look on her face.

"I'm just asking you to be perfectly honest, Miss Troy. What did Mrs. Prescott tell you verbatim?"

Monique became nervous and shifted her position in her chair. "Well, uhm, let me make sure." She looked down at her notes. She searched the prepared list for a few seconds. "She said that she would cut my baby out of my stomach. She said that I'd better watch out..." Monique sighed. "She said that my death won't be an accident."

Darren waited before speaking, to make sure that she was done. "Okay, so, did she say that she murdered Dante?" He stood up and sat on his desk, crossing his arms in the process.

"Well…"

Darren sat back down and leaned back in his swivel chair. He didn't believe that the wife had given a confession to murder. That didn't mean that she didn't murder him, but a confession he wasn't buying. He looked at Monique who he thought resembled the R&B singer, Mya, only a lot taller. He studied for a moment as he did all his witnesses and suspects. He'd prided himself on having good judgment in the past, and if his senses were correct, Monique seemed to be a needy woman.

"Look, I know she killed him. I sent pictures of me and him to her. She was pregnant. I'm pregnant. She killed him," Monique ended in a matter of fact tone.

"Okay, is there any other evidence that you have that I can use to determine if we can pursue this as a case?"

"Did you see the pictures that were sent to her home of me and Dante?"

"No, I wasn't on the case; however, I can go to the evidence room and look them up." Darren moved swiftly toward the door as if the interview was over. "Miss Troy, I will talk to the Sergeant and if we need you we'll contact you. Write your information on this pad for me."

Monique stood up, quickly wrote her name and numbers down, grabbed her Prada bag and walked out, slamming Detective Lewis' office door behind her.

Janay and Brielle made their way toward baggage claim with Brielle still holding onto the sonogram picture of her baby, Summer. Janay noticed it but refused to comment.

"Wake up, girl," Janay said as they walked the corridor. "You already slept the whole flight." She bumped against Brielle to wake her up a bit.

"Oh, trust me. I'm ready to have a good time and spend some of my dead husband's money. At least he was good for something. If I would've known what I know now, I would've chopped him up a long time ago." She ended with a psychotic chuckle.

Janay stopped dead in her tracks and grabbed Brielle's shoulder bag making her stop.

"Listen Brielle, I'm not going to listen to you make jokes about what happened with Dante. What's wrong with you? Was it an accident?" she asked, glaring into her cousin's face. "I need to know."

"Yes Janay, of course it was an accident," Brielle responded. "But because of him there will be no Summer," she added, looking at the picture.

"I understand about Summer, but stop with the jokes, I told you that before. You never know who could hear you say that. I'm serious Brielle, you're scaring me, acting like you're crazy and shit. You're either cracking jokes or crying hysterically every minute of the day."

"Oh my God! I'm fine. Really," she added, stepping onto the escalator. "Okay, I'm gonna stop now for real, because you're starting to think I need help. But I don't. I won't do it anymore."

"Seriously Brielle," Janay said, giving her cousin a stern look.

"I said okay, damn, alright."

Brielle pulled her arm to release her bag from Janay's grip and started walking swiftly ahead. After making it to baggage claim, she looked for her bags and took them off of the conveyor belt with Janay getting hers as well. Afterwards, they silently walked outside to the cab stand, got in the next available taxi, and were on their way to the Havana Beach. Brielle decided to go there because when she was at the travel agency, she was told that the Soul Beach Music Festival goes on Memorial Day weekend in Aruba every year. She hadn't told Janay that there would be a weekend of performances by Common, India Arie, Alicia Keys, and Jamie Foxx to name a few; along with comedy performances and dance shows.

Just what the doctor ordered, she told herself.

Minutes later, they got out of the taxi at The Amsterdam Manor Beach Resort, a property close to where all of the activities were going to take place. The resort was beautiful but quaint.

Brielle didn't want to stay in a high rise hotel like the Hyatt or Hilton; she chose something cozy with its own small beach. The resort was a three story Indian/Caribbean inspired design. They both opened their mouths widely at the fabulous site of it all.

"Wow!" Janay said, "This is beautiful."

"Damn straight! I should've been coming here with my daughter."

Janay's eyes bulged, but she didn't say anything. "Girl, let's go. We're going to take this island by storm," she said, changing the subject.

They rushed inside, checked in, took quick showers and threw their bathing suits on. They both looked nice and sexy, with Brielle ready to show that she'd lost the majority of her baby fat. She had on a white Dolce & Gabbana bikini that had gold chains along the sides of the bottoms and on the top.

"Girl, that bikini is hot. What size is that, maybe I can squeeze into it one day while we're here," Janay said.

"It's a seven and you're a nine, so it's not gonna happen. And anyway that's nasty, I don't share bikinis."

They both laughed.

"You skinny girls always hating on bangin bodies with meat. It's okay, just eat a little more, you'll be alright." She pushed Brielle jokingly as they walked out the room and threw the lobby. "No, but seriously, you lookin' hot with that wavy-ass weave, and the white bathing suit. If you still have curls when that shit gets wet, I might have to hate on you a little bit."

"I know bitch, so fall back," Brielle stated, stepping foot on the white sand outside the hotel.

They both laughed as they grabbed two lounge chairs, and called out to the waiter for drinks.

Meanwhile, Detective Lewis knocked on Brielle's door in Fort Lee. After realizing no one was home, he turned his attention to the mailman who was approaching the mailbox with more mail.

"Excuse me, I'm a detective. It seems like her mail has been piling up. Can you tell me how many days it's been like this?"

"About five...maybe six. It's been so long I'm starting to lose track," the mailman replied, putting the new mail inside the screen door, instead of the full mailbox.

Detective Lewis' forehead creased a bit. He marched to Brielle's next door neighbor's house and rang the door bell uneasily. When no one answered, he strolled over to the home on the other side of Brielle's house and rang that door bell as well. Finally, a young, dark-skinned woman came to the door holding a newborn baby. He took his badge out and showed it to her through the screen door after seeing the funny expression on her face. She still didn't unlock the door, but motioned for him to go to the window instead. Finally, she appeared at the window and opened it.

"Yes?" she said curiously.

"Uhm, my name is Detective Darren Lewis and I was wondering if I could ask you some questions." He walked closer to the window.

"About what?" she asked, patting the baby's back.

"Your next door neighbor, Mrs. Prescott, have you seen her?" He returned his badge to his pocket.

"I saw her leaving a few days ago."

"Was she alone?"

"No, she was with two ladies. I have to go." The young woman began pulling the window down.

"Excuse me, is everything okay? I was just hoping to get some information." He waved his hand to try to stop her from closing the window.

"I've given you all I have." She slammed the window, locked it, and moved away from it.

Lewis whipped out his phone and called the Newark Airport hoping Brielle had chosen the nearest airport to her house. He spoke to a manager of public relations after verifying his identity. After several minutes, he found out that Brielle had traveled to Atlanta. He called his superior at the station and was told to return home, pack a week's worth of clothes, and book a flight to Atlanta to investigate a little further.

He returned home and packed a bag within the hour. Suddenly, he got the idea to call the airport in Atlanta to find out if he would be taking a worthless trip; and on a holiday weekend at that. She could have possibly been on her way back home by now. After faxing his law enforcement credentials to the supervisor at the Atlanta airport. he was told that Brielle Prescott had traveled to Aruba that day. Like clockwork, he too booked a flight to Aruba.

∾Chapter 7∾

Brielle and Janay were laid out on the beach, gawking at every sexy man who crossed their path. It didn't take long for Janay to realize there were an awful lot of black people on the beach, and at their resort.

"Damn, doesn't it seem like there are a lot of black people on this trip with us? I mean even on our flight?" Janay seemed to be in deep thought as Brielle shook her head and laughed.

"You still don't know...huh?"

Janay responded with a confused look.

"Girl, we're here for the Soul Beach Music Festival."

Suddenly, Janay sat up, looked around and smiled at all of the people of color around her. It finally clicked. "What? We are? Who's performing? Please say Eric Benet girl, I want to help him with his sex addiction."

They both burst into laughter.

"I don't know, supposedly every year plenty of extra performers come on down and jump on the bill. And they have surprise performances. All I know so far is Common, India Irie, and Jamie Foxx. Oh, and I think Robin Thicke."

"Ooh, Brielle, we gotta make this memory last forever. Let's go back to the room and figure out what we wearing to the show tonight."

They got up excitedly, and grabbed their beach bags before heading back to the hotel. It was only four o'clock in the afternoon, but Brielle decided she needed a nap if she was going to party half the night with Janay.

As they slept, Detective Lewis' flight landed safely in Aruba. He wasn't on official business as Brielle wasn't a suspect but as his boss stated, a *person of interest*. After Darren had recited Monique's version of the story, his boss gave the approval for Darren to do some snooping. He wasn't sure how he would find Brielle, but decided to do what he did best, detective work.

After visiting Aruba twice himself, he was familiar with the music festival, so he decided to visit the hotels that were in closest proximity to the area where the main concerts would be held. Havana Beach wasn't too large, and was mainly one strip of hotels across from the ocean. He started with the Divi Aruba then the Aruba Phoenix Resort, and lastly the Aruba Bucuti Beach Resort. None of them had a Brielle Prescott listed. As the sun began to set, he seemed to get a bit frustrated. The more time passed, he found himself wanting to turn in for the night. He figured his last stop would be the Boardwalk Vacation Retreat where he would also check in. Of course, there was no Brielle Prescott listed there either.

Inside the room, Darren took some time to study the photos he'd brought of Brielle before changing into a nice pair of shorts and a short sleeve embroidered shirt. The shirt was a gift from his wife, so instantly he was reminded of her. Unfortunately, he was in the process of going through a divorce and promised himself that he would remove her pictures from his desk when he returned to work. He hoped to replace her soon with someone who understood him more.

A few hours later, Brielle and Janay were dressed and ready for the show. Brielle had on a white Nicole Miller strapless dress that was just above her knees, with white Etienne Aigner flip flops. And Janay looked just as good wearing an orange, mini-Valentino dress.

After looking at themselves in the mirror for the hundredth time, they finally left the hotel and made their way to the beach with the thousands of other party-goers.

"Oh, I can't wait to see Robin Thicke," Janay said with enthusiasm. "I heard he likes black girls, too." Janay smoothed her dress out like he was right there checking her out.

"His wife is black. And he's married Janay. Stop acting so damn desperate." Brielle sucked her teeth and took a deep breath. "Just in time," she uttered, "he's coming on now!"

They found a nice spot to watch Robin Thicke's performance. Throughout the show, they were approached by various men trying to hook up with them, but their eyes were glued to the stage. As soon as Robin Thicke went off, a short, chubby guy in his twenties tried to get Brielle's attention, but she shooed him away like a worrisome fly.

Suddenly her cell phone rang. It was a blocked number again. She answered, even though the MC had just introduced Frankie Beverly and Maze.

"Bitch, you gonna get yours for doing what you did," a voice said into the phone.

Brielle hung up and ordered a drink, hoping Janay didn't see her mood change. She figured it was Monique or Boss Lady. She was going to make sure she started to sleep with Dante's gun when she returned home because knowing Dante it could've been some woman she'd never found out about.

The remaining acts seemed to move in slow motion as Brielle thought about Dante, Monique, her father, and the many awful nights from her childhood. Janay could see that Brielle wasn't enjoying the music anymore, so as soon as the show ended they headed back to their hotel. When they strutted into the lobby it seemed like a party was going, so Janay got excited.

"Bitch, since you cock blocked me earlier, I'm going to make sure I make up for it now. I'm not going upstairs. I'ma meet me a man." Janay started walking toward the bar.

"Well, I'm going to bed. I'm tired, and not in the mood for these scavengers." Brielle turned her nose up at all the men within her view. "All these fools are looking for is a quick fix so they can get on a plane and go back home to their wives. I'm going to bed."

Janay shook her head. She didn't want to seem too desperate so she decided to get a drink from the bar away from all the happenings. She found a lounge chair near the pool, then sipped on her drink a few times trying to be cute. She even pulled a book out of her purse to look as if she wasn't at all interested in her surroundings just before a man approached her.

"It's too early to be reading, you should be snuggling right now."

She looked up and saw a handsome man standing in front of her. He was short, and sorta snoody looking, not her type....but hell he was a man, she thought.

She smiled. "Oh really, is that your pick up line?"

"No, not at all. It just so happened that I was walking to my hotel next door, but decided to come to this hotel bar for a drink, and that's when I spotted a nice, attractive woman."

He sat down in the chair across from Janay.

"So, why don't you go find her," Janay suggested.

"I did. Actually, I'm talking to her."

"Oh, so you mean there haven't been *any* nice looking attractive women in all the girl groups walking around that you could've picked through?" Janay joked. She put her book back in her purse.

"Wow, you make it sound so bad. I'm not trying to pick through a litter, I follow my vibe and my vibe told me to come and talk to you. And look how lucky I am, I didn't have to pick through a group to find you. You're here all by your lonesome, just for me." He popped his collar.

"Well, actually, my husband is in the restroom," Janay replied.

"Oh, okay, well tell him he's a lucky man," the man said standing up.

"Wait...you didn't tell me your name, so I could tell him that I met you."

Darren paused and turned around. "Oh, my name is Darren, Darren Lewis."

"Well, Mr. Lewis, I was just joking. I'm actually here with my cousin, but she was tired and went to bed. I was here waiting for you."

Darren smiled. "Well, here I am." He spread his arms in a charming sorta way just before sitting down next to Janay. "I don't want this to sound like a corny line but did anyone ever tell you that you look like a model? I mean you thin from your head all the way to your hips. Even your lips," he added as he stared intently.

"...Well if there's any place to have some weight, I'd rather it be my hips and ass." She smiled.

"You really do have a nice shape. Like a Coca-Cola bottle," he said with a smirk."

Janay was flattered. Most men commented on how slender she was at the top and how she was phat in all the right places. So for her, being a sized nine was perfect.

"Well you kind of remind me of Stephon Marbury a little bit, with your caramel complexion and you kind of have the same nose. You favor him a little minus the athletic body. So, I guess you're a celeb."

He leaned forward then smiled. "Can I get your name?"

"My name is Janay Terry."

"Where are you from Janay?"

"Atlanta. And you?"

"I'm from New Jersey," Darren admitted.

"Oh, yeah, my cousin that I came here with is from Jersey."

Detective Lewis tried not to show his strange expression. He wondered if it was a coincidence that Brielle had traveled to Atlanta then Aruba and now he was meeting a woman from Atlanta who had a cousin from New Jersey.

"Oh yeah? What part?" he tried not to sound eager.

"Fort Lee."

His eyebrows raised a bit and his adrenaline sky rocketed. "So, what's your cousin's name?"

Janay developed a strange feeling. "Huh? Why you wanna know her name? You need to fuck somebody from Jersey?" She crossed her arms.

"Oh, I'm sorry, I might know her. That's all."

"Her name is Brielle," Janay revealed, showing him every tooth in her mouth. "Where do you live and what do you do?"

"I'm an auditor for an Accounting firm in Palisades Park."

"An auditor? If I had to guess, I would say you were a detective?" she said jokingly.

Darrren displayed a slight grin. "That's funny. No, numbers is the line of work I'm in." He tried to change the subject. "So, tell me about yourself."

"Let's save that info for our first date. I'm really tired. We can exchange numbers if you want and I'll call you tomorrow," Janay suggested as she rose from the chair.

Darren quickly put her number in his cell phone and kissed her cheek lightly before leaving. He walked back to his hotel room with his hands deep into his pockets as he thought about Brielle, and how he would approach them in the morning. The Amsterdam Manor was the only resort he hadn't checked earlier so fate must've been on his side.

The moment Darren returned to his room, he took out the pictures of Brielle and studied them intensely. They were evidence from the many domestic disputes stemming back to 2006. Some revealed black eyes, while others showed bruises covering her firm arms and legs. In one picture she had a busted lip, which also showcased her usual reddish-colored lip gloss. It seemed to be a favorite of hers as it was seen in several of the photos. Obviously, the color appealed to Darren as well as he focused his attention on her sensual lips.

Even with the bruises he thought she was beautiful…striking…something about her that he really adored. "Okay Darren, she's pretty, but she's your suspect," he told himself, before turning out the lights.

Chapter 8

Wanting to get a jump start on their day, Brielle and Janay woke up early the following morning, got dressed, and made their way down to the lobby. Both rocked skimpy jean shorts, bikini tops and a shit load of sun tan lotion. The two women strutted out by the pool to have breakfast and to decide what their itinerary would be for the rest of the day.

"So, did you find a baller last night?" Brielle said sarcastically. She read the menu to see what she wanted.

"I met some dude from Jersey. He looked comfortable, not too stacked up with paper though. He's an auditor. I have to look into how much they make. Do you know?" Janay raised her eyes above the menu to look at Brielle with pity.

"No, I don't. I also don't care about finding a man with money anymore, cause I'm about to have a whole lot of it myself. Now, I can find a nice guy without worrying about what he can do for me," Brielle answered in a sarcastic tone.

"Oh Brielle, guys with money aren't nice? I hate to say it, but it seems like Dante really screwed your head up."

"Hell, he did. I just think that men with money are worse because their egos grow with their wallets."

Before Janay could respond, a short black man in a Hawaiian print shirt walked up to them a flashed a cheesy grin. "Hello, beautiful ladies. My name is Desmond, and I'll be your server. Can I start you all off with a beverage. Maybe some orange juice?"

"I'm ready to order actually. I would like the western style omelet and pancakes." She and Dante both loved omelets.

"And I will have the same," Janay added. She handed her menu to the waiter and adjusted herself in her seat before he walked away. "Well, worse is a man with no money who treats you like shit. At least...never mind. I don't want to talk about that. What are we doing today?"

"I figured that tonight we could go see the rest of the performances, and tomorrow night is the comedy show. Today we could go on a Lobster lunch cruise after we go parasailing."

Janay agreed at first. "Hold up...I don't want to go parasailing."

"Then don't go. You asked what we were doing." Brielle picked up a brochure of island attractions that she'd brought downstairs and began to thumb through it for the third time.

"Well, maybe I'll call Darren and see what he's doing," Janay said, watching Brielle's expression change.

"Oh, so I brought you down here so you can dip off with some guy?" Her voice began to rise.

"No, we can both hang out with him. I was just saying I was gonna call him, that's all. Stop being so testy enjoy your damn vacation. You know all you need is a stiff dick, and you'll loosen up."

Brielle started laughing. "You know Janay, I'm not going to doubt you, you might be right. Let's eat and go and enjoy the day. Maybe I'll find me a stiff dick on the beach lying around somewhere and I can just put it in my bag and take it up to the room."

Both women laughed simultaneously before Brielle's cell phone began to ring again. Knowing it was probably a good idea not to answer, she answered it anyway. "You should've died instead of him. Watch your back," the caller ended and hung up. Brielle's face dropped.

"What's the matter?" Janay looked concerned.

"I think that bitch Monique is having someone make these threatening calls. It's not her voice, but I know it's her." She shook her head.

"Are you sure, Brielle?"

"Yeah, unless Dante had another bitch on the side whose mad at me, too. It's probably Monique, though."

"Damn...Well, if you're really concerned, hire a body-guard."

"No need," Brielle spoke with confidence. "I got something for whoever comes my way. Dante had a registered gun and I'll be keeping it close to me." She smiled nervously.

"I don't think you need to go that far."

"I am gonna go that far, especially if she keeps it up." Brielle displayed a blank stare for a few seconds before looking back at Janay. "Enough about that dumb shit, are you gonna go parasailing with me or what?" Brielle tried to put the negative thoughts out of her mind.

"I guess," Janay said, shrugging her shoulders. Then suddenly her eyes shifted as she noticed someone watching her.

"Hey, beautiful," Darren said, walking up to the table.

"Hey, Darren." Janay instantly started blushing.

"How'd you sleep?" he asked.

Janay nodded up and down. "Good. Can't complain." When she noticed Darren looking at Brielle, she continued. "This is my cousin I was telling you about. Brielle, Darren, Darren, Brielle."

He extended his hand. "Nice to meet you, Brielle," he said, softly shaking her hand. "You ladies must have a beautiful family." They both looked at each other, then back at him. "That was a compliment," he said bashfully. "You're both stunning, that's all I meant."

"Thank you," they both chimed, then laughed.

"You look like Stephon Marbury a little bit," Brielle said.

Janay nudged Darren, "I told you."

"Where are you ladies off to?" He looked at Brielle instead of Janay.

"We're about to go parasailing," Janay emitted. "I was actually about to call you because she's trying to force me to commit suicide," Janay said, pointing to Brielle with an attitude. "I was hoping you might have something better for us to do. I mean where are your friends?" Janay asked curiously.

"Oh, my boy's wife stopped him from coming at the last minute," Darren stated pitifully. He licked his plump lips.

Strangely, his eyes were still fixated on Brielle.

"Awwww, so now you must hang out with us. You're all alone. He can come with us, right, Brielle?" Janay said, giving her cousin a stern look that said not to be mean.

"Sure, he can come," Brielle replied, showing little emotion. "But let me finish eating first."

"So, I hear you're from Jersey," Darren interrupted.

"Yes," Brielle said, without turning to look back at Darren. "Fort Lee," she added.

"I dated a girl from Fort Lee once."

"Are you dating now, Darren?" Brielle asked him abruptly.

"Actually I'm married, but going through a divorce."

Brielle looked at Janay, while Darren kept his eyes on Brielle. It seemed that Janay was starting to become more attracted to Darren the more he talked, but she noticed the extra attention he was giving Brielle all of a sudden.

"Any chance of you getting back with your wife?" Janay asked with a sexy smirk.

"Oh, no. My wife is not the faithful type. And I'm more of a one-woman man." He directed his comment toward Brielle, which immediately sent Janay into competition mode.

"So, Darren, what can you and I get into today?" Janay asked, making everyone at the table uncomfortable.

Without hesitation, Brielle stood up. "Let me let you two get better acquainted. I'll be back."

Brielle got up without returning Darren's blatant eye contact and walked away. Janay didn't try to stop her and Darren knew it wouldn't look right if he tried to either.

"Keep your cell phone on, Janay. I'll call you before I go back to the room to see where you are," Brielle stated.

Brielle pulled her shades off her head and walked away with a slight sway of the hips. She could feel Darren watching her backside but refused to look back.

"Is your cousin married?" Darren asked Janay.

Janay sucked her teeth. "Would you like me to call her back and ask her. I mean I can disappear?"

"Oh no, I was just asking."

"Cut it," she snapped, showing her anger. "Soooooo," she sang slowly, trying to get her attitude right. "What do you want to get into?" Janay asked in a suggestive manner.

"Uh, I don't know, whatever you want to do?" he answered, feeling trapped.

"We could go back to your hotel room, if you like."

Darren was shocked, but like the average man, he allowed his dick to answer. Before he knew it, they were on the beach headed to his hotel room. The walk was a quiet one while Darren thought of the best way to get information from Janay about Brielle. The fact that Janay kept touching his ass every chance she got was pissing Darren off.

Janay knew he was uncomfortable, but didn't care. She was horny and Darren had the stick to cure her problem. She wasted no time. As soon as they got in the room, her shorts were coming down her legs, and the bathing suit lay across the floor.

Janay could tell Darren was hesitant, almost like he'd never had pussy before, so she started strong. In less than five minutes she'd fingered herself artfully, and seduced Darren into taking off his linen shorts. It didn't take long for her to plunge her head into his lap giving up a sloppy blow job.

Darren couldn't resist letting out a moan. Unfortunately for him, the minute Janay heard the possibility of an orgasm on the way, she hopped up, ready to get a bit of his stiff dick. Darren's eyes grew larger as he watched Janay commit rape. She went wild like she was on set at a porno shoot, while Darren moved very little.

As soon as Janay released, Darren hopped up and rushed into the bathroom turning on the water in the shower. By the time he got out, Janay was back in her bathing suit with a silly grin plastered across her face.

"So, what are we going to do now?" Janay asked.

"Well, I actually have a timeshare tour that I scheduled."

"You're so straight-laced." She laughed. "Oh, well I'll go meet up with Brielle, and we'll hook up with you at the concert." She smiled. "You do go to concerts, right, straight boy?"

"Yeah, I party a little."

"I guess I found myself a nerd. Give me a kiss, baby." She caressed the side of his face. "What you just got was just a taste of what's in store for you. I can help you get over your wife."

Darren stood frozen with a blank look on his face as Janay waltzed out the door.

Brielle tossed and turned as she slept. That dream…the re-occurring dream of her father and mother bothered her greatly.

They both sat in her parent's bedroom while her mother did her hair. Suddenly, her father marched in without saying a word. She remembered him swiftly moving toward the closet, coming out with an overnight bag. Her mother yelled, "You going some-where?"

"I'm going out of town to visit my family. I'll be back in about a week," her father responded.

"Take your daughter."

"No, I'm going with my brothers down south. No kids al-lowed."

Within minutes, he'd left with no other explanation. That's when another day of Brielle's torture began. With force, her mother yanked at her head and hit her forcefully with the handle of the brush.

"That hurts! That hurts!" Brielle screamed in her sleep.

For minutes, she shouted. Fortunately, Janay walked in re-alizing her cousin was in the middle of a bad dream.

Janay nudged her several times, "What's the matter, Brielle? Wake up!"

Brielle opened her eyes, realizing she was in their hotel room, and safe from her mother's torture. "I was having a bad dream. I'm okay now." She breathed heavily and hopped off the bed like everything was cool. "Did you have a nice time with Daaaa-ren Dahling?" She laughed.

"Yeah, I had a nice time. He's alright. What do you want to do now?" Janay changed the subject.

"I want to eat, of course, and then go to the concert, it starts in two hours, and it's already five o'clock." Brielle slipped her thigh-length dress on while rushing Janay. "Girl, hop in the shower so we can go."

Hours later, the girls were on their fourth Apple Martini, dancing to the sounds of Alicia Keys. They'd already seen Common and India Arie, and planned on being totally intoxicated by the time Jamie Foxx took the stage.

It was obvious they were drawing attention by the way every guy stopped and stared when they neared their space. Janay knew that Brielle felt pretty drunk by the way she danced up on a muscular, cute guy who walked up and started dancing with her. They danced for a while, then talked a bit until Jamie Foxx hit the stage singing, *Blame it On the Alcohol*. People went crazy. One man even grabbed Janay's hand and started dancing with her like he'd known her for years.

As one of his friends approached Brielle, Darren appeared out of nowhere and beat him to it by pulling her from behind. When Brielle turned around, she saw that it was Darren.

"Oh, you ain't making my cousin mad at me," she said, nodding in Janay's direction.

At that moment, Janay and Brielle locked eyes. She asked Janay without words if it was okay. Janay reluctantly shrugged her shoulders and continued bouncing her ass on her dance partner's dick. Brielle took Janay's body language as "I don't care" and started dancing freakily with Darren. She was clearly tipsy and feeling good.

When they danced their way a few feet away from Janay, Darren whispered in Brielle's ear "So, why have you been so mean to me since I met you?"

"I haven't been mean to you; you're my cousin's interest." She moved with him in unison.

"I only met her before you, I didn't propose."

They locked eyes.

"What are you saying?"

"I'm just saying, you two beautiful ladies are out here to have a good time and I met her first, but I want to hang out and get to know both of you."

"And why is that?" Brielle asked and then turned around to look at the stage.

Darren moved up close behind her and gently wrapped his arm around her waist. Jamie Foxx was singing one of his ballads as Darren whispered in her ear again. "Because I do. Now, you never told me if you were married."

"No, I'm not. Besides, that's enough questions right now. Let's just enjoy the music."

"I hear you loud and clear," Darren said, as they continued dancing. Darren didn't know if he was sincerely attracted to her or if it was just the possibility of cracking a murder case.

Soon, Darren and Brielle got lost in the crowd and made their way toward a bar in a more secluded area. Darren ordered Brielle another drink, then began with his undercover investigation.

"What do you do for a living, Miss Prescott?"

She raised her eyebrows. "I never told you my last name."

"Yes, you did." He lied.

"No...I don't remember telling you my last name."

Darren began scrambling for words and quietly cursed at himself. "You did. How else would I know?"

Brielle still looked suspicious. "Anyway, I'm an interior designer. I work for a design company, but I've been on a leave of absence. I'm about to start my own company actually."

"That's cool. Do you have children?" He gently rubbed her belly.

"No, do you?" She moved his hand away with ease.

"No, not yet. I want them badly though." He smiled.

"Is that why you and your wife are separated?" They clutched their fingers together.

"Well, it's one reason. She had an affair, and then another one, and then another one; get the picture?"

"Yeah, my hus…I mean, I know what you mean." She pulled her fingers away from his.

"Oh, so you are married huh?"

"Not anymore, my husband died."

"I'm sorry to hear that." *Now, we're getting somewhere*, he thought.

"I'm not." She downed her drink.

"Huh?" he asked. "You want another drink."

"No, I want to vent. My husband was horrible to me. He cheated on me repeatedly and I guess God punished him for being such an evil bastard. He took him out of my life and I'm glad He did."

"Wow, he must've hurt you really bad for you to want to see him dead. I just don't want to be with my wife. But I can't say that I want her to die."

"Well, good for you. He tried to kill me. He killed a piece of me every time he betrayed me. He made me lose three babies." Brielle fought back tears.

"Oh, I thought you meant he tried to literally kill you," he pried.

"Did you hear me say that I lost three children because of him? Do you know that I could've lost my mind behind just that alone?"

Darren shook his head after seeing Brielle lose her cool.

"I loved him very much and tried to keep him happy and all he did was hurt me. I hate him and I'm glad he's dead." She wiped a single tear running down her face.

"How did he die? If you don't mind me asking."

"I really don't want to talk about it anymore," she returned calmly. "Look, I gotta go," Brielle downed her drink then placed her empty glass on the bar."

Darren didn't protest, but did steal a quick kiss on her cheek. "I hope to see you soon," he told her as she walked away.

"You will." She blushed.

"What's your number," he yelled above the crowd as she began to walk away.

Brielle mouthed each number slowly while moving backwards at a snails pace. It wasn't until she bumped into an over-weight transvestite that she turned around and strutted away bashfully.

The next day, Janay and Brielle were sitting on the beach talking about Corey, Janay's new, young victim. She was telling Brielle how they'd danced the night away and ended with a bang when Brielle's phone rang.

"Oh, let me get it, so I can curse the motherfucker whose been playing on your phone!" Janay didn't even wait for permission before answering. "Yeah."

"You never said goodbye last night, it's Darren."

"This isn't who you think it is Darren. Hold on," Janay replied, before handing Brielle the phone. She then put on her sunglasses so she could eye her cousin's expression discretely.

"Hi Darren…" Brielle said, then smiled unconsciously. "Cool. I'll lock your number in and call you later. Bye," she said, like a smitten school girl. She looked over to see Janay shrugging her shoulders. Even though she was happy that Darren called, she didn't want the drama.

"I don't care Brielle, you can have him," Janay said, rubbing more suntan lotion on her almond colored legs. "Tonight's our last night here, so believe me, me and Corey are gonna make the best of it. Besides, Darren's a 9 to 5 nerd, and Corey's a paid thug."

Hours passed and Brielle found herself back in the room, asleep, and alone. With Janay nowhere to be found, she hopped up, got dressed and then called Darren. Immediately, he dropped what he was doing and met Brielle at a cozy restaurant about a quarter of a mile from her hotel. Darren knew he only had that night to make some kind of impact on her. He wanted her to want to see him when they got back to New Jersey. After all, he only had a month to see if she would confess to murdering her husband.

They dined at The Sunset Seafood Terrace. It was on the water and they had a private booth that was closed off on one side with a thick, mahogany curtain and a spectacular ocean view.

"How are you feeling today? You seemed upset last night," Darren stated.

"I was drunk. I couldn't do anything but go to sleep. I felt good when I woke up though. I was glad I didn't have a hangover this morning." She looked over the menu.

"Yeah, I was pretty drunk, too. So, am I going to be able to see you when we get back to Jersey?" He reached over the table and touched the tip of her fingernails.

"I guess. What is it that you're looking for from me any-way?" she questioned.

Darren paused for a moment thinking that she was referring to the case, then it clicked. "I'm looking for someone who's look-ing for what I'm looking for."

"And?" She started laughing. "What is that supposed to mean?"

"I don't know. What do you want from me?" he shot back.

"Anything different from my dead husband."

"Brielle, not to be funny but, you talk like you would've killed him yourself if you could have."

She paused and remembered what Janay had told her about being careful how she spoke about Dante.

"Let me clear something up. I loved my husband and I do miss him in a way. But, I'm more angry with him for doing me wrong and then dying, instead of doing right by me and giving us a wonderful life together."

Darren took her hand and started rubbing it. He seemed to be sincere, and spoke to Brielle caringly. Suddenly, he picked up his glass and motioned a toast. "Here's to a healthy mind, body, and spirit."

She toasted with him, feeling good inside. She was starting to like Darren a little bit, but there was something about him that wasn't right. It was clear that he didn't have the right height, or the domineering personality that she was used to. But he was cute, and she especially liked the smooth hair that he'd grown and trimmed neatly along the sides of his face. Still, something wasn't right, yet didn't reveal itself as they chatted through dinner.

When they left the restaurant two hours later, they walked along the beach holding hands. The companionship was good for them both; especially Brielle. She contemplated kissing him, hoping he wouldn't take it the wrong way.

Darren, on the other hand, fought hard between the feelings developing for Brielle and the detective side of him. He was supposed to be doing his job, but it was hard. He knew he'd better not try to sleep with her even though he desperately wanted to. If she did confess to murder, and was charged she could use a sexual encounter against him in court.

However, before he could contemplate any further, Darren's feelings got the best of him. He stopped Brielle in her tracks, pulled her close, and gave her a warm kiss, with all of his tongue. She needed it. It relaxed her deeply, yet she didn't want to read too much into it. She'd promised to take her life one day at a time, and not commit to another relationship so soon. They did agree to see each other once she got back home and to talk on the phone until she got back from Atlanta. Darren seemed very interested in knowing when she would return, but she told him she didn't know.

By the time they reached Brielle's hotel, they'd kissed over twenty times. When Darren walked away, Brielle stopped and remained in deep thought. She then prayed to God, which was something she never did because she didn't really know if she actually believed in God.

God, please forgive me. I know I had no right to do what I did, but I just snapped. Please don't let me go home to be tormented, and help me find peace. Oh, and a man, too.
Amen

⚙Chapter 9⚙

The flight back to Atlanta arrived shortly after 2:00 p.m. As soon as the ladies got back to Janay's duplex, Janay revealed that she was leaving for the evening. She'd gotten a call from someone whom she obviously wanted to keep as a secret.

"I'll be back later," Janay quickly told Brielle.

Brielle figured it was a guy she'd met at some club. She didn't understand how Janay could see so many different men at one time. Nonetheless, Brielle felt lonely so she called Peyton to tell him that she was back and had made it safely. They'd talked twice since she had been in Aruba and promised they could see each other as soon as she returned.

"I wanna see you bad. Can I come by right now?" he pleaded.

"Peyton, I'm tired. But we can get something to eat. That's it."

"Whatever I can get," Peyton said, in a humorous voice. "I'll be there in twenty."

Brielle hung up and called Darren instantly. She wanted to make sure he'd gotten home safely as well. As soon as she heard his voice, her heart warmed. She kept the conversation short but at least they agreed to see each other as soon as she got back to Jersey.

Brielle hung up excitedly, and got ready for her date with Peyton within minutes. It was clear she anticipated their quick date. She paid extra close attention to her make-up which she hadn't done in years. It confirmed even to her that she really liked him. It was the first time she cared about the way she applied her foundation down to every piece of clothing she put on.

When Peyton pulled up, Brielle's entire disposition changed. She was stunned to see that he had the same type of truck that Dante had, a black Tahoe. She shuddered before getting in as Peyton's music blared. He pulled away from the curb with a wide smile on his face, but as he drove away, Brielle kept looking over to make sure it wasn't Dante driving. She knew her mind was playing tricks on her, because he looked nothing like Dante.

Their first hour at the dinner table was uncomfortable as Brielle continued to think of her late husband. But before long, she started lightening up and sharing personal business with him even though he hadn't asked.

After dinner, they returned to Janay's where Peyton asked the ultimate question.

"Can I come in for a while?"

Brielle thought about it for a moment. Janay still wasn't home and Brielle thought twice about taking a man into her cousin's spot. She was really starting to be curious about what Janay was into. She seemed very sneaky, and always kept everything to herself, like she was working for the C.I.A. Janay never talked about what guy she was seeing, or who she was really interested in. She simply kept her business to herself which prompted Brielle to decide a little company would do her no harm.

"C'mon in," she told him.

After walking inside, Brielle and Peyton hadn't been on the couch long before he slipped his arm around her neck and started caressing her shoulders.

"Yessssss, that feels good. There's nothing like a man who knows how to give a good massage." She moaned for several minutes as he worked her neck and the upper part of her back.

Way too soon, Peyton moved closer, then hopped on top of Brielle pressing his hefty body against hers. He started kissing Brielle aggressively, but she was instantly turned off.

"Peyton, why are you moving so fast?" she asked, while sitting straight up on the couch. "We've got time."

"I know but you're just so beautiful, I want you."

"Yeah, well, don't rush me." She picked up the remote and started channel surfing.

"It's all about you, beautiful lady. I'm just a man, that's all."

"Are you in a relationship?" she asked, although when they met he said that he wasn't.

"I told you before, no. I'm just coming out of one, too," he responded with his hands upright.

"Well, I'm not ready to sleep with you, yet." She stopped turning the channel when the movie, Pretty Woman displayed on the screen.

"No problem. I gotta go to work in the morning anyway," he said, sorta disinterested in the movie. He stood up and signaled Brielle to walk him to the door, but not before sneaking a quick kiss.

Janay waltzed in shortly thereafter with a bunch of different designer shopping bags. "That was the guy from the club, right?"

"Yeah, that was him. Peyton, remember? Damn, did you rob the mall?" Brielle asked.

"I tried to, but money makes it so much easier; especially when it's not your shit." She laughed and took her bags to her room. Brielle followed and talked to her as she put her new things away.

"What is that supposed to mean? I mean…what exactly do you have going on down here?"

"You ain't ready to find out what I got going on, but I can surely hook you up when you're ready. You're used to being someone else's woman. But me…I'm my own woman, and it's so much more fun that way. Try it. You might like it," Janay smirked.

"I'll pass. Juggling men ain't my thing."

"Believe me when I tell you, your way is more of a headache, but do your thing," Janay replied. "Anyway, how'd your date with Peyton go?" She took her Manolo Blahnik peep-toe stilettos out of the bag. "Girl, are these shoes hot or what?" She passed them to Brielle.

"Ooh, these are really cute. Don't get mad if I copy." She passed them back, then watched as Janay placed the eight-hundred dollar shoes in her closet.

"Brielle, you couldn't be me if you tried. You're too naïve, gullible and nice. That's why Dante took advantage of you so much. I always knew he was a damn dog. Anyway, I hate talking about Dante. What's up with Peyton?" she quickly changed the subject so that Brielle wouldn't react to her comment.

"Good, he's really funny." Brielle smiled and thought about the time she and Peyton had just spent together.

"Sometimes I think you're too needy Brielle and you don't have to be. You should've left Dante's ass years ago, but you were scared to be alone. Believe me, being alone is better than being with a loser…you know."

"I know." Brielle confessed. "I guess I was used to the abuse from my parents. My father used to call me all kinds of names, beat on my mother and degrade her; and my mother would beat on me because she couldn't beat him back."

"Yeah, your father was an evil man."

"Yeah, but at least I had a father," Brielle snapped, then re-canted. "I'm sorry Janay, I shouldn't have said that. I hate that I'm so bitter."

"I told you you're evil."

"No, I'm not. I'm as sweet as pie, if you don't cross me," Brielle added, just after shooting Janay a weird look. She then walked away when her cell phone rang, noticing that it was Peyton.

For two weeks straight, Peyton spent every available minute with Brielle. He would leave straight from work and they'd either go out, or chill at Janay's place, cuddled up. She had even considered moving down to Atlanta permanently to be with him. One day she asked Peyton why he never invited her over to his house. He explained that his mom had been living at his place for the past couple of years. She'd been diagnosed with Multiple Scle-rosis and had to retire early. Brielle thought that the story sounded like a crock of shit, and continued seeing him without even want-ing to face the truth. If she couldn't go to his house, she knew that meant that he lived with a woman, not his mother.

Strangely, a few days later she received the invite she was waiting for. When they pulled up to the small, two-bedroom house, Brielle was taken aback. She expected something larger, even fancier. As soon as they walked inside, Brielle's eyes surveyed the place. Old photos of him and his siblings when they were younger lined the walls. And the furnishing reminded Brielle of her grandmother's taste, not that of a bachelor.

The décor seemed to have been that way for a long time, not the couple of years that his mother was supposedly living with him. Brielle wanted to meet his mother, however, she was in Maryland visiting Peyton's younger sister. She didn't want to seem superficial, so she left the issue alone, and followed him to his bedroom.

As soon as the door opened and her eyes set in on the two double beds, she turned to Peyton, "You don't have to lie to me. I know this is your mother's house." She kissed his cheek. "At least it's not another woman."

At that moment, Brielle fell hard for Peyton. She started spending more and more time at his place. And soon after about three weeks the relationship became intimate. Brielle told Peyton to his face she was ready to make love. Peyton quickly planned a weekend getaway at a local Hilton Renaissance Resort. They arrived on a Friday night where Brielle spent the early part of the day getting pampered and the later part of the evening pampering her new man.

With help from the first installment from Dante's pension check, she decided to surprise Peyton that evening with three different gifts. The last gift would be the best treat of all, probably sending him into orgasm heaven. Brielle had it all planned until she got the call Saturday morning, informing her that Peyton had to rush his mother to the hospital, and that he would be back to her first thing in the morning. She was disappointed, but glad that they'd spent Friday night together, alone, just the two of them- no Janay.

Brielle enjoyed her day alone. She stayed in her hotel room, ate popcorn, and watched movies all night. However, she was more than happy to see Peyton the next morning. He came in as she was stepping out of the shower. Her first instinct was to get dressed quickly, then she realized a towel would do. Brielle's main concern was to give Peyton his gifts. She took a neatly wrapped box out of her purse and placed it in front of him.

"That's for you, baby," she said, pointing to the box.

He looked surprised and hesitated before picking up the box. "For me?"

"What's the matter, you don't like presents? It's for you. I appreciate you," Brielle continued.

Peyton became nervous. He opened the box and his eyes widened at the sight of the five thousand dollar Rolex watch that was inside.

"Brielle, you bought this for me?" He was shocked.

"No, I bought it for that guy over there." She pointed to Maury Povich, who was on television.

Peyton laughed nervously. "Are you sure? I mean, thank you."

He didn't know how to react. He did however know that she'd spent a pretty penny for the watch, and he didn't deserve it. He also knew that he had a secret to clear up, but decided he would cross that bridge when he got to it. Peyton took the watch out of its case and put it on his right wrist.

He figured there was only one way to thank her. Sensually, Peyton grabbed Brielle and charmed her into his arms showing just how much he appreciated his gift. After ripping off his clothes, he pulled the towel away from her body and pushed her onto the bed. Peyton was big on teasing his women so he started with her breast sucking and licking his way toward her stomach. Brielle kept opening her legs wide, hoping he would continue licking toward her wet treasure. Slowly but surely, he tasted her, proving to be a pro at eating pussy.

"Oh my Goodness!" Brielle shouted. "I love you Peyton! I swear I do."

She lied, and continued to yell out passionate words until she climaxed, leaving Peyton at the foot of the bed, watching her intently. It seemed that he studied his victim before climbing on all fours like a tiger about to devour his prey. He entered roughly, dick rock hard. As he pumped, Peyton began pulling Brielle's hair. He moaned, groaned, and pulled even more. Brielle didn't know why, but she liked the way he was being rough with her. He continued to work the middle, pushing Brielle's legs behind her ears and pumping forcefully. Just as Peyton was about to explode, he began choking Brielle causing her to pull back from their session.

"Stop, stop!" she began.

"Why?" he asked kissing her just beneath the neck, continuing to pump.

Before she could answer, he released all over the bed. "See, I wanted to show you how much I liked my gift." He grinned.

Strangely, she grinned back. "On round two, I'm on top." Brielle fantasized that they were already married. They made love two more times in five different positions. Peyton was laying pipe long, and hard. Of course, Brielle needed it. She let her guards down and gave all of herself to him without holding anything back. They panted, moaned, groaned, and released many times over.

By the time three o'clock rolled around, Peyton got another alarming call. He said that he had to leave to go back to the hospital to speak with the doctor on call about his mother. When he dropped Brielle back at Janay's, she was walking on cloud nine.

Janay noticed the glow on her face as soon as she hit the door. "Umph.Ummm," she said, clearing her throat.

"Oh Janay, I didn't know you had company." Hell, she was even surprised that Janay was home. "Your hair looks good. You added more red, huh?"

"A little something something." Jany patted the short, tight curls that lay perfectly in the back of her head before making the introduction. "Brielle, this is Stacy my co-worker. Stacey, this is my cousin, Brielle."

"Hi. Nice to meet you." They gently shook hands.

Just then, Janay's cell phone sounded. She hoped it was one of her clients. "Hello," she answered.

"Hey, how are you, beautiful?"

"Who is this?" she snapped.

"Darren. Darren Lewis from Jersey, by way of Aruba." He

laughed. "Remember me?"

Janay shot Brielle a funny look then covered the phone slightly to tell her it was Darren. "Yeah, I remember you," she uttered with attitude. "Why are you calling me?"

"I was calling to see how you were doing. It's been a month since the trip and I was thinking of you."

She rolled her eyes. "Thinking of me. Huh? Your ass should be thinking of Brielle."

"How is she, by the way?"

"She's fine…just been hanging out with her new man," she teased.

The information bothered Darren instantly. "Oh really," he said, trying not to show his feelings. "I was wondering why she hadn't called me."

"You know…late nights…good dick," she joked.

"Oh, well, ask her to give me a call when you see her. I've been calling her all weekend."

"I sure will," Janay ended with a deceitful tone.

As soon as she hung up Brielle burst into laughter. "You're crazy girl. "But I really did have a fabulous weekend," she sang with a grin.

"That dick must've been off the chain, because you look like you about to lose your mind. But remember, it's only been about a month Brielle," Janay preached. "You always jump in head first. You need to tread lightly." Janay shook her head in disgust.

"Whatever. I had a wonderful time with Peyton." Brielle took some juice out of the refrigerator and began to pour it.

Janay's friend looked like she'd seen a ghost, "Peyton, who?"Stacy asked.

"Rowe. Why? Do you know him?" She put the juice container back in the refrigerator and closed it hesitantly.

"Peyton Rowe? The only Peyton Rowe I know is married to my friend, Gina Rowe. I hope it's not him. Does he drive a Black Tahoe and work for the phone company?" Stacy inquired.

"Yes, he does," Brielle answered, thinking immediately about the Rolex she had just given him.

"Oh, my God. I don't wanna be the one to give this type of

bad news, but they've been happily married for eight years."

Brielle couldn't believe it. However, she tried to play it off. "Well, we all know about happily married men. They are happy in the presence of their wives, but tell a sob story of being unhappy when they're out on the prowl. Oh well, I guess another one bites the dust," Brielle commented with sadness in her eyes. "I don't wanna mess up a happy home on my account. I'll just leave him alone. I'll be going back home to New Jersey soon anyway, so don't even mention this to your friend. It'll probably destroy her," she uttered, leaving the room.

Her goal was to get away from the kitchen swiftly so they would not see the anger she'd built up in her face. Brielle quickly walked upstairs to the guest room and closed the door behind her. The tears flowed as she lay sprawled out across the bed. She pulled out her cell in a fury. Peyton had the audacity to send her a text saying he was falling in love with her. She'd also gotten a text from Darren saying: *just tryna see you soon*.

The moment she got the bright idea, her tears dried up within seconds. The first step was to call Peyton from a blocked number. When he surprisingly answered, Brielle told him to meet her at his house. She told him that something had come up and she would be leaving to go back to Atlanta in the morning.

Luckily, Peyton agreed to meet her there. She was hoping that his mother really was in the hospital. She had something important to do and she didn't want to do it with his mother there. After they hung up, Brielle began to pace the floor.

"Bitch, must you be so stupid? You ain't even known this man two months and you bought him a damn Rolex. Janay is right, you are so gullible," the voice in her head sounded.

At that moment, Brielle rushed back down the stairs pretending to act normal. When she re-entered the kitchen, Janay noticed that her face had turned a fiery reddish tone.

"What the hell is wrong with you?"

"Hot flashes. Girl, I need your car. I need some tampons."

"You mean my Lexus? I don't let anybody drive my shit," Janay returned.

"Stop showing off. Where are the keys? I'll be right back."

"The keys are in my purse, and you better put some gas in it, rich lady," Janay joked. Deep inside, Janay hated that Brielle's was about to be paid from Dante's death.

"Oh, where are those pills you were taking last week for insomnia? The one's that knocked you out cold," Brielle questioned.

Janay seemed puzzled. "In my purse, why?"

"I've been restless lately, and was wondering if I could borrow some."

"You're not supposed to take other people's prescriptions. You tripping," Janay replied.

Brielle was running out of patience. "Janay please, I just need some sleep not a damn lecture."

Even though Janay was skeptical, she agreed. "Alright, but don't say I didn't warn your dumb-ass. Those pills aren't to be played with. Shit, the side effects are powerful- hallucinations and they'll put you out, quick. Hell, you already crazy as hell."

When Brielle shot her a look, Janay smiled. "Just kidding."

"Oh, and I need to stop by the mall, too. Shopping always makes me feel better."

"Look, just have my shit back in a few hours, and it better not be one scratch on it," Janay replied.

Brielle said goodbye, noticing that two other women had shown up since she'd gone upstairs. They all looked like rich housewives or mistresses of rich men. Each and every one had an expensive bag, manicured nails, and jewelry that looked like it all cost thousands per piece.

They gotta be high-class prostitutes, Brielle thought.

She wanted to pull Janay to the side, but decided against it. Instead, she left the house doing sixty in a thirty-five. On her way, Brielle stopped by the store and purchased a large scented candle, and a small pack of baby wipes. Next stop- the liquor store, where she rushed in to buy a bottle of wine.

Like a race-car driver, she jetted to the mall, parked Janay's car, and ran in to buy an outfit. She bought herself an outfit and something for Janay as well. Going to the mall and purchasing clothes was only an alibi to show her whereabouts...nothing more. After putting the bags in the back seat, she called Peyton again with her number blocked and told him to pick her while Janay was still shopping.

When Peyton pulled up ten minutes later, it seemed the word liar had been spray painted across his forehead. Brielle motioned for him to open the door for her, as she had tons of items in her hand. Peyton reached over, opened the door from the inside, and grinned extra hard when she got in.

"You know I couldn't let you leave without giving you some one more time. I wouldn't want you stepping out on me so early in our relationship," Peyton said, with a cheesy grin.

It took a lot to hold her composure. "I doubt if I'll be stepping out on you," Brielle admitted seductively. "I'm starting to fall in love with you... so I figured we might want to get married one day." She rubbed his neck which was very tense as he continued driving.

"Well-l-l-l-l-l-l," Peyton stuttered. "I'm not interested in getting married. Now, that I think about it, maybe we are moving a little fast," he said with conviction.

"You think so? Okay, then I'll fall back a little. Actually, I'll give you some space. Let's just go to your place," she said, in a crazed tone, followed by a blank stare. I need to fuck. Hard."

Is this bitch crazy? Peyton asked himself. He was unsure if Brielle was being honest or if she really had a few mental issues. He remained quiet and drove with speed to his mother's house.

❦Chapter 10❧

Peyton sensed that something was wrong with Brielle. They'd been inside his mother's house many days where she was hesitant about even moving off the couch. Yet today, out of the blue she danced around in the middle of the living room floor listening to old Luther tunes, and taunting him with her exposed, hardened nipples.

It had to have been the wine. She'd drank two glasses in front of him, and possibly some before he picked her up at the mall. Her whole demeanor was different and had been over the last hour.

"Drink," she told Peyton, standing above him trying to force the ridge of the glass into his mouth.

He sipped, then whipped his tongue out like a snake, hoping that his obedience would get him some ass. Brielle was already half-naked with no bra on at all, accompanied by some tight crop pants, and heels. She looked sexy as hell from where Peyton sat, so his patience had run out.

"Let me run to the bathroom. Be ready when I get back," he teased.

Brielle knew he was probably speeding off to find a condom. But there was no need. He would never fuck again if she had anything to do with it. The moment that he was out of her sight, Brielle sprung into action.

With force, she crushed six of Janay's Zolpidem pills, enough to put a horse out, and mixed them into his glass of red wine. When Peyton returned, Brielle rushed to his side again.

"I missed you," she said rubbing up against him. She then rubbed the back of his head.

"Damn, I just left." He grinned at her comment and at the feel of his manhood expanding in his pants.

"Drink," she said, picking up the glass and pushing it toward his lips.

Peyton drank, then kissed Brielle sensually. He drank again. And again. And again.

"You want me," she said lifting her glass from the table, and taking a sip.

"D-a-a-a-m-n, str-ai-i-i-ght," he slurred.

Brielle grinned devilishly. Only fifteen minutes had gone by and she'd already had him where she wanted him.

"Whoa, I'm feeling a little woozy."

Peyton stumbled back, allowing the back of his knees to rub against the couch. His eye sight became blurry within minutes, yet his focus remained on Brielle's breast rubbing against his chest.

"Ooh, b-a-b-y that feels g-o-o-d."

"I know," Brielle mumbled as she massaged affectionately.

The moment he leaned backwards, Brielle gave him an extra push, with both of them landing on the couch.

Brielle giggled like a woman on top of her man, while Peyton could barely keep his eyes open. Brielle knew it was time. She straddled him and removed his white, extra starched shirt, while talking dirty to him the whole time. When she stopped getting a response, the voice called out.

"Get the baby oil, stupid."

Brielle hopped up, grabbed the bottle of baby oil from her bag, and rubbed it all over his skin. "Liars deserve to be burned to a crisp," the voice sounded abruptly.

Brielle rubbed intensely. Faster and faster. Her eyes reddened and memories from her past invaded her mind. As Peyton fell into a deep sleep, Brielle lost control of her plan. Something…someone…had a tight grip on her mind. She sat in the middle of the floor crying like a baby while Peyton slept like one. She thought about her mother, the day she beat her to a pulp for dropping the carton of eggs all over the floor.

"Get up bitch!" the voice said.

Brielle continued to cry, but finally hopped up, ready to execute her original plan. With speed, she removed the Rolex watch from Peyton's wrist and spit directly in his face. She grabbed him by the collar, asking him "Why," repeatedly. "You live with your fuckin' wife! And you lied to me! You lied!" she screamed. "Why the fuck do all men lie!"

He was gone. Didn't move at all.

Quickly, she unzipped his pants and squeezed the rest of the baby oil into the hole of his boxers, and onto his limp penis.

Brielle quickly switched into clean up mode. It was already after eight, and the sun had almost set completely. There was no way she would allow another police officer to ask her questions about a death. First came the glasses. She washed the glasses that they drank vigorously, and put them back into the cabinet. Next, the candle. She lit the candle and knocked it off the coffee table purposefully. Lastly, the fire. It started the moment the candle's flame caught the carpet fibers. It took a few minutes for the fire to catch the way she wanted, but she was indeed satisfied.

Brielle bent down and used the lighter to set Peyton's pants on fire. As his pants caught fire she gathered all her things and ran to the back door, hoping she hadn't forgotten anything. Carefully, Brielle took out a baby wipe and opened the door slowly.

She walked from his back yard through another yard behind his house. Although it was dark, her senses said someone was watching.

Brielle crossed the street and walked about a quarter of a mile down the road. As soon as she'd made it to a main road, Brielle threw the empty bottle of wine into an open trash bin next to a bus stop. She was thinking ahead just in case an autopsy was ordered.

It didn't take long for her to hail a cab back to the mall. She'd carefully chosen a drop off point near the entrance, and decided to walk through like the others to the parking garage.

The drive was serene for the first ten minutes. What she had done didn't really hit her until she was only five minutes away from Janay's place. Her adrenaline still pumped, yet she appeared to be in a daze.

As soon as she was safely inside, her hands shook. She sat down on one of Janay's wobbly chairs in the kitchen and began talking to herself. She thought back over the scene back at Peyton's, hoping it was a clean job.

She couldn't believe she'd committed murder again, sending her into a frenzy. She paced the floor calling out to Janay, knowing she wasn't home. Finally, she came to her senses. She snatched the phone from the base and called Janay on her cell phone.

"What's up Brielle? You back home from shopping?" Janay asked, sounding tipsy. "How's my damn car?"

"I'm home and your car is fine. Where are you?" Brielle asked, trying to hide her upset mood. She could hear the loud music blasting in the background.

"I'm out handling some business? What's wrong?"

"I'm a little upset, thinking about Dante, can you come and get me?" She sat down at the table, and started digging her nails into her skin.

"No, but I can send a car to pick you up. Come to where I am. And when you get here, don't be acting all scary and stuck up. You hear me?" Janay shouted.

"I hear you."

"And wear something sexy. You can't get in unless you're a hottie." She laughed.

Chapter 11

It didn't take Brielle long to shake her nervous state of mind. Two drinks later, she'd stopped the shivering, taken a quick shower, and thrown on a baby blue Marc Jacobs mini dress with a sexy pair of Enzo pumps.

Before she could even apply her make-up, a black Jaguar with a driver pulled up to the house and blew the horn. Moments later, Brielle got inside and rode for about thirty minutes before pulling up to a circular driveway of an enormous brick mansion. Brielle stepped out in awe. She looked great, not like a woman who'd just killed someone.

When the butler opened the door, he took Brielle to a large room where a social event was taking place. Janay grinned, waved her over, and introduced her to the small group of people that were there listening to a pianist play. There were only white men in the room whom all looked like pedophiles. One of them called Janay over out of the blue and whispered in her ear.

When she finished talking to the man with two strands of stringy hair hanging over his forehead, she walked back over to Brielle. "Listen cuz, that man over there wants to have a private hour with you. He will pay five thousand for the hour. I get two of that five." Janay's expression verified that she was serious.

"What? Oh hell no Janay, I'm about to have all the money I need soon. What would I do that for?" She looked over at the old, stringy-haired man who grinned at her with a naughty look.

"Brielle, it starts at five, and then the more he requests you, the more money you will get later on," Janay said persuasively.

"I don't need money. I wouldn't let that shriveled up man touch my pinky, let alone my pussy!"

"Look Brielle, this is my business, you better not mess up my business. Stop acting like you so upper class, you come from the ghetto girl," she whispered in Brielle's ear.

Brielle looked at her cousin. "So, this is what you do?" When Janay didn't respond she kept going. "Look, I have let my past ruin my life and money won't fix it. I have money coming. I don't need some strange man breathing in my ear and humping on me." She paused to look Janay in the eye again. "You should've told me this shit over the phone and I wouldn't have even wasted my time."

The old man was still smiling, waiting.

"I wasn't gonna tell you at all because I know you're not strong enough to handle this type of business. The salary that I make at the PR firm is not enough and since all of the clients there are rich, I do this side hustle and it's great pay."

Brielle shook her head in disbelief.

"Oh, now you're judging me? You try to play like you are a goody goody, but I know the truth. Dante is not your first victim."

Brielle froze.

"Janay, what the hell are you talking about?"

"Listen, I don't have time to be your counselor, you need a real one chick. Go back outside and tell the driver to take you back home. I'll see you later."

Janay left the room in an instant. And it took nearly five seconds for Brielle to head back toward the front door.

Back in the car, she silently cried uncontrollably, hoping the driver would mind his business. She needed to go back to Jersey, but also wanted to see if the death of Peyton would be on the nightly news.

Janay knew she was dating Peyton so Brielle didn't know how Janay would act when she heard about his death. The best plan was to stay a few more days so that Janay wouldn't get suspicious. Janay already told her that she felt that Brielle killing Dante was no accident. She wanted to talk to someone badly, but didn't know who to call. She picked up the phone and called Darren.

"Hello?" he said in a surprised tone.

"Hi, Darren," she said desperately.

"Hey, Brielle, I've been thinking about you. Did Janay tell you that I called?"

"No, Janay doesn't tell me anything. She's got too many tricks up her sleeve."

"How are you doing? Janay told me that you had met someone in Atlanta who you were getting serious with and that's why you haven't answered my calls."

"No, I did meet someone but it didn't go anywhere." The voice jumped out at her. "Brielle, it did go somewhere. Well, it did go up in flames." The voice laughed. Then Brielle laughed lightly.

"So, when do I get my chance?" Darren questioned.

"I don't know. I don't know about you men."

"Brielle, every man is not the same," he said sincerely, as he flipped through some pictures that they took in Aruba together.

"I will let you know when I come back okay, I'm tired. I was just thinking about you and called to say hello. I'll be home soon, I'll call you then."

"You sure?" he asked, sounding like a beggar.

"Okay, in the meantime, I want you to know that I've been thinking about you. I've been concerned; and I'm here for you. If you need to talk, call me," he persuaded.

"Okay, thank you. Goodnight," she ended softly.

"Goodnight."

Yes, Darren was on the case, but he was not lying to her. He was starting to believe that she had not killed her husband intentionally, like Monique Troy had claimed. She seemed like a good person who just had a troubled soul. A soul he wanted badly to take care of.

Early the next morning, Brielle woke up in a panic. Sweat stuck to her backside as she ran from the guestroom to the kitchen. Janay was in the kitchen preparing for work.

"So, how long have you been a madam?"

"I'm a pimp, shit. A chick with balls." She poured Brielle some tea, as a grin slipped from the side of her tightened lips.

"Yeah, but Janay, what if you get caught up?"

Janay smiled. "Believe me, I have information on each and every one of them fuckas. I've got it covered, trust me. They are indebted to me, believe me." She checked her cell phone and threw it in her bag.

"Janay, what I saw last night was enough for me."

"That's why I keep my mouth shut. I don't talk the talk, I just walk the walk." When her house phone rang moments later, Janay snatched it. "Hello... what? Get outta here! Are you serious? Wowwwwww. Okay." She hung up and looked at Brielle strangely.

"What is it?" Brielle knew what Janay was about to say.

"I don't know how to tell you this, but Peyton died in a house fire last night." She put her plate in the sink and allowed her eyes to scan Brielle's demeanor.

"What? You can't be serious? Oh my God! What is it? Everyone I care for dies." She shook her head and paused. "But then again, God don't like ugly," she said, which gave Janay a strange thought after Brielle made that comment.

"Are you celebrating another death Brielle?" Janay stopped what she was doing and looked at her cousin for a reply.

"No, I'm just saying, God don't like ugly."

"Okay, well, you were at the mall last night, right?"

"What are you saying, I set the fire? C'mon Janay, I didn't even know he was married, how would I know where he lived?"

"Yeah, right, bitch?"

"No, really. I didn't care about him like that. I was mad that he led me on and lied, but I wouldn't want him dead, I barely knew the man," she said without giving Janay eye contact.

Janay still seemed leery, bur decided to drop the subject. "Well, I gotta go. Call me later."

As soon as Janay left for work, Brielle made herself some breakfast. Brielle's cell phone rang. It was an Atlanta number.

"Hello?" she answered nervously.

"Yes, may I ask who I'm speaking with?" the voice asked.

"Who am I speaking with? You called my phone."

"This is Detective Lowell, Atlanta PD."

Her heart raced. She knew that she had blocked her number right before seeing Peyton. She figured they may have gotten his phone records to see who he may have spoken to recently.

"Oh, my name is Brielle."

"Well, do you know a Peyton Rowe?"

"Yes, I do."

"Can you tell me what your relationship is with him?"

"We're friends. That's it." She knew she could lie easily over the phone.

"Have you seen him lately?"

"I saw him the other day, in passing. Why, what's going on?"

"Well, Mr. Rowe died in a fire last night and we're just trying to talk to people he knew, to rule out any foul play, like arson. I might call you back again if I have any further questions?"

"Oh my God, that's terrible. Of course you can call."

"Thank you," the detective said innocently.

"No problem," she said firmly. Yet she hung up and cried hysterically.

❧ Chapter 12 ❧

Brielle tossed and turned as she slept, drifting from one bad dream to another. Her memories took her back more than twenty years where she and her mother were sitting at the table waiting for her father to come in for dinner. Young Brielle began to get nervous as her mother watched the clock and waited for her father to show up. She was very hungry and didn't want to wait because it was near 9:00 p.m., and she knew that he wouldn't be coming anytime soon. "Mommy, maybe Daddy had to do something?" she said innocently.

"Do what? Or do who? Dorothy? He's probably having dinner with Dorothy."

"Mommy, don't be sad. Maybe he had to do something with Uncle Chuck." She tried to calm her mother's nerves.

"Oh yeah? Well, since everyone is more important than us, I guess he won't have anything to eat when he comes home. And you won't either. She started taking the pots of food toward the garbage and throwing it away bit by bit. Brielle started crying.

"Mommy, please, I'm hungry!" she shouted as her stomach growled.

"Is that so? Okay, well here you go." Her mother reached into the pot of mashed potatoes and smeared a handful all over Brielle's face.

Brielle jumped up and started running from the kitchen, but her mother quickly pursued her. Within minutes, she'd grabbed the frying pan out of the sink and pushed Brielle onto the living room floor. Brielle screamed and covered her head as her mother beat *her arms and legs ruthlessly.*

She screamed, "You stupid bitch! You don't tell me what to do with my food that I paid for! You're as worthless as your father." She continued to beat her until Brielle's arms and legs were swollen and black and blue. Brielle's pleading for her mother did not stop her. When she was out of breath and tired of swinging she walked back into the kitchen, threw the pan back in the sink, and sat back at the kitchen table to smoke a cigarette.

Soon, her dreams took a turn for the worse. Brielle saw herself as a young girl, just a year older, yet not more than eleven. She sat in a rowboat on a deserted lake with someone familiar, but couldn't see his face. Although his back faced her, she knew he was older. His voice was deeper than most, and the hairs on his face scared her even more. Without warning, the boy stood up and began rocking the boat back and forth maliciously. Brielle screamed for her mother. But no rescue came. Her mother had deliberately sent her with him even though Brielle protested. She'd told her mother the things he'd done to her, and how he made her feel, but to no avail she was alone with him once again.

Out of the blue, the boy stood, unzipped his pants and told Brielle that he would tip the boat over if she didn't stick his dick into her mouth. She panicked. Then called out for her mother again. Again, no one was in sight. Brielle fought hard as the hefty boy grabbed her by the hands and pushed her frail body to the bottom of the boat yanking at her pants.

"Nooooooo!" she screamed as she tossed and turned. "Get off!"

They tossed and tussled as Brielle prayed to God for help. Finally she was able to pull herself up. She stood in the middle of the boat and firmly gained her balance pretending to open her mouth wide. As soon as he charged her again, ready for his sexual pleasure she pushed with all her might. He fell...backwards off of the boat, and into the murky water.

The sound of the splash woke Brielle up instantly followed by Janay bursting through the bedroom door, singing "I Ain't Saying She's a Gold Digger."

Brielle stretched then asked, "Why are you so damn-happy?"

"Because I'm going to Houston in exactly five hours. It's 10:00 a.m. and you're still sleeping. Get up." Janay tapped Brielle's hip beneath the covers. "If you weren't so stuck up, you could go to Houston, too." She shot Brielle a smirk.

Brielle sat quietly letting Janay know it was a possibility. Deep inside, she wanted to get away. The Peyton situation really had her on edge. "I gave the insurance company your address so they could forward my check. I've been waiting for weeks, so maybe I should stay here."

"Stay if you like, crazy girl. What company do you think would send the killer the check?" Janay stopped fiddling with her long, colorful fingernails, and gave Brielle a funny stare.

"What?" Brielle's mouth hung open.

"You know I'm playing." Janay gave off a plastic smile. "Get packed if you going. I'll charge you a ticket in a few minutes. No need in staying in the ATL."

As soon as the ladies arrived in Houston, Janay started trouble. They ended up at Scott Gertner's Skybar, a rooftop club that was supposed to be a hot spot. There appeared to be many well-off men in the place and Janay was checking around to see who she could scout out.

"What's up Brielle, you game yet to make some money?"

"Janay, I have money coming," Brielle responded, using her proper voice. "Don't bother me with that bullshit again," Brielle said disgustedly.

"It's not about the money, it's about the game. These sorry-ass men need to be taken for whatever they're worth." She downed her drink. "You're so fuckin' goody two-shoe. It makes me sick. Play the game, bitch. Play the game!"

"Well, that's a game that I'm not interested in playing."

"Since when did your crazy ass become righteous? You need to go and see a shrink instead of trying to analyze situations."

Janay walked away, while Brielle watched her scout the two men at the bar. After about a half hour of drinking, Janay was grabbing her purse, and saying her goodbyes as if she were leaving with the men.

As they walked out one of the men said, "Aren't you going to tell your cousin that you're leaving?"

"She can see that with her own eyes. I asked her if she wanted to dabble."

"She said no?" the younger gentleman asked, while examining Brielle.

"Yep. C'mon. Don't worry about her, I can handle the two of you. But it's going to cost you double since I have to satisfy you both."

"How much are we talking about?" one of them asked. "Cause we might need to convince your cousin. She's beautiful. The long, full hair, the petite frame, and my favorite, the red lipstick."

"Listen, she killed one of our cousins when we were smaller, but she doesn't remember. Now, if you want to possibly get shanked tonight, let's call her over."

Both guys glared into Janay's face, realizing she was serious. Neither said a word, just looked on in shock.

Janay leaned over to whisper something in the shorter guy's ear. They both turned to look at Brielle as Janay continued to whisper. When she was done she clarified the amount. "I'll stay with you guys 'til the morning for fifteen hundred a piece, and then you can deduct the three hundred after what we discussed is done."

"Wow, what you gonna do for that much money?"

"It's like T.I. said, 'You can have whatever you like'," she sang and started laughing. "I pride myself on knowing how to show successful men a good time since they work so hard. So, if the price is out of your league, let me know now." She stopped and got ready to turn back toward the bar.

"We got you baby," the other man cautioned. She moved his hand away.

"Listen, I'm not a whore. I'm a business woman with a great commodity, and I will not be disrespected." Janay held her hand out. "I want my money up front." Janay was very drunk and her speech became more slurred as she walked.

"Hey. Hey. C'mon now. Let's go to your room," the older gentleman grinned, showing Janay a sneak peek of the stack holding down his pant pocket.

Within minutes, the threesome had left the bar without Janay ever officially telling Brielle where she'd gone.

As Brielle was about to get up and go to her hotel room, a desperate looking man walked over.

"Hello, beautiful." He sat down just three feet away.

"I'm sorry, but I'm not interested." Brielle turned her head in the other direction.

"Interested in what? I just wanted to buy you a drink." She got ready to decline his offer, but decided to be nice and accept one drink from the guy. She wasn't ready to go back to the hotel just yet.

"Oh, I'm sorry. You can get me a screwdriver, a vodka and orange juice."

The man walked away and came back with two drinks, which was the last thing Brielle recalled. When she woke up later on that night, she was naked and in a cheap hotel room with the stranger sleeping next to her. It was crazy how she knew nothing about him, not even his name. She knew that he must've drugged her. He must've put something in her drink and walked her out of the club before she was totally passed out.

She thought about calling the police and having him arrested, but he probably would say that she had gone freely after having drinks with him. It would be her word against his. She had no idea who he was and how she had gotten there. For the third time, she had been forced to take matters into her own hands.

She noticed that there was an open dollar bill on the night stand that had drugs in it and an open bottle of liquor. Brielle grabbed the bottle and broke it on the edge of the nightstand loudly. The stranger jumped up, but unable to protect himself before Brielle lunged, cutting his throat like a professional hitwoman. She jabbed the broken end of the bottle into his neck and twisted it from side to side, while drooling from the mouth at the site of the blood. His eyes nearly exploded, feeling her slice him like a can opener. Blood squirting, he made a few gurgling sounds before his eyes closed permanently.

"You raped the wrong bitch, Motherfucka," Brielle said quietly, watching his body jerk for the last time.

As his sounds faded, Brielle ran into the bathroom, quickly washed the blood from her hands, and walked out of the room as if she'd done nothing. Once outside the door, she wrapped the bloody bottle top in a washcloth and slipped it in her bag to dispose of later. Within seconds, she'd walked a few blocks from the hotel with her head downward before hailing a cab back to her own hotel. She was furious and scared all at the same time.

Brielle couldn't believe what had happened to her. All she wanted to do was get away and have some peace of mind and she ended up the victim. At that moment the light bulb came on. She wondered if Janay set her up. "Nooooo," she said to herself loudly.

"Yessssss," her inner voice sounded.

Brielle felt confused and decided she would ask Janay about leaving her. When she got back to the room, she banged on the door crazily wondering why Janay wouldn't let her inside. "Open the damn door, Janay! I hear you," she shouted.

Janay heard the knock on the door, but ignored it. She was in the middle of a sandwich, her favorite position. Janay lay flat on her back on top of gentleman number one gyrating him while he was inside of her anally. Gentleman number two was inside of her vagina, moving in stride. Janay had no intention of stopping, because to her she was in paradise. And getting paid for it. She figured Brielle was coming to ruin her party so she shouted, "Come back in thirty!" She laughed crazily.

The next morning, Brielle awoke early, finding herself in the lobby on a couch near the bar. She stretched, then turned to see if anyone was nearby watching her. In a dash, she'd gotten up, and rushed upstairs with an attitude only to find the door wide open.

Janay was nowhere to be found. Brielle packed her bag in three minutes flat hoping no danger would come to her.

She'd already booked a flight from Texas to New Jersey the night before, and figured that whatever was at Janay's she could send for later. *If the bitch is still breathing*, she thought.

Within ten minutes flat, Brielle found herself in a cab, at a light next to a nice black family; a mother and father with a son and daughter. She wished that she had what that woman had. All she ever wanted was a family. All she ever wanted was to be loved. At that moment she decided anyone who'd ever hurt her would pay...even Janay.

Chapter 13

Back in Jersey, at one o'clock in the morning, nestled deep in darkness, Brielle sweated like a disgruntled pig. The graveyard was where she stood in the midst of the gloomy field where her mother's dead body was laid to rest. With each thrust into the dirt she struggled to dig deeper. Her eyes were glued to the shovel, yet her mind was somewhere far away. Somewhere back in time; a time where her mother abused her regularly. A time where her life was destroyed. Tonight, her hope was to dig deep, deep enough to resume her body and beat her into another life.

With her hands wrapped tightly around the newly pur-chased shovel, she vowed to dig until the morning light, hoping to resurrect her mother's grave. She'd decided that she had words to share with her late mother; some things that needed to be taken care of. The frown on her face had been planted for hours as thoughts played back in her mind of her childhood. She'd returned from Texas just hours ago after having a meltdown on the plane. It was another bad dream, one where her fellow airline passengers knew something was deeply wrong.

Brielle cried loudly into the darkness, throwing dirt all around as the dream replayed once again.

Her mother was talking to Aunt Janelle on the phone and young Brielle listened closely.

"Janelle I'm not like you. I don't feel for Brielle, the way you feel about Janay. I don't know what it is. Maybe I just wasn't meant to be a mother. I don't feel that motherly thing."

"Don't say that, Sis," Janelle shot back.

"Hell, it's true. I should've listened to Johnny when he said not to have the baby. We probably would've still been happy. It's all her fault."

Janelle instantly became quiet. "Shhh, Brielle may hear you."

"Who cares! I just wish I had never had her. You want her? Cause if not, I'm thinking about giving her ass up for adoption."

The thought of her mother spitting those words from her mouth sent Brielle into a frenzy. Her heart rate increased as she sobbed uncontrollably and drove the shovel deeper. Tears fell into the two foot hole she'd created giving her even more motivation. And even the site of the corner of a black coffin made her smile.

Suddenly, that smile turned into a frown. The lights flashed and Brielle instantly froze. Brielle's first thought was to check her car that had been parked near the exit. It seemed to be fine, untouched and ready for her escape if needed. Her eyes widened as she re-focused on the small truck as it drove along the path leading to the gravesites. The bright, shiny lights held her captive. *Who in the hell would come to a graveyard at one o'clock in the morning?* Brielle thought. She continued to throw questions at herself while running for cover.

With speed, she dropped the shovel and darted behind a tall headstone, near the back fence just yards from her creative work. Brielle's eyes grew drastically as she measured the distance between her car, the exit, and the position of the truck that had suddenly stopped.

The situation had her on urge wondering who the driver was and why he was there. From afar, it seemed as if he were reading from a paper. Brielle took advantage of the situation and tip-toed her way over near the pavement. As she crossed each grave, she shouted her frustrations of not being able to finish digging up her mother's grave. "It's something that must be done," she told herself, rushing toward her car near the bottom of the hill.

With each huff, she prayed she wouldn't hear the start of the truck's engine. All was going well, until she stuck her key in the door, and the lights blinked from the truck pulling closely behind her.

When Brielle arrived home, uneasiness took over her body. There was a feeling of emptiness; and most importantly death in the house. It was bad enough that she'd spent an extra hour pleading to the overnight worker at Harmony Graveyard. He'd pulled up behind her, saw Brielle crying, and listened to her plead her case as to why she had entered the facility after hours.

Luckily, the shovel had been ditched near the fence, and she had cleaned the dirt that splattered her cheeks. Brielle recited a fake name for her deceased relative and prayed he wouldn't get a good look at her license plate once someone saw the damage she'd done the following morning. The graveyard incident was just the beginning of her mental meltdown.

Everything seemed to be going wrong, and her emotions had collapsed. She wondered how her best friend, Dante had turned into her arch rival; how their love had turned to hate. And how her mother had betrayed the bond between a mother and a daughter.

On the ride home she had already decided to block her mother from her mind, forever. Now it was time to put Dante to rest, the only way she knew how. It took hours, but Brielle managed to remove all of Dante's belongings to the garage in a huge pile. She'd even stopped for a few minutes to make an important call.

It didn't take long for her to get the sanitation department and the Salvation Army on the line telling them about her new pile of junk. Both were to send a pickup truck out that day, before five o'clock. Of course that meant staying home all day. Yet getting rid of Dante's memories seemed worth the wait. She already worked for nearly six hours, and there was plenty more work to do. Quickly, she gained momentum again. Brielle rampaged through the house frantically, removing exercise equipment, clothing, personal items, electronics; simply anything to do with her ex.

Pacing through the living room, Brielle spotted something

that couldn't be resisted. She decided to grab their wedding album from the shelf. As soon as the first page was turned, tears began to flow, and gushed for hours. It caused so many mixed emotions that Brielle found herself walking through the house with her wedding dress on. She pranced for minutes admiring the sleeveless, elegant styled dress with the satin beaded train. Every now and then she would grab hold of the train, pretending to lift the material from the floor as she was serenaded by Dante.

Step by step visions of the ceremony from start to finish infiltrated her mind. Then the next step was the alcohol, which she knew would send her emotions on a mission. This was one of many emotional rides she'd been on throughout her life; yet most had gone unnoticed by others.

In the kitchen cabinet, Brielle managed to find the last bottle of champagne that was left from their big day. It had a youthful picture of both she and Dante taped to the bottle, a gift from the photographer who'd taken the wedding photos. Brielle studied the bottle for minutes, switching from smiles to frowns over and over again.

Finally, she popped the bottle and poured it into one of the monogrammed champagne glasses they'd also received as a gift. Slowly, almost in a mesmerized state, she walked into her living room, and turned the Ipod system on. As the music played lightly, Brielle drank and glared at the over-sized African Art portraits on each wall as well as a picture of the wedding party.

Once again, she smiled. But crazily. Next thing she knew, she'd located all the songs from their wedding reception, and danced an imaginary first dance as each song played lightly in the background.

When *You and I* by Jodeci started, Brielle became extra emotional. She leaned back as if Dante himself were dipping her in the middle of the floor. She lifted herself back up and kissed the air as if she were kissing his lips. Things spiraled down hill quicker than expected. Her arms were suddenly wrapped around her own body as she squeezed a tight hug, like a circus act. Oddly, there were no tears, simply joy from the memory of someone wanting to marry her.

Brielle danced and reminisced for nearly three hours. She'd finally faced the fact that he was gone. In order for her to move forward, she'd have to let go of the ill feelings in her heart. Brielle had made the decision that it was time to say goodbye and put Dante to rest forever. He'd wasted enough of her life while he was alive, and she wasn't about to allow him to torment her in death.

Abruptly, Brielle turned off the music, removed the wedding dress and added it to the large *Dante pile* in the garage. Standing at the doorway to the garage, Brielle realized she wore panties and a matching bra, compliments of Dante. But it too had to go. Every memory of Dante had to go. Within seconds, she'd taken the bra and panties off then threw them on top of the pile as well.

She stood ass-naked, staring at what she considered garbage thinking about every memory she'd ever shared with that man. Seconds later, Brielle walked back into the living room and turned the television set up extra loud to override any thoughts that might enter her mind about her late husband. She felt a break-down coming and knew she needed help. It was that chemical imbalance again…the one she knew existed. Her intuition said call Janay. The voice said, "No! Invite Monique over."

Brielle lifted the receiver. She called her aunt.

"Aunt Nelly, I need you to be honest with me about something," she said when her aunt answered the phone.

"Yes baby, what about?"

"When I was young, did you ever have a phone conversation with my mother where she told you that she wished that she didn't have me, and that she couldn't love me like you love Janay?"

Her aunt stuttered before slipping into silence.

"Aunt Nelly, you can tell me. I had a dream about that conversation and I feel like I really heard that when I was little."

Janelle still didn't respond.

"Aunt Nelly, please. I already know that my mother didn't love me but I just want to make sure I'm not going crazy, please tell me."

"Yes baby," her aunt started crying, "And I'm so sorry. I asked her to let me take you plenty of times, but she thought that

Johnny would leave her for sure if you came to live with me."

"So, I was just a pawn? To my own mother?" She stared out of her kitchen window playing with the hairs on her pussy. "You know she used to abuse me, right?"

"Brielle, the past is the past, let it go baby. Dante is gone. He can no longer hurt you and neither can your mother. Love yourself baby."

Brielle listened to her aunt cry on the other end while she wiped the tears falling from her very own eyes.

"Why you crying, Aunt Nelly?"

"You've been through so much, baby. Some things I'm sure you remember. Other things I'm not so sure," she added in a bizarre tone.

"Aunt Nelly, whatever that means, keep it to yourself," Brielle responded hesitantly. "I can't take anymore. I'll be okay sooner or later."

"Yes, you will. You just have to make the best of your life now and move forward. I love you, Brielle."

"Me, too." Brielle hung up the phone thanking God for her aunt. The only person who seemed to care for her.

She wiped her tears and quickly tried to switch to a new attitude. First, she started with slipping on a pair of shorts, and an old t-shirt stopping near her navel. Brielle decided to rearrange her home to help bury the past. It took hours but she managed to move furniture, and replace curtains and trimmings with ones that were being stored in her closets. She decided to throw most of the old curtains onto the big pile of garbage in the garage, never to be used again.

Soon, the house had taken on a slightly new look and was becoming a home again. She realized that she had really been unhappy for a long time, but had ignored the truth way too long. Brielle stopped momentarily to scan the living room, and breathe a sigh of relief at what she'd accomplished. The makeover seemed to please her, but not that inner voice. "This is bullshit," the voice sounded.

At the same moment her doorbell rang. She shook her head swiftly in an attempt to ignore what she'd just heard. Brielle proceeded to the door, opened it, and saw the most gorgeous hunk of a man standing on the other side.

He was from the sanitation department and although he was in a dirty uniform, she could tell that he was a diamond in the rough, and would shine with some fresh gear on. He was beautiful. He was about 6'4 and about 280 pounds resembling a body builder. His long, thick braids attracted her the most and kept her from saying anything to the gentleman.

"Mrs. Prescott?" he questioned.

"Yes, that's me." She looked him up and down from head to toe in an exaggerated way so he would know that she liked what she saw.

"We're here to remove your garbage."

"Okay, well, it's in the garage. And please pardon the mess. My husband passed away and I'm trying to start over. I kind of just threw all of his stuff in a pile," she said apologetically.

"Well, Miss, I'm sorry to hear that. It's okay. We'll take care of it."

"I'll meet you at the garage door," she said, noticing his freshly trimmed beard and moustache.

"Tell'em you'll meet him in your room. Or are you scared?" the voice asked. "Yeah that's it, you always have been worthless."

Brielle hit herself in the head in an attempt to get the voice to stop. She ran faster than she even imagined to grab a comb, hoping to smooth out her four-week-old wavy weave that had lost most of its curls. She wanted to look her best; even pulled lip gloss from her purse.

When her hand pushed the button to the automatic garage door, it didn't take long for it to open and for Mr. Right to appear again. She didn't know how, but knew that she had to have that man. He looked too strong, and too handsome to be single.

When the door was completely up she saw his face again. He looked like the model, Tyson Beckford, but way manlier and more built. He was standing there with two other men who paled in comparison. They were invisible next to the "Mandingo Warrior."

"I'm Shawn by the way," he said, introducing himself formerly.

The three men walked into the garage and started picking up Dante's belongings, moving the items to the truck. Brielle looked at Shawn from the corner of her eye to see if he was checking her out. Sadly, he didn't appear to be. After they had made about four trips back and forth without Shawn even looking in her direction, Brielle retreated back into the house. She knew they would be at least a half hour so she went in the kitchen to waste time.

"Masturbate, bitch!" the voice said.

Brielle pressed her hands against her eyes hoping to make the voice go away.

"No, really. You can't keep a man. Why not just fuck yourself?"

Again, Brielle rushed to turn the television up to block out the sounds. About twenty minutes later, there was a knock on the front door. When she opened it up, Shawn was on the porch wearing a warm smile. Even with the sweat rolling down his burly face, he looked good enough to eat.

"Okay. We're done Miss. It was nice meeting you." He paused. "Here's my number if you ever want to talk. I lost my wife two years ago in a car accident, so I know how lonely that can be."

"Oh, I'm sorry to hear that. Thank you," Brielle said modestly. "I will definitely give you a call. Would you guys like some iced tea or something?"

"Uh, no thanks, we have a lot of jobs today and we're kinda behind schedule. But make that call, beautiful."

"Okay Shawn, I will," Brielle said, smiling seductively.

She watched him walk away and get behind the wheel of the sanitation truck and drive off. "Uhm uhm uhm, I'm ready for my new beginning and I want him to be in it," she told herself as she was closing the door. She noticed her neighbor, Talia, walking up the driveway with her baby. She walked up onto Brielle's porch.

"Hey Momma, how are you?" she asked Talia.

"Girl, I'm having a rough day. Nigga problems."

Brielle laughed hard. Talia laughed even harder. "That's men for you. They all lie," Brielle replied.

"Hey, that reminds me, a detective came here looking for you not too long ago. He gave me his card; it's in the house, I have to find it. He was asking me where you were, and said that he had some questions for you about Dante. How are you holding up?"

"Girl, it's been up and down. One day I'm good, the next I'm having nightmares. I just don't know. Hopefully the trip did me some good."

"Where did you go? I thought about calling and telling you about the detective, but I didn't want you to be burdened with more stress. You know I don't fuck with police anyway, so I didn't even entertain his conversation. Are they giving you problems?"

"No, girl, they're just doing their job. Had I not defended myself you would've been coming to my funeral. I just did what I had to do and they're just doing what they gotta do. I was visiting with my cousin in Atlanta and then for a few days over the Memorial Day holiday we flew to Aruba for the Soul Beach Music Festival. Let me show you the pictures."

Brielle walked into the kitchen and grabbed her digital camera off the table then walked back toward the porch. She then gave the camera to Talia while Brielle took her son from her arms. Talia started looking at the pictures and then made a jaw dropping expression.

"Oh my God, that's the detective!" Talia yelled.
"Who?" Brielle stopped smiling at the baby to see who Talia was talking about.

At that moment, Talia pointed to Darren in one of the pictures with her and Janay. Even though her blood began to boil, Brielle decided to keep her composure.

"Are you sure?" Brielle asked in disbelief.

"Yes, I'm positive. That's him." Talia pointed her finger at Darren.

Brielle bit her bottom lip to try and calm herself down. "Wow. He tried to act like he was interested in me."

"Brielle, do they think you murdered Dante?" Taila questioned.

"I guess they do."

"Pay him a visit Brielle," the voice stated firmly.

❧ Chapter 14 ❧

Brielle punched the buttons on her cell phone frantically. She'd planned on ignoring Janay's phone calls for a few days to get a breather from her wild cousin, but now her plans had changed. Even though she still wasn't sure if Janay had anything to do with the altercation in Houston, they were still tight and from what she thought, always had each other's back.

Janay answered, "Yeah bitch, I could be dead right now."

"Well, that would be your fault, freak. Anyway, you not gonna believe this! Girl, Darren is a detective!"

"What the fuck? I knew there was something shady about his plain-ass. He was asking too many damn questions about you. That's why I fucked him and put him on you."

Brielle's mouth dropped.

"What? And you didn't tell me? Why are you so damn grimy, Janay? Why wouldn't you tell me?"

"I'm sorry, cuz. Sometimes I get overly horny. But when I realized he really liked you, I had already fucked him. Just so you know, the dick wasn't all that," she sighed then added a sarcastic, "umph."

"Liked me? Shit, he was probably just trying to get information about me and Dante." Brielle's voice trembled slightly. "I hope you didn't say anything off the wall to him about Dante."

"Hell no! Girl, I didn't say anything.

"I can't believe he tried to play on my emotions so that I could incriminate myself."

"What do you mean? How could you incriminate yourself if you didn't do anything wrong?" Janay asked.

"Well, I'm angry and the things that I've been saying about Dante could be taken the wrong way, like you told me yourself," Brielle responded.

Janay instantly stopped talking.

"Janay. You there?" Brielle asked.

"I'm here," Janay said in an odd tone. "So, how did you find out?" she continued.

"My neighbor came over here to tell me that some detective was asking about me. So, when I showed her the pictures from Aruba she was like, "That's him!" Brielle breathed heavily. "I cannot believe this."

"Well, at least you know and didn't start seeing him on some romantic shit. You could've fallen in love with him and told him what really happened."

"What's that supposed to mean?"

Janay ignored Brielle's comment, and continued to rant. "Then he would've ended up throwing you in jail for murder. Now, *that's* a reason to kill somebody," Janay said, with a thunderous laugh. "But don't get any ideas crazy girl. Just be glad you found out beforehand. Now, I gots to go. I got a hot date with Corey. You remember him from Aruba, right?"

"Yeah, the seventeen year old. I remember." Brielle frowned.

"He's not seventeen. He's nineteen and got a dick like a thirty year-old horse. Anyway, he's down here for the week. I might just fall in love for a change...ha ha...Hell no! Gotta go!"

"Wait Janay. Send my stuff to me please?"

"Okay, call me later," she said and hung up abruptly.

Brielle placed the receiver down for just a few seconds, then lifted it to call Darren. After the fourth ring, his voicemail finally picked up. She thought about going to the police station to see the look on Darren's face when he saw her there, but she knew that only would interfere with her revenge.

She left him a message, "Hey Darren baby, I'm back. I want to get together with you. Call me ASAP; I can't wait to see you." She hung up and pulled a hammer from the drawer. Immediately she began to beat against the furniture, attempting to pull fixtures from the wall for no apparent reason. Then just as the thought of the camera hit her, she grabbed it, and began demolishing the digital camera with the hope of destroying Darren's pictures from Aruba, and soon destroying him forever.

At that moment, Brielle could feel her mood changing. It was a scary feeling; one where she needed companionship, medication, or just something to set her mind at ease. She paced the floor for several minutes wondering how she could curb her anger against Darren. "Let it go, Brielle," she kept telling herself.

"Hell no! Don't let it go," another voice countered.

Brielle rushed over to her purse throwing item after item around. Frantically she seemed uneasy as she fumbled through pieces of paper. Her thought was to add up monies in her bank account that she shared with Dante, in addition to the first installment from Dante's pension.

With a devilish smirk she finally spoke, "A car. That will cheer me up. I'm buying myself a car," she said with confidence.

And just like that Brielle headed out the door with intentions on lightening her mood with a new ride. As she pulled out the driveway she couldn't help but cross her fingers as she stopped, hopped out, and rushed to check the mailbox for the anticipated life insurance check.

The mailbox was yanked open with speed, but her heart sank faster. Still no check. Little did Brielle know, the check had been put on hold, compliments of the Fort Lee Police Department.

❧ Chapter 15 ❧

June was hot and typical in the south. The Atlanta heat had been smoldering most of the day, and Janay was about to hit the heated streets. Corey had just gotten on a plane to fly back to Brooklyn, and she and another girl had a hot date with a multi-millionaire from Russia. Janay had met him the day before when he was in her boss' office finalizing some contracts. He gave her a suggestive look that she knew all too well, so when she saw him leaving she jumped on the elevator with him and slipped him her number. She called Kourtney, one of her "girls" that worked for her after he called and requested her and a white girl. Kourtney was from a rich family, but she had a mean addiction to prescription pills that she used her body to pay for.

They met and all dined at the exclusive Pompei restaurant where they consumed great food and plenty of drinks. Afterwards, they accompanied the Russian mogul to his hotel room at The Four Seasons to have an evening of kinky sex that would pay $2,500.00 a piece to the two women. Janay began calling the shots immediately instructing Kourtney to change with her in the bathroom. Quickly, they changed into their lace and strings, then waltzed out of the bathroom where Mr. Slavikt was waiting in his bed already naked.

He gave them orders and they obliged. He wanted to see the two women have sex with each other. They followed all of his requests. He wanted Kourtney to ride him while Janay performed sex on him with a dildo in his ass. He was a deviant man with a mean streak for pain. He wanted to be whipped and clipped and so the two girls met his every demand. Soon, he found himself on top of Kourtney, riding her like a raging bull.

Janay got up to use the bathroom and while she was in there she heard a scream and what sounded like a scuffle from inside the room. She quickly finished using the bathroom and went out to see what was going on. Mr. Slavikt was choking Kourtney and she was struggling to release his grip. Before Janay could make it over to Kourtney, her body fell limp in the man's grip. Janay tried to make it to the door but as soon as she turned to run he was on top of her choking her, too. She noticed her purse on the couch within reach. She reached for her purse and pulled out her .380 with special hollow point bullets, shooting him point blank range in the temple. He rolled over and landed on his back, limp.

"Oh my God!" Janay screamed.

She immediately ran over to Kourtney and shook her. She checked for a pulse and couldn't find one. Janay panicked. She didn't know what to do. She knew that she couldn't call the police, especially since she was the one who'd arranged for Kourtney to be there in the first place, ultimately leaving her responsible for her co-worker's death. Janay knew that Mr. Slavikt probably had a wife who would want to see her held responsible for his death as well.

It didn't take long for Janay's instincts to kick in. She wiped the gun and then cleaned up as much as she could to remove any evidence of her being there. Moments later, she turned the television's volume up as loud as it would go. She then wrapped a hand cloth around her hand before placing the gun in Kourtney's hand. After silently telling Kourtney that she was sorry, Janay pulled the trigger so that the gun powder would be on Kourtney's hands. She dragged the pervert's body over to Kourtney and made it look as if Kourtney had killed him in self-defense. Once her cover up was done, Janay quickly got dressed and left. She knew that the hotel had cameras so she looked down the whole time until she made it out of the hotel. She realized when she got into the car that she should've taken both of their cell phones.

The next morning Brielle was awakened by the constant ringing of the doorbell. She was shocked to see Janay in Jersey, standing with a worried expression plastered across her face.

Janay brushed past Brielle with a hard nudge before she could step to the side. "What are you doing here?"

"Brielle, I killed one of my clients in self-defense," Janay informed nearly out of breath.

Brielle looked at her in disbelief.

"I swear it was self-defense." Her hands were high in the air as she paced the foyer. "But he's rich and he killed the white girl that I had paid to come along with me… so I'm gonna be the blame."

"Why did you run, girl? That shit makes you look guilty!"

"Shut the door, crazy! I have to get a lawyer, fool. And whose car is that in your driveway?" Janay started looking around the house for any sign of company. She seemed overly tense.

"Mine."

"Bitch, you bought a Bentley? Even with Darren trying to find you guilty of murder?" she asked, dropping her bags down in disbelief.

"Does me buying a Bentley make me guilty of murder?" Brielle turned her back to Janay.

"No, but you watch plenty of crime shows. As a matter of fact didn't I see you on an episode of Snapped," she joked, followed by extreme laughter. "No really, I got myself into some serious shit." Janay followed Brielle into the living room and sat on the couch wanting to discuss her problems.

"Janay, Dante tried to choke me to death and I stabbed him, that was it. There is no other story. I need something in life to cheer me up. A 2009 Continental GT Bentley was what the doctor ordered." She paused to shoot Janay a smirk. "Besides, I financed it. I haven't officially gotten the insurance check yet. Now, let's focus on you. What are you gonna do?"

"I just have to get my defense ready. Girl, can you pay for a legal team for me?" Janay asked with ease.

"What? Janay, all that money you were making at work and with your extra curricular schemes. Where is it?"

"Brielle, you can't help me out? You been getting a little money. Plus, what about Dante's bank accounts?" Janay developed an instant attitude.

"Janay, forget money, what the hell happened?"

Janay breathed heavily, then commenced to telling Brielle exactly what happened. In the end, Brielle told her that she should turn herself in and tell the true story to the police. Janay decided she wasn't going back until she found a good lawyer. Brielle told her that she should stay up north in a hotel, but she said that she was going to stay with her flavor of the month, Corey. Corey would be picking her up that evening to take her with him to Brooklyn.

Janay admitted that her lifestyle had finally caught up to her, but wanted to know more about Brielle's situation. "So, have you talked to Darren?"

"Hell no, why?" Brielle asked aggravated.

"You said you didn't do anything wrong, why are you worried about it. Maybe you should still date him; he seems like a nice guy. Just let him know that you know he's a detective. And tell him that you are innocent and then give him a chance. I think he really likes you."

"Whatever. I met my new husband. He's gorgeous."

"What's his name?"

"His name is Shawn, and you'll never meet him. Maybe at the wedding, but not before that. You know you're a hater. Besides, your ass might try to fuck him behind my back."

Just then Brielle's phone rang.

She rolled her eyes when she saw the name pop up. "You talked 'Jersey's Finest' up. It's Darren." She answered dryly, "Hello."

"What's up with you beautiful?"

"Oh, I was just getting rid of my husband's belongings so I can start to move on with my life."

"Uhh, well that's good, it makes room for me," he said with a slight chuckle.

Brielle rolled her eyes up into her head. "It sure does," she said playing along.

"When can I see you?"

"Oh, maybe this weekend. Friday I'm free," Brielle chimed.

"Okay, I'll pick you up at eight."

"You know where I live?" she asked.

"Uhh…no actually," he stuttered, "You can tell me when I call you."

"Talk to you then."

Janay had made her way over to the couch in the living room and had started calling some lawyers back in Atlanta. They all told her that they would need to meet with her to discuss her case. Janay huffed and puffed and mouthed each conversation with the lawyer to Brielle.

The end result was that she would stay up north for the rest of the week and return to Atlanta the beginning of the following week. Janay and Brielle sat and mapped out the best plan for Janay. They talked for hours about the worst case scenarios until Janay's ride showed up.

As soon as Janay left, Brielle got comfortable on the couch and decided to call Shawn.

"Hello," he answered sounding sexy.

"Hello, Handsome," she said as forward as possible.

"Who am I speaking with?" Shawn asked.

"This is Brielle, from yesterday. You were at my house."

"Yeah, right. Mrs. Prescott. I've been thinking about you since I saw you," he replied.

"That's good to know. But call me Brielle. "So, how long have you been a garbage man?" she blurted out, wishing he were a top executive at a Fortune 500 company somewhere.

"Well, we like to call ourselves sanitation technicians," he said laughing, " but I worked for the company for two years before becoming a supervisor and then eight years later the owner of the company died and left the company to me. So, I'm actually the owner."

"Oh, so you're the owner?"

"Yeah, you sound surprised." He laughed. "I just hired my two cousins to work for me, so I've been showing them the ropes."

"Really? That's great," she said cheesing.

"Enough about me. How are you holding up since your loss?"

"I'm okay. My marriage was not the best, so I hate to say it but it's a relief not to have him around. He was abusive."

"Sorry to hear that. If you don't mind me asking, how did he die?"

"Well, he tried to kill me, so I stabbed him and he died. I was pregnant and lost my daughter, too." She wanted to be as honest with him as possible.

"Wow." Shawn paused for several minutes. "Are you going to counseling?"

"No."

"I'm not trying to be funny, but even when my wife died I had to go to counseling for a little while. It really helps to talk to a neutral party who is a professional. Sometimes we harbor things that we don't realize, and it interferes with our ability to move on in life."

"Yeah, my cousin and my aunt suggested that I see a therapist. I'll take it into consideration."

"Well, maybe I can be your counselor. You can talk to me," he said sincerely.

"Yeah, I'd like that. I might even pay you," she said suggestively.

"That sounds good. You can pay me until we become intimate and then I'll do it for free." They both laughed. "Can I see you soon? I have something fun that we can do Saturday if you're not too busy."

"Okay, I'm game. What time?" she asked eagerly.

"Let's say three. I'll pick you up. But I'll call you tomorrow anyway."

"Sounds good, Shawn. I'll see you on Saturday." She counted on her fingers. "Three days. Damn!" she said beneath her breath.

"Sleep well, sexy."

Brielle couldn't wipe the wide smile from her face. "Okay, you, too."

❦ Chapter 16 ❧

Brielle woke up Thursday morning with a new attitude, elated that she didn't have any bad dreams the night before. She was in a great mood, and decided she needed style to match her frame of mind. She put on a silver, sleek ensemble by KLS; a pair of capri's and a matching sleeveless top with glitter covering the front, all in an attempt to match her new ride.

Brielle stepped away from the mirror when she received an alert on her phone showing that she had a hair appointment at five. That would give her enough time to get some new bling from her jeweler, and trade in old pieces given to her by Dante. Plus, she could show up to the beauty parlor flossing in her new whip. It was definitely her time to shine and allow the new Brielle to take center stage.

It didn't take long for Brielle to leave the house. She visited her jeweler first, and gave the sad account once again of what actually happened to Dante. She cried out telling the jeweler of his many abusive tirades, and that she needed to get rid of any memories that *his* jewelry would give her. He agreed to take her pieces, and gave her a credit of $19,000.00 to use toward what new jewelry she chose. She knew he was getting the better end of the deal because her engagement ring and wedding bands alone had cost seventeen grand. But she didn't care, it wasn't money out of her pocket, and her insurance check would be coming soon.

"Dante owes me," she told herself.

She picked a diamond band that had baguettes and princess cut diamonds. It was extremely extravagant along with a bracelet to match which totaled roughly $5,000. In total, her bill came close to $22,000. Without hesitation, she whipped out her bank card and charged the rest to the game. The game was fun, she thought with a wicked grin. She wished that she could've benefited from Peyton's, or the asshole in Houston, as well. But her reward was knowing that they'd gotten the ultimate pay back.

Brielle chose her jewelry boxes for her new bling, but kept the jewelry on. She felt like royalty walking back toward the parking lot. By the time she'd zoomed out of the lot and onto the highway, she felt unstoppable. When Brielle pulled into the lot of the hair salon a few minutes later, she parked by the window so all the hatin' ass, catty women could see her get out of her car. She absolutely loved the feeling as she walked into the shop.

"Girl, don't tell me that's your car?" her stylist, Roxanne belted. She too tried to hide her envy.

"Yes it is. You like it, don't you?" Brielle said boastfully.

"I love it! Oh my God, that's beautiful! I want a ride right now."

"No girl, I need my hair done first. I want the works. My weave is loose as hell."

Roxanne struggled to run her fingers through Brielle's hair and said, "Yeah girl, you ain't lying. Come on, get on in my chair."

As Brielle's weave got cut out, she surveyed her surroundings. She said her hellos to a few of the other stylists, just before a face that she did not want to see came walking from the back shampoo room. Taken to a chair two seats away from Brielle was a very pregnant Monique Troy. She looked to be twelve months pregnant.

"Well, I see that you're having a hard time getting over my man," Monique said scornfully.

Brielle knew that Monique's attempt to start with her was because she had an audience, and she also knew that Monique was trying to provoke her. However, she remained calm and decided to use her material possessions as get back.

Brielle put her hand out, looked at her finger and wrist and said, "Well, I know one thing, my husband is still taking care of me, even in death. I have a fabulous new car and exquisite jewelry to match." She stopped and shrugged her shoulders. "He wasn't that bad I guess. I know how hard it is for a man to resist the constant advances and despair of a desperate whore. But please, let's have some respect for Roxanne's shop. I apologize, Roxanne."

The women in the room along with the stylists were shocked. Their mouths were all open and headed to the floor.

"Ladies, do remember what goes around comes around so watch how you do people." Brielle shook her finger at them and preached a little more. "Whores will be whores."

"So, is that why you killed your husband, to get him back for being in love with me?" Monique provoked.

"I killed him because he tried to kill me," Brielle said hatefully, then smiled. She winked at Monique without anyone else noticing.

"You know…Dante never liked dark meat. He loved red bones like me. But you know that, right? Even his other women were light-skinned. I guess that was what he really wanted," Monique teased.

"No, he fucked redbones and married me. Real men like a little color."

Monique broke quick and easy. "I've got to get out of here. I'll get my hair done some other time." Monique choked up in front of everyone. "Brielle, I know you murdered Dante! You can say it was self-defense if you want to." Monique got up and stormed out without saying another word.

All of a sudden, the mood in the shop turned sour. It was so quiet you could hear a pin drop. Brielle watched to make sure that the bitch, Monique didn't do anything to her car because pregnant or not, she would get dragged all over the parking lot if she did.

Brielle knew that the women wanted to ask her questions but were probably scared that she might've given them a similar tongue lashing. So, most carried on trivial conversations until Brielle's hair was done.

When she looked in the mirror, a smile daunted her face. Her hair color had been touched up and pulled back into a long dramatic ponytail down her back, allowing her high cheek bones to be seen more clearly. She really looked good considering what she had gone through over the last month or so.

Brielle stayed in the shop for nearly three hours making herself extra beautiful. It didn't take much to make her look the part. From make up to fake lashes, to even the wax job, she looked gorgeous. In her heart, she knew it was time to reel Darren in for the kill.

❦ Chapter 17 ❧

"No mommy! No mommy, please don't go!" Brielle pleaded.

But no sooner than the last braid on her long, thick hair was done, her mother shoved her away. *"I'm leaving for the evening! My motherly duties are done. Besides girl, I'm sick of seeing you and I told you Tony's coming."*

"Can I go to Aunt Janelle's? Pleaseeeee Mommy. I told you Tony hits me. He touches me, too!"

"Don't tell me what to do little heifer! I'm a grown-ass woman. Now take your ass in there and sit down." Brielle's mother, Rochelle, lifted the receiver, called her mother, and told her to send Tony over to watch Brielle. Not even five minutes passed before Tony walked in the door in his usual grimy attire with a smirk on his face that signaled trouble. Just like that, her mother turned her head.

"What the fuck possessed me to have a child, I'm out," Rochelle chanted.

"Mommy pleaseeeee."

Without warning, Tony pushed Brielle's ten year old frame onto the couch while her mother shrugged her shoulders and opened the front door with ease. No sooner than the locks turned, Tony turned into a horny savage. Roughly, he grabbed Brielle by the neck, landing her into a tight chokehold near the bottom of the couch. He pulled her ear toward him harshly, *"It's our time again, pretty little cousin. It's timeeeee."*

Brielle began to cry just as she always did. But nothing

would save her. Tony was taller, stronger, and seven years older.
So, with his free hand he strong-armed her left hand and placed it
firmly on his crotch. With each moan, he scared Brielle more and
more.

"Make it feel good, damn it!!! Make it grow!" he de-
manded. Her tears had no effect as Tony unzipped his zipper, and
shoved her hand into his pants to caress his growing dick.
"Squeeze, squeeze, squeeze," he sang loudly, while his eyes rolled
to the back of his head.

Brielle shouted, "Get off of me! Get off of me! I'm only
nine years old!"

Brielle rocked and rocked in her sleep so much that she'd
finally fallen off the bed. The moment that she snapped from her
dream, her mind traveled from one bad experience to a sick idea
playing out on the television.

The television had been on all night and as Brielle moved
around on the bed, an episode of "Cold Case Forensic Files"
caught her attention. There was a story on about a wife who killed
her husband by putting antifreeze in his food. She learned that
there was an active ingredient in antifreeze that was hard to detect
if the doctors aren't specifically looking for it. The ingestion of it
could cause sudden death. Brielle decided at that moment to use
antifreeze to kill Darren. She knew that she would probably have
about an hour after they ate together to get him home before his
food was digested. On the television, the lady's husband had begun
making frequent emergency room visits and was continuously released and diagnosed with gastrointestinal problems. The husband
finally died after weeks of ingesting anti-freeze yet it was ruled
cardiac arrest. The wife would have gotten off Scott-free, but years
later she told a boyfriend what she had done. The boyfriend told
authorities, and her husband's body was exhumed. They looked for
that special ingredient and it was found.

Just like that, Brielle picked up the phone and called Darren. "Hey," she said when he answered, "are we still on for tomorrow?"

"Of course we are. I'm gonna take you to my favorite
restaurant."

"Oh no, I wanted to cook dinner for you and stay in." She knew he wouldn't turn that down, thinking that he might be able to get some ass.

"Oh really? Well, I have no problem with that. I'll see you around eight? Is that okay?"

"Sure," she said.

"Goodnight, lady."

"Goodnight, Darren." She hung up, slamming the phone down angrily.

She decided to make lasagna; the perfect dish, cheesy, messy, and hopefully deadly. She traveled to Edgewater, nearly thirty miles away and bought some antifreeze. Soon after, she took the drive over to Hoboken to buy the ingredients for the dinner. She made two different pans so that she would be able to eat with him. Passionately, she mixed the antifreeze inside the food while blasting, Junior Mafia's old song, "Get Money" and sang with Lil Kim, "*Payback's a bitch motherfucka believe me, not I ain't gay this ain't no lesbo stuff it's a little something to let you motherfuckas know...my bitches get money, my niggas get money.*"

She laughed wildly and repeated the song and sang that part about ten times until the meal was done. For the first night in years, she walked upstairs to her bedroom a happy woman.

Brielle woke up Friday morning excited about what was to come. She couldn't wait to see Darren. She made two fruit salads and put antifreeze in one of them as well as two containers of iced tea, with a touch of antifreeze in one. She took a little taste of each to see if anything was noticeable, but nothing tasted funny.

She called Darren and told him that she would be out at eight so she would pick him up instead of him coming to her house. A decision Brielle made so she wouldn't have to try to get rid of his car. Once she noticed him getting sick, she would offer to take him back home. Darren said it was fine and gave her his address. He then asked her if she liked Gin and Juice.

Yeah, you think I'm gonna get drunk and let you have some, but I have a surprise for you, Detective, she thought to herself after telling him to bring the alcohol, and then hanging up the phone.

Brielle had everything prepared and ready to carry out her plan by 7:30. She left home dressed seductively, and picked Darren up from his condo.

Darren hopped inside, "Wow, is this your car? Is it new?"

"Yup, I bought it with the life insurance money."

Darren seemed uncomfortable when she made the statement. He knew his boss had been talking back and forth with the insurance company and decided to delay honoring Dante's policy until the police gave the okay. She was still a person of interest, and wasn't sure whether she would be officially charged.

"So, how have you been holding up?" Darren asked, switching the subject.

"Fine," she replied.

"Well, I have a confession to make." Her stomach tightened.

"I heard about what happened with your husband. You told me that he died, but someone who knows you told me how he died."

"Okay, and? What's your point?" Brielle shot him a blank look.

"I just wanted you to know that I knew in case you want to talk about it," he replied.

"Nope. I'm good." She paused then changed the subject to Janay. They talked about her crazy ways for nearly twenty minutes until Brielle interrupted, "We're here," she said, pulling into her driveway.

As he got out of the car Brielle noticed him look over at Talia's house. She started laughing.

"What's so funny little lady?"

"Oh, nothing."

Once inside, they sat in the living room, watching a special on MTV about top grossing couples. Brielle got up to make them both gin and juice, but put way more gin into his cup than hers. She put the food in the oven for it to warm and brought out two small bowls of fruit salad. He ate it all, which of course immediately put a smile on Brielle's face.

She made small talk with him while they watched more T.V. She made sure that he was tipsy before getting back up to make their plates. Brielle smiled from ear to ear as she brought the plates into the living room, with his deadly food and laced iced tea.

They ate and talked a little bit about Darren's fake occupation. Brielle wasn't interested in anything that he had to say and was barely listening. She felt that he was not someone to be trusted. His main goal was to put her in prison for murder. As far as she was concerned he was her enemy, and she would get him before he got her.

About an hour after they finished eating she noticed him dozing off. She didn't know if it was him being drunk or if the concoction was starting to affect his body. She told him that she had to go to the bathroom and quickly came back and said, "Oh Darren, I'm so sorry. I just threw up. My stomach is hurting. Maybe the meat in the lasagna was bad. I think I should take you home. I don't feel well."

"Yeah, my stomach is cramping a little bit, too. Damn girl, the first date and you poison me?" he said laughing. She didn't laugh. "I'll make it up to you, come on." She hoped the potent dose would be enough to put his lights out permanently.

On the way to his house she noticed him dozing off again. "Are you okay?" she asked and gave him a nudge.

He jumped and said, "Huh, uh, yeah. I just feel a little dizzy, that's all."

She pulled up into the driveway of his building. "Well, I hope you don't get sick, too. Call me tomorrow."

"Okay." He leaned over and kissed her cheek. She hoped the kiss would be their first and last.

With a devious grin, Brielle drove home and called Shawn immediately.

"Hello beautiful. I was just thinking about you. How was your day?" His voice put an automatic smile on her face.

"Oh, it was okay. I wanted it to go by fast so tomorrow could come and I can see you. I just called to say goodnight."

"I can't wait to see you either. I can't wait to get my first kiss, Pretty Lady."

"Okay, well I'm gonna soak my lips in gloss tonight so they'll be nice and soft for you."

"That's what I'm talkin' bout. See you at three. Oh, and wear something comfortable, we're going to Central Park."

"Okay, Shawn."

Brielle cleaned up, throwing away all of the laced food and tea out. She changed into a t-shirt and a pair of Dante's boxers that she had been wearing for years. At that moment, something stopped her in the middle of the floor. It was a flashback that she so desperately wanted to forget.

The day her mother died, she was by her mother's hospital bed. Death was near, and they both knew it. Brielle was crying dreadfully. But even on her death bed her mother despised her.

"What the hell are you crying for? I'm the one who's gonna die, thanks to you and your no good father. I gave my life to you two and for what? I should've left you with him and his girlfriend years ago. No, I shoulda sucked your ass up with a vacuum at the clinic. One rotten motherfucker deserves another, she told Brielle to her face. He never loved me the same after you were born. And he never wanted children. But I had you anyway! And then he fell in love with Dorothy and now Marilyn. And I don't even get to live to see fifty years old. You should be the one dying Brielle, not me! You should die for being born, and ruining my life." Brielle started crying instantly, and then walked toward the door of the hospital room. She turned around and looked at her mother but her mother wouldn't even look in her direction. "See you in hell," was all she said.

Suddenly, Brielle realized she stood frozen in a pool of sweat wondering if it was her mother's voice she had been hearing all along, or if it was indeed another dream. For the first time in months, she realized it was her mother's voice that she heard daily. It was her mother, her dead mother who was giving unworthy advice. Brielle calmed her nerves a bit and rushed upstairs to bed thinking she would go down for the night. To her surprise, she was awakened just three hours later in a panic. She glanced at the clock. It read 3:00 a.m. Brielle turned over, hoping to sleep through the night, but awoke to another bad dream.

This time her father was berating her. At eleven years old they were sitting in the car one of the many times that they were going home from Dorothy's house.

"You're gonna be nothing but a worthless woman just like your mother. She thinks making me take you out is gonna stop me from seeing the woman I love." He grabbed her by the shoulders and peered into her face. "You better know how to please a man when you get older and not be an evil bitch like your mother. She only had you to keep me. I didn't love her anymore and she knew it so she had you. And you turned out to be just as ugly as she is. Dorothy is gonna be my wife one day, I'm gonna leave your mother one day so I can be happy." Brielle sat quietly sobbing while her drunk father made her feel unloved once again.

She woke up again, and the clock read 4:00 a.m. This time she pressed the button on the remote and flipped channels frantically, hoping to see some breaking news about Darren. One channel after another…nothing.

"Damn!" she shouted and threw her head against the headboard in anger.

∾Chapter 18∾

The following day, Brielle didn't get out of bed until noon. Her mood had turned sour, something that needed to change before it was time to go out with Shawn. Moments later, her phone rang startling her. Anxiously, she reached to answer without looking at the caller ID.

"Hello."

"That food had my stomach in a war with itself."

She punched her pillow with a strong pound when she heard Darren's voice. "Yeah, I know. I had a bad stomach ache, too."

"Well, once I started feeling the cramping, I made myself throw up."

"I'm so sorry, Darren. I'll make it up to you."

"It's not your fault. I'll cook for you next time. You can come to my place. How about tomorrow? I have to work today?"

"Ahhh," Brielle stuttered. "Ahhhh, okay."

Brielle knew she had to see him soon to offer some more medicine to his body, before it could rid itself of the first round of dosing.

"Uh, let's say I'll pick you up at two. My church lets out around one. Unless you'd like to go with me to church?" Darren's offer was casual but sincere.

"Just pick me up after you get out of church."

"Okay, I'm gonna give you another chance since you almost killed me on the first date." He laughed. "I'll see you tomorrow."

Brielle hung up, showered, then threw on some True Religion jeans with rhinestones and a matching t-shirt. She really wanted the day with Shawn to be special. She was determined not to let her lack of sleep interfere with her day with him. She made herself an English muffin, then commenced to getting dolled up. She started with lip gloss and mascara, then made sure her ponytail was neat before sitting in the kitchen window waiting for Shawn's arrival.

Shawn pulled up shortly after in a burgundy 2008 Mercedes Benz CLS 550 with chrome rims, and a mild tint on the windows. She couldn't wait to see him without that dirty sanitation uniform on. When he stepped out in his Ed Hardy jeans with a matching t-shirt, Brielle's heart melted. He was even more handsome than before.

Before Shawn could even approach the porch, the door swung open, and Brielle started with the praises.

"Damn, you look good," she said while blushing. "You obviously work out."

"I do, but you lookin' sweet, too. C'mere, let's get this out the way." Shawn grabbed her and pulled her close, kissing her softly on the lips.

Brielle kissed back, feeling like she was already in love.

"So, what do you have planned for me?" she asked.

"You'll see. You ready?"

"I was born ready."

"Don't speak too soon," Shawn told her. "You don't know what I have planned," he said laughing. She reached for her large new Gucci bag until Shawn stopped her. "Oh, you won't be needing that. You can leave that here. Just bring yourself and your keys. And of course your cell phone. But maybe I should tell you just in case. Do you have your own rollerblades by any chance?"

Brielle was excited. "No, I don't know how to rollerblade. I'm ole school. I have roller skates though. I'm glad you told me because I hate skating with rented skates."

Brielle followed Shawn out to his car while smiling from ear to ear. The short drive was filled with energy as they talked about their past relationships. Before long, Brielle noticed they

were near the George Washington Bridge. Shawn took the upper
level across the bridge giving Brielle a chance to look down at the
Hudson, recalling the many times she and Dante took ferry rides,
spent time at the lookout park, or went jet skiing in the Hudson.
She still couldn't understand what had happened to the happiness
and closeness that they had had in the beginning. Shawn broke her
concentration.

"Hey, you okay?" he asked.

"Yeah. I'm just enjoying the view," she lied.

"Are you hungry?" he inquired.

"I ate a little bit before you came. I'm good for right now."
She reached over and rubbed the back of his neck.

"Okay, because you're going to be hungry after I dust you
in the skating ring."

"Oh, no you're not. I'm a pro, I've always loved to roller
skate," she said and then realized that she was sounding too excited. Janay always said she seemed so desperate.

"That's good. I do this twice a month in the spring and
summer. Let's go," he announced, after parking the car on Central
Park West.

They walked into Central Park with their skates over their
shoulders noticing people everywhere. It looked like one great big
outdoor party. When they walked over to the roller rink, it was
jamming. The DJ was playing, "Roll, Bounce, Rock, Skate" and
the people were making their rounds while dancing, jumping,
twirling, and bouncing to the music. Moments later, Brielle and
Shawn put their skates on and joined the fun. They both took off
on their own until Shawn came up and started skating closely behind. The scene was dreamy and became more romantic once
Shawn grabbed her hand softly.

"I had to see if you could skate first before I attached myself to you."

They laughed like two long-time lovers, then skated hand
in hand, backward and forward, and intertwined. It was a great ice
breaker, but after about six songs they agreed to go sit on the grass.

While sitting side-by-side, they watched the other skaters,
and talked and laughed. The day was beautiful and Brielle felt the

same way inside. She listened to Shawn talk about himself, his childhood, and how he'd grown up in the Bronx, NY. Of course she didn't have much good to say about her childhood. She answered whatever questions he asked, and asked him questions back. That was it.

She did find out that Shawn was thirty-four and had only been married three years when his wife died. He had an eight year-old son who lived in Harlem with his mother and was hoping for more children soon. Shawn lived in a brownstone in Harlem by himself. He and his wife had been trying to get pregnant before she died, but were unsuccessful. She didn't tell him about her other two miscarriages.

"So, I don't know how to put this so I'll just ask. Do you feel bad that your husband died at your hands?"

At first Brielle thought intently about how to answer the question, but then just blurted out the truth. "No. I'm sorry, I don't. I've been having bad dreams though. It's not that I'm glad things ended that way it did. It's just that when someone hurts you so bad over and over you get numb and you start to hate them. I thought I still loved him and was happy with him, but now looking back at all that he did to me, I was just holding on to a lie and now I'm just glad he's out of my life. It hasn't really hit me that he's dead. He's just not around. Does it make you look at me in a funny way?"

"Well, it's a first. I mean, you're not going to meet many people who can say that they killed their spouse and they're not in prison, unless it was self-defense. You had to do what you had to do, I guess. What do your friends think?" He took her hand in his.

"I kinda shut myself off from everyone. I haven't called my friends or taken their calls since the funeral. I need this time to myself. Just so you know, I stayed because I loved him. I didn't love myself enough to know that I deserved better. We were together for six years so I became used to the mistreatment and abuse."

"That's not good. Did you grow up in an abusive household?"

"Yes." Her answer required no further explanation.

"Well, that explains some of it as well."

Brielle let out a half of a smile. "Did you go to school for psychology or something? You really want to be a counselor, huh?" She wrapped his arm around her and sat under his wing.

"Well, to tell you the truth, I did want to be a psychiatrist when I was growing up. I started college, but I got into some trouble and dropped out."

"Wow. Tell me more." She moved to lay on her stomach and peered up at him while he sat.

"Enough about the past, we are in the present and you're with me now. Are you hungry?"

"Yes, indeed. Didn't you hear my stomach?"

They laughed as they gathered their things and started walking through Central Park to Central Park East. They ended up at BBQs on 72nd St. and 3rd Avenue.

They got a table outside at BBQ's and had Texas Sized drinks and continued getting to know each other. He was a Capricorn and she was a Taurus. She didn't know much about Capricorns, but she hoped that they would become star-crossed lovers. By the time they finished dinner it was 10:00 p.m. Brielle didn't want the night to end, but she didn't want to be a first date "trick". She wanted to make a good impression.

They walked back to his car hand in hand with their skates over their shoulders like teenagers. He didn't ask her if she wanted to go anywhere else. He drove her straight home, and didn't ask her if he could come inside either. He said, "I really enjoyed your company today, Brielle. I'll call you tomorrow and if you don't mind, I wanna see you again real soon. Okay, beautiful?" He took her chin in his hand and pulled her face to his.

"Okay," she replied without pouting.

He leaned over and gave her a long kiss goodnight igniting strong feelings inside; feelings Brielle hadn't felt in years.

"He'll never love you!" a voice said.

"Shut up, mother!" Brielle shouted. "You're not going to ruin this one."

Shawn jumped back and frowned showing several crinkles on his forehead. "You okay?"

"I'm fine. Kiss me again?" she pleaded.

Shawn did just that. Not once…not twice…but for minutes

at a time. For Brielle, it was perfect.

Chapter 19

The next morning Darren woke up feeling drained and weak. He sat in his office deciding whether he should take the rest of the day off when the Sergeant walked in.

"Hey man, you look horrible, what's the matter with you?"

"I've been having some stomach problems the last couple of days. I think I might need to go home and stay in bed the rest of the day."

"Sure, go home. But what's going on with The Case of the Murdered Cheating Husband? Any more leads?" the sergeant laughed.

"No, not yet. I haven't spoken to her since the Aruba trip," he lied. "And I haven't found out any more information. I've interviewed a few people at Dante's job, but they didn't ever recall hearing anything bad about Mrs. Prescott." Darren stopped to clutch at his stomach. "One guy did know that Mr. Prescott was a heavy cheater and mentioned that he knew that Dante was physically and mentally abusive to her. She had the chance to tell me in Aruba. She had had quite a few drinks and she was talking about him but she never said that she did it on purpose." Darren looked through his notes as he spoke.

"Well, maybe she wasn't drunk enough," The Sergeant said laughing.

Darren was surprisingly offended, but he couldn't show it to his boss. "Well, Sergeant Wiley, I don't believe his mistress. I think she may be looking for some money, maybe a civil suit or something to help her support her child. She seemed to have it out more for Brielle than the other way around."

Darren closed the notebook reluctantly.

"Oh, *Brielle* huh? Not Mrs. Prescott? Am I sensing that you fell for her in Aruba while laying on a white sandy beach looking into her poor lonely eyes? You sure she didn't do a job on you?" Sergeant Wiley patted Darren on the back.

"Why would she? She was on a faraway trip. Most people tell things to strangers that they would never tell to their closest friend. The opportunity was there." He huffed. "How much more time do I have?"

"You have about a week left, but from the look in your eyes, I would say that you might as well let the week run out. Detective Shields and Detective Roberts have been on her trail, sniffing around to find any cause to charge her. They've come up empty handed, too. Looks like the bastard was an abuser; and she really did retaliate in self defense." He sighed, then watched Darren's reaction.

Relief covered his face, "You did your job; we have some other heavy cases piling up," the sergeant said and then noticed more relief in Darren's eyes.

"So, then she's fair game right?" Darren asked.

"Absolutely. She's no longer a suspect. You're free to fall in love fella. Just don't keep any sharp knives around if you decide to cheat," the Sergeant joked.

"I wouldn't cheat." Darren leaned back in his swivel chair.

"Yeah, you're a pretty good guy. You probably would give her the happiness that she needs. And you'd make a great father, too. Go for it. But first go home. Take a few days. Go to the doctor if you need to. I'll see you when you're feeling better." The sergeant walked out of his office then swiftly peeked back in.

"Hey, I almost forgot. Call the insurance company, tell them Mrs. Prescott is no longer a person of interest- it was self defense."

Darren felt better just by hearing the news that he could see Brielle without having to go against the rules at work. He had long forgotten about the case. He didn't really care if she had killed her husband in revenge or not. From what he had heard about Dante Prescott, he didn't deserve to have Brielle at all. He was glad however that she had not confessed to him in Aruba, because he would have had to fulfill his call of duty.

He didn't know what it was about Brielle, but he knew that whatever it was, he was falling in love. A few more months and he'd be shopping for an engagement ring, he joked to himself. Darren could tell that all she really wanted and needed was love. She seemed so sad, deep down inside. Darren wanted to change that, and he wanted to snag her before any one else could.

☙Chapter 20☙

The next morning Brielle got up early plotting on Darren. Although she thought there was a pretty good chance she'd found true love with Shawn, Darren still needed to get his. She'd asked herself over and over again, why she wanted to kill Darren. It was because he had tried to use her heart to frame her.

"Let's go then, bitch," the voice said.

"Stop it, mother!" Brielle shouted, stumping her foot against the floor. "Go away. I have a chance to be normal again!"

Brielle got dressed and made herself some Eggo waffles hoping to keep her emotions and mental issues under control. She put on a yellow and pink tye-dye sleeveless t-shirt and some BCBG pink velour sweat pants with yellow stripes and some pink and white Nike's. She was pondering how to get the antifreeze into Darren's food, at his house. She didn't even know what he was going to cook for her.

She looked through the drawer of utensils in her kitchen and tried to find something that could contain the antifreeze. At that moment, she noticed a turkey baster. That would keep the liquid in and allow her to squeeze the antifreeze out and onto the food on his plate. She took the turkey baster out of the drawer and sucked the antifreeze out of a pan and into the tube. She put the turkey baster into her large Gucci bag, then sat down to watch T.V. awaiting Darren's call.

At 2:15 her cell phone rang. It was Darren. Her stomach churned. "Should I really go through with this?" she asked herself.

"Yes, whimp," her mother suggested.

"Hey, Darren," Brielle answered.

"Hey, sexy," he replied, "I'm on my way."

"Good. I'm hungry. What are you making for me?" she asked.

"I made baked turkey last night with stuffing, macaroni and cheese, and collard greens. Oh, and homemade gravy," he added teasingly.

The gravy is the ticket, Brielle thought with wide eyes. The meat will absorb the antifreeze, and the gravy will just cover it up.

"Sounds good to me, is your gravy thick or like water?" She paced back and forth contemplating her attack.

"It's nice and thick. Don't worry, you'll enjoy the meal."

"Oh, I'm sure I will." She smiled.

"I'll be there in a half."

"Okay, I'll be waiting," Brielle said and hung up.

She put the bottle of Zolpidem pills into her purse, just in case she needed them. She knew that this would have to look like a natural death, all the way because she didn't know whether he was reporting to the department every time he saw her or not. Brielle had a good feeling about her developing relationship with Shawn. She was going to make sure that it worked. Or at least try her best to so that he wouldn't end up being victim number five. She needed Shawn to be genuine. She needed him to save her from the mess.

Her phone rang from Darren's number, prompting her to look outside where she spotted a black Dodge Charger with nice rims and dark tint. She opened the door to see if it was Darren. He rolled down his window and motioned for her to come out. She told him one second and rushed to get her purse which contained her needed chemicals.

As soon as Brielle got in the car, Darren leaned over and gave her a kiss on the lips. She shuddered inside. She couldn't stand him; hated to even be near him. To her he was just a snake, nothing more. She couldn't even feel him, she was numb in his presence.

"How's everything with you? You okay?"

"I'm fine, what makes you ask?" She looked out of the

window, ignoring his stare on her.

"Just checking on you honey, that's all."

"Please don't call me honey." She gave him a mean look.

"Okay. I'm sorry. You seem a little tense."

"No, I'm good. I just hate that word. My husband used to call me honey after he would beat me and that would make me want to kill him." She was purposely messing with his head. She wanted to see if he would bite the bait. He turned his radio down and tuned in.

"So, what actually happened, Brielle the day you killed your husband?" He moved his ear closer, leaning to the side while driving.

"Huh?" she said, looking at him with an attitude. She didn't expect him to be that forward with it.

"I'm sorry. I just know it must be really hard for you right now. That must've been a horrible day for you. To find out that you *accidentally* killed your husband."

"I didn't *accidentally* kill my husband; I killed my husband in self defense. Accidentally is pulling out of the garage and not seeing him laying in the driveway, and driving over him."

Darren cleared his throat. "I apologize again."

"I'm trying to move forward, not backwards. I told the police what happened. They haven't been back so I guess they believe that it was self-defense, so I guess if you look at it that way, it is considered an accident since I didn't plan to do it. I didn't kill him on purpose, so I apologize for being snappy, but I really would like it if you didn't ask me about it again."

"You're absolutely right," he replied as they pulled into the driveway of Darren's condominium complex. She didn't see any visible cameras in the parking garage, yet figured there were some since the complex was new.

His apartment was on the fifth floor. It was nicely furnished and was nice and neat. It had a woman's touch. So of course Brielle wondered where the woman was.

"How long have you been separated?" She looked around.

"About six months."

"Oh, so you're a neat man. That's a plus." She surveyed his

kitchen and living room.

"Good? You mean I finally earned a point? I seem to keep striking out with you." He shook his head pitifully.

"So, feed me, so I can give you two points," she said eager to get out of there. She wasn't able to pretend that she liked him much longer.

"Would you like to have a drink?" He smiled. "We gotta loosen up, this conversation is too tense."

"What do you have to drink?"

"I made some Pina Coladas. I'll put the food in the oven to warm up." Darren strode into the kitchen, while Brielle walked into the living room and took a seat on the couch.

"Okay, that's fine." Brielle kept her purse up under her arm.

Within minutes, Darren brought out the drinks and passed one over. He sat on the couch tensely and picked up the remote.

"Before you get comfortable, can you get me a paper towel, please? This glass will start sweating on your coffee table."

He jumped up and said, "Oh, yeah. Anything for you."

As soon as Darren walked out Brielle quickly sprung into action. She took out the turkey baster, leaned over and squirted some antifreeze in his glass, and stirred the Pina Colada with her finger. With speed, she jumped back over to her seat and slid the baster back inside her purse. Darren waltzed back into the living room, passing her the paper towel as if nothing happened. Brielle sat with an odd look about her face.

"Brielle, there's something about you that I really like. You are very mysterious."

"I'm like a good 'whodunit' right?"

"Yeah, you're like a Nancy Drew novel." Darren turned the T.V. on.

"Oh my God, I used to love Nancy Drew books when I was in elementary school. I read all of them in grammar school."

"Well, I was a boy so I read The Hardy Boys. I knew Nancy Drew was better than them, but I had to be on the boys' side."

"Did it make you want to be a cop?" She looked in his eyes with a smirk.

"I'm not a cop. Who said I was a cop?" he said nervously. He wanted to tell Brielle the truth, but on his own time.

"I said did it make you *want* to be a cop? Calm down."

"Oh, yeah, when I was younger. You?"

"No, I don't like cops. I feel like they use their badges as a right to break the law, or to do whatever they want to do to people.

Darren flipped through the channels nervously. He thought about just telling the truth. "Let me go get the food. What kind of salad dressing do you like? I made salad, too."

"I like Italian." She thought of Shawn and his inheritance from that Italian man and smiled.

"Okay, be right back." Darren left the room to get the salads and she gave his drink another two shots of antifreeze.

He came back with two salad bowls. She started eating and he stopped her. "Can you wait a second? Let me say Grace first girl, don't ever forget to thank God," he said seriously. "Lord, we are blessed to have this food to eat. We are saved from dangers seen and unseen. Please, if there is any unseen danger in our food, take it out Lord," they said Amen and she continued eating.

"Are you a believer?" he asked and she looked at him blankly. He rephrased the question. "Do you believe in Jesus Christ? Are you a Christian?"

"I believe there's a God. I don't know how true Jesus waking from the dead to perform miracles is. How come there aren't any more miracles like the Red Sea?" She looked at the television set not very interested in his answer.

"There are miracles everyday. Jesus is real. And He can help heal your pain if you ask Him."

"Okay, I didn't say He wasn't I just said I don't know about it. I wasn't brought up in church and as a child and a wife, I prayed to God and he must not have heard me because shit stayed the way it was."

"Well, you have to be faithful. You can't just ask for stuff for nothing, not even believing that he'll do it."

"I feel you," Brielle said, trying to cut that conversation short. She wasn't in the mood to talk about God. As far as she was concerned, Darren was trying to play God by judging her and prosecuting her.

"Well, I have some movies. Pick which one you want to watch." He passed her a handful of DVDs.

She started looking through the pile of movies that he had passed to her. She finished eating her salad and passed him the bowl. *Get out of here so I can give your ass another dose*, she thought. He put her bowl on the coffee table and finished his salad. He got up to go into the kitchen again to prepare the dinner plates. She dosed his glass up yet again.

Darren came back out with two plates of turkey and stuffing with gravy, macaroni and cheese and collard greens. It looked delicious. He put the plates down and excused himself to go to the bathroom. She shot up his gravy on top of the turkey and the stuffing, which also had gravy on top of it. She finally emptied all of the antifreeze out of the baster and returned it to her purse for the last time. He came out of the bathroom a few minutes later.

"Man, I wouldn't go in that bathroom if I were you. I just blew it up and I didn't even eat yet. I don't know what has been going on with my stomach these last few days. Maybe you have my nerves shot. You got me all anxious and intimidated." He rubbed his stomach.

"Maybe you're just full of shit," she joked.

"Real funny. No, seriously I really like you." He stretched, trying to shake the stomach pains.

"Is that so? Why?" She crossed her legs and moved her top leg up and down.

"Because you seem real. You seem like you are a loyal person, not full of games."

"Oh, I'm no joke, trust me." She changed her position and sat half Indian style.

"Yeah, I don't like a whole bunch of fluff around a woman and then when you get to the bottom of it, there's really nothing there. Brielle, you have substance."

"I have something, but I don't really know what it is myself. I don't think like most people think. I take most things to heart. That's not always good though," Brielle admitted.

"Yeah, because most people don't take anything seriously.

Everyone is going for self so no one really cares about each other anymore," Darren explained.

"I know. We are a world of individual people who have their own goals and will hurt whoever we need to hurt to accomplish those goals."

"Well, there are still a few good people left in the world. You might have that person staring you right in your face and don't even realize it," Darren said and leaned close to her. He stared into her eyes.

Brielle took a bite of her turkey, prompting Darren to take a few bites, too. "Yeah? And people have secrets that they know would ruin their chances if they told on themselves."

He seemed interested to hear what she was referring to.

"So, you're saying that there's something about you that you think I wouldn't be able to handle?"

"All I'm saying is that people don't always tell you the truth about themselves, that's all," she said matter-of-factly.

"Okay…" Darren stopped talking and ate with moans in between. "Your conversation is deep."

"Yeah, you're not ready for me. Just eat," she added. "Watch this movie you chose. *A Family That Preys*, I heard that was good."

Within minutes Darren was done. He'd cleaned his plate entirely. "You must like my food, you're almost done, too. Do you want some more?"

"No, but I'll have another glass of Pina Colada."

When he got up to refill her glass, Brielle reached for her bag, but suddenly remembered that she didnt have anymore antifreeze left. A few seconds later, he returned to the room and passed her the glass.

Darren leaned forward and kissed her, sticking his tongue deep into her mouth. She let him move his tongue around with not much response at first, before pulling back and kissing his lips.

"Uhm, I could do that more often," he said.

"Now I know I gotta get rid of you. I was not feeling that," she told herself.

"Stop wasting time," her mother sounded from the right

side of her brain.

They continued watching T.V. until Darren started caressing her shoulder and playing with her hand. All of a sudden he grabbed his stomach. "Aw man, my stomach is cramping up. You gotta excuse me again. Man, I might have gall stones or something."

Darren got up and sped toward the bathroom. Brielle instantly got nervous. Both her heart and mind raced for fear that he might die right there with her in his place. Then her senses kicked in. She figured that it would take time for his body to absorb the deadly ingredient in the antifreeze and maybe have a heart attack in his sleep. That would probably be the only way there would be no suspicion of his death.

For nearly twenty minutes, Brielle switched bodily positions, and changes in her plan, while sitting on the couch waiting for Darren. She thought of an alibi just in case she was ever questioned after his death. Then he appeared out of nowhere saying, "Do you think you can ever love again?"

"No," she snapped. To her, he was unbreakable.

"I wanted to forget about love too, until I met you," he admitted, plopping down on the couch next to her. Brielle instantly became uncomfortable about the way he was expressing his feelings for her.

"I agree. It's like your loved one giving your enemy the gun to shoot you with. It's the most painful thing to find out about someone you love. But, I'm not ready to hear this right now Darren." She focused on the T.V. screen but wasn't really watching it.

"Well, I'm ready to say it, Brielle." He turned her face to look at him.

"Okay, well, let me get something to drink. Do you want something?" she asked.

"Yeah, I'll take some Ginger Ale, thank you. And don't think you're going to get out of this conversation. I've been waiting for the right time to tell you this."

She rushed into the kitchen and stood by the sink for a few minutes with her thoughts playing ping pong inside her mind. "This wasn't supposed to be a part of the plan," she told herself, crossing her arms tightly "He wasn't supposed to be talking like this." She thought some more and shrugged her shoulders, "He's lying. He's trying to get me to trust him," she decided. Then hit herself on the forehead harshly.

"He wants me to fall for him so he can fuck me over," she said to herself.

"Let's go Bitch, handle this business, he's nothing but another twisted man," her mother taunted.

Brielle rushed back into the living room and sat down uneasily.

"Let me have some of you, Brielle. I really want you." Darren damn near attacked her with his tongue. Yet strangely, she couldn't resist it. She kissed him back. She didn't know why. He started to feel good, and Brielle wondered if his little spiel was starting to work on her mind. He kissed her breasts and sucked on them hungrily, sending Brielle into horny heaven. Her guard was coming down more and more with every kiss on her body.

Suddenly Darren let out a loud, painful yell. He hopped up as fast as he could and stumbled toward the bathroom again. "You okay?" Brielle shouted from behind. Darren could only wave her off with his hand as he entered the bathroom and closed the door.

Brielle took advantage of the moment. She had to cover herself. Quickly, she got up and covered her tracks. She plotted hard and thought of every instance where the police could interrogate her. Soon, thirty minutes had passed so Brielle decided to walk down the hall to knock on the door. Unfortunately for her, she heard the toilet flush. When Darren opened the door, Brielle held her breath. "Are you okay?"

"I'll be right out," he said. He looked flush and sick and very faint. His eyes had sunken in, that fast. She panicked and got ready to call a cab. She closed her cell phone back up. She thought that wouldn't be smart to call a cab from there.

Darren walked back into the room with some basketball shorts on instead of the jean shorts that he'd had on when he picked her up.

"Pardon me, Brielle. I really think I might go to the Emergency Room."

"Yeah? You feel that bad? You probably should just lay down. I called a cab already. It should be outside in a few minutes. Maybe you should see how you feel by the morning and then go to the hospital."

"Yeah, you might be right, but I've never felt cramps in my whole life like this and it's not just my stomach muscles, it's like all the muscles in my body are tightening and contracting. Like I'm being suffocated. I can't explain how I feel; it's a really weird and painful feeling. But, it's calmed down for a minute."

"Okay, well, I'm gonna go home now. I'll call to check on you in the morning."

"Do that," Darren uttered, trying to force a smile. "Hey, wait!" he struggled to say. "I have to tell you something, Brielle. I can't go any further without telling you the truth because then everything I tell you will seem like a lie when you find out."

"What?" she said with a confused expression. Her keys were in her hand and she was nearing the front door.

"When I met you in Aruba I was there to find out about you. Monique Troy came into the Fort Lee Police Department and accused you of murdering her lover, your husband. I'm a cop. I was given a month to find out if she was telling the truth." Brielle just sat there listening, with no reaction. "So, I traveled to Aruba and found you. I befriended you. I listened to you talk and tried to see if you would confess. I was there to catch a killer and caught feelings for you before I left Aruba."

She still had no reaction.

"You're not mad?" He was confused.

"Mad? No, I'm not surprised. All of you men are liars and cheats." She shook her head and opened the front door.

"Brielle, wait. I'm for real. After I met you, I knew that it couldn't be true. I started falling in love with you the moment I started being in your company. I left Aruba with the intentions of making you mine. Brielle, I love you."

"Darren, come on, you don't even know me." A tear came to her eye. She really wanted someone to love her. "I'll call you to-morrow," she said, shutting the door behind her.

∾Chapter 21∾

Brielle left Darren's place uneasily, and rushed home to clean up the evidence. She walked in the house damn near in tears and put her bag down on the counter near the refrigerator. She took the turkey baster out of the bag and soaked it in dish detergent, in the kitchen sink then headed for the backyard. Outside, she mumbled to herself, then breathed as much air as she could. Things were getting hectic and the stress had taken its toll. She had only been out on the deck a few times since spring had come and it was already summer.

Something told her to open her cell phone. It was time to call Shawn, so she dialed his number. She needed to hear his soothing voice.

"Hey, beautiful," he answered.

"Hey, baby," she said smiling.

"What are you doing?"

"I'm sitting on my back deck, thinking about you." She then looked down at the hot tub and imagined her and Shawn inside.

"Oh yeah? Well, I'm down to sit on the deck with you. Can I come?"

"For real?" She nodded her head wildly knowing he could not see her. "Sure you can."

"Yeah, I'm out here in Jersey anyway. I had to go to the office for something. I just want to see you for a minute. I'm going to take my son to the movies at 8:30, so I have about an hour and a half." He started driving toward her house.

"Come on over and see me. I'm glad I called you."

"You're not going to believe this, but I honestly was just about to call and see if I could come by and see you. I probably conveniently had to come to the office so I'd have an excuse to come and check you."

"You don't need an excuse, handsome. I'll see you in a few."

"You hungry, Pretty Lady?"

"No, I'm just hungry to see you," she said sweetly.

"Oh, that was smooth. You get some points for that one. I'll be there shortly," he said just before hanging up.

Brielle hurried back inside, took a bottle of wine out of the cabinet, and poured some into two glasses. She took a sip and waltzed back out to the deck to escape her problems again. Her backyard was huge, and was decorated with elegant lounge furniture on the lawn, and a top of the line grill beyond where the Jacuzzi was.

Before long, her doorbell rang and she rushed to the door patting her ponytail into place along the way. When she opened the door, she became moist almost instantly. Shawn was standing there looking like a cross between Idris Elba and Carmelo Anthony. He had on light blue Nike basketball shorts and a white and blue, Nike t-shirt, perfect for exposing his bulging bi-ceps.

Shawn wasted no time. He grabbed her and stuck his tongue deep, into her mouth. Oddly, she sucked on it, while he twirled his tongue inside in her mouth just as Dante had done in the past. The few short minutes felt good to Brielle until, Shawn pulled back and kissed her full lips. He squeezed her, and held her hands lovingly just before pulling back and stopping to stare her into the eyes.

"Damn, you're such a brown cutie. You are so sexy. Girl, I haven't stopped thinking about you since I met you." He rubbed his thumb along her thick eyebrows stopping on the side of her cheek.

"That's good. Because I've been thinking about you, too. Come on, let's go outside. She walked through the living room and turned on the CD player. The CD from her and Dante's wedding was still in the CD player and "Cupid" by 112 came on.

Shawn grabbed her from behind, before she could even make it to the sliding door. He pulled her back and turned her around. He started dancing with her to one of her favorite songs. And he sang softly in her ear, "*Cupid doesn't lie, but you won't know unless you give it a try…True love, doesn't lie…*" He had her hand up and his other arm around her waist. He dipped her and brought her back up. They danced cheek to cheek until the end of the song.

When the song finished, Brielle led him out to the deck and down the stairs. He followed suit and picked up the wine bottle after seeing her grab the two glasses. They moved seductively down the stairs and onto the lawn chairs. Brielle held her glass up, and Shawn clanked his glass against hers. She nodded for him to say something.

"To new beginnings. To forgetting the past. To forgiving and letting go."

They both sipped their wine and chatted for hours. Shawn talked to her about his father. They had gotten on the subject because he told her that his father's birthday was coming up in a couple of days. He said that he appreciated his father so much for raising him. He had grown up with so many men who had no example at all growing up, of how to become a man. He knew that he was a different person than who he would have been had his father not raised him. He did start to stray at a point when he thought he was grown and he almost ruined his life by trying to be "down". But his father had to step in and save him right before he reached the point of no return.

Brielle didn't interrupt his conversation by asking questions. She just let him talk. It appeared to be good therapy. He talked for a good hour, telling of different experiences with his father and his family. She wished that she had good memories like he did. She wished that she could recall from such evidence of love from her childhood, but she couldn't.

He checked his watch and realized that he had to go and get his son.

"Aw Ma, I hope I didn't bore you with my stories. I wanted to give you my undivided attention, but I ended up talking about me." He stood up and he pulled her up by her hands.

"It's all good, Shawn. I enjoyed listening. That's good that you have fond memories like that. That way you can always pick things to smile about when thinking about your dad." She pulled herself close to him and wrapped his arms around her, still holding his over-sized hands.

"That's true; I have nothing to be upset about. He was a great father. Now, let me go be a great dad to my son. I'll call you either tonight or tomor…"

His cell phone rang causing him to check the phone screen then step back. "Hello," he answered hesitantly. "Oh, what's up with you? Nah, I've been a little busy lately. I can't talk right now, I have to call you back." Shawn hung up and pulled Brielle close to him again.

"Who was that?" she asked accusingly.

"Nobody important."

"Well, it was obviously a female. Are you sure you're going to get your son?"

Shawn looked at Brielle strangely. "Brielle, relax, jealousy is unbecoming of you."

"But damn, you couldn't talk in front of me, so that must mean that you're seeing someone else."

"What it means is that I'm a grown man who can handle my own business. Now I gotta go. I'll call you either tonight or tomorrow. Okay, baby?"

"Okay." She walked him to the door wanting revenge on both Shawn and the woman who called. She made a mental note to start checking his phone when possible.

Brielle got up early the next morning and called Darren only to get his answering service. She paused slightly before putting the receiver down, wondering if he was still alive. He should've told me the truth a long time ago, she told herself convincingly.

As soon as she placed the phone down, it rang loudly startling Brielle.

Was it Darren calling back? Brielle wondered in fear.

"Hello," she answered hesitantly.

"Damn, you haven't even tried to check on me! I could be in jail!" Janay shouted.

"Bitch, if you were in jail, I would've gotten a phone call. Stop it. You ain't even leave Brooklyn yet. You said you were leaving tomorrow and I know why I haven't heard from you. Yo' ass is out there skeezin' with Corey. I hope you ain't doin' what you was doing in ATL."

"No, I've just been with Corey but it goes down in Brooklyn. Every night we are doing something in the hood. It's crazy over here."

"Yeah, it's more your league. You were trying to be something you were not with all them fuckin' white people and now you see what that got you right? Stay in your lane."

"Brielle, shut the fuck up. You pretend that you are so upper class and yo' ass is from Paterson. You only live in Fort Lee bitch, don't forget where you came from," Janay shot back.

"Whatever. Call me when you get settled. You can't go back to your house?" She sat up higher in the bed.

"I don't know. None of my friends have called me, yet. I said I was in the Bahamas to a few people who have called me this weekend and I told my job that I was going to California for a family emergency so I'll see if they call, asking me any questions. The phone that I use for business is a dummy phone so when the cops start calling on that line, I'll know to start worrying. I'm good for right now. I'll call you in a couple of days. Love you, Brielle."

"Love you too, Crazy," Brielle answered.

"Look who the hell is talking. A'ight, talk to you later."

Brielle hung up from Janay, but picked it back up to dial Shawn's number.

"Hey handsome, how'd you sleep last night?" she asked leaning back on her pillow.

"I'm good. But it's you I have to worry about now."

"Oh really?"

"I just want to help you feel better. I know that you're still hurt. And I want your mind on me and me alone."

"Why do you say that?"

"Because you're scared and you have a reason to be. You've gone through a very traumatic experience and it doesn't go away over night. It takes time. I have all the time in the world, don't feel like you have to rush to make me feel good."

"What about my competition?"

"There is no competition. No rush. You have my undivided attention. You have my shoulder to lean on, my ears to listen to you, and my arms to hold you."

Brielle blushed. "Oh my God, you're making me melt over here."

"Well, then I guess I have to give you my hands to scoop you up off the floor. Look, I gotta go. I'll call you later, okay?"

"Oh, okay. But I was calling to tell you that I'll be staying in Paterson for the next few days. My grandmother is not feeling well and needs to go to the doctor and stuff. So I'm gonna be over there." She crossed her fingers and hoped that he wouldn't catch her in this lie because that would not be a good look.

"Okay, well make sure you have your cell phone."

"Uh, okay." She hung up after saying goodbye.

She hung up and called Darren again. Still no answer.

❦Chapter 22❦

Vodka and pineapple juice had become Brielle's best friend. Two days had passed since she left Darren's and still nothing. No word. No sign of anything. She sat on her king-sized bed, in the same pajamas she'd slept in, and sipped on what had become her favorite drink. She felt different; different from other times when she'd killed a man. Almost an overwhelming sense of guilt.

Out of the blue she began to bang herself in the head, telling her mother, "No. No more!" It was a hard battle keeping the voices out, but something she'd committed to doing. Brielle even considered going to see the psychiatrist recommended to her from the hospital. She'd talked to her aunt Janelle earlier in the day and promised to look into it.

As she sat and thought about the events of her life, the phone rang. She got antsy, took off toward the window, then darted back over to check the caller ID for fear that it would read Darren's number. Once again, it was Shawn. Strangely, she didn't even want to talk to him. She felt that he would know that she wasn't the same woman he'd been getting to know. But even more fearful that he would be able to tell something was suspicious.

"Hello," she said as if he had woken her up.

"Hey, beautiful. Did I wake you? It's two o'clock in the afternoon."

"I just got back from my grandmother's."

"Oh, I forgot you said you weren't going to be there. I was in the area and I wanted to see you," Shawn said.

Oh no, she thought, "Baby, I'm so exhausted. I would love to see you, but can you come by tomorrow?"

"Bet. That's why I called to tell you that I wanted to take you on a boat ride tomorrow night."

Brielle figured she'd be okay by then. "I'd love to go."

"Okay, so call me later, beautiful."

"I will," she said unenthused.

She hung up and made one more drink to relax her nerves, ready for another nap. She didn't know if she'd be waking up to a news story about Darren, or a knock on the door by the police. Darren wasn't expected at work the next day so maybe he wouldn't be found for a few days.

"I cannot do this again. I cannot ever do this again. If I get away with this, I will never kill again," she announced to the open air.

"You will!" the voice crept through.

"Mother, you're done. You can no longer have an effect on my life!" Brielle shouted, followed by a shot of vodka.

Brielle's situation was becoming more bleak by the day. The fact that she'd taken a leave of absence from her job, and hadn't done the leg work to starting her own design company made her vulnerable to too much time on her hands. It was too much time to think about all the negative things in life, and too much time alone.

For days, she'd been drinking like a wino, and barely eating. And even though she took sleeping pills throughout the day, she couldn't get her mind off of Darren. The torment of what had been done to him remained in her mind. She kept having nightmares about Darren and Shawn meeting one another, and then in another dream they became boys. She just couldn't get her mind together. She was paralyzed with guilt for what she'd done and fear that she would be caught.

The next morning Brielle woke up bright and early and told herself that she must try to move forward. She started with finally taking a shower, and getting out of her pajamas. She decided that she needed Shawn in her life to help her move forward so she picked up the phone to call.

"Well, look who's back from the dead," Shawn said after hearing Brielle's voice.

"Well, I'm back and ready to see my Gent." Her voice seemingly held excitement again. "I'm sorry that I've been kinda distant over the last couple of days. I was feeling a bit depressed."

"I know. It's okay."

"So, if you knew that, why didn't you say anything about it?" Brielle asked with attitude.

"Because Ma, you're a big girl. There are some things that you're gonna have to go through on your own. I knew that once we got together I would make you feel better. I had to let you deal with it until I could get to you and take it from there."

"You're lucky you came up with a good answer," Brielle countered.

"No, it's the real answer. When you can't wipe your own tears, I'll wipe them for you. But you gotta be strong so you can have my back, too. If you can't handle stuff on your own, then how you gonna hold me down when I have to lean on you?"

"I got you baby."

"Okay, well be ready at six, I'll be there to scoop you."

Brielle's smile returned to her face. She felt relieved to be feeling like herself again. It was her hope that it would last until Shawn arrived, but she had her good friends, Vodka and Pineapple juice nearby just in case.

She spent hours getting ready for her anticipated date. From the hair down to the make-up she looked hot. And of course once she threw on a cream Chloe dress, Brielle knew her curves would drive Shawn crazy. It was both stylish and sexy which made her throw on her four inch heels.

By the time five o'clock rolled around, she was dressed and found herself drinking again out on her deck. For some reason, she couldn't shake the nervousness. She felt like she was hiding a deep dark secret from Shawn that he would soon uncover. And of course, leave her.

Out of the blue, Brielle poured the rest of her drink off the top deck. The thought of being drunk when Shawn arrived had her extra jittery. For moments she breathed inward like she was doing an exercise that she had been taught.

Breath after breath she inhaled then exhaled until the doorbell rang. She walked through the living room and opened her front door surprised at what she saw. Shawn looked like an angel sent from heaven, only instead of white, he wore pale orange cuffed slacks and a tan embroidered button down shirt. Almost flawless, his braids were freshly braided in a criss-cross style toward his neckline, and his teeth shined as if he'd come straight from the dentist. Brielle wanted to rip his clothes off and have him carry her upstairs to what would be *their* bedroom soon.

"Damn baby, you clean up well. I want three kisses right now," she said, smiling from ear to ear.

"No doubt." He obliged while squeezing her ass.

"Alright, well, anything to make you happy. So let's go."

They left the house just in time to make it to the pier shortly after seven. Shawn had told Brielle all about the boat ride they were going on, and bragged about how he was going to show her the best time of her life.

It didn't take too long for them to board. Shawn claimed a table with another couple he knew, and introduced Brielle to them as his lady. They shook hands, and the ladies hugged just before Shawn ordered Don Perion champagne for the table. It didn't take long for them to pop the bottle, and start drinking just as the boat set sail. Then D. J. Kid Capri started rocking and the crowd started partying instantly. It was a nice crowd, mostly mature except for a few younger ladies who had googly eyes for Shawn's body. Brielle had to have a pep talk to herself. She promised not to ruin the evening.

Brielle was already feeling good when Shawn grabbed her hand and took her to the dance floor. They started dancing and getting close. He held her tightly, while looking into her eyes and kissing her softly. T-Pain's "I like the Bartender" came on causing him to start dancing with speed and spinning her around. Shawn made her laugh doing silly stuff, so Brielle followed suit, imitating him. Soon, the other couple joined them, where they eventually switched partners. Brielle pretended to like it, but clearly did not. She watched Shawn disapprovingly dance with his man's girl while her body moved slower and unenthusiastically.

Before long, they switched back and some brown-skinned

girl started dancing behind Shawn. He turned around, acknowl-
edged the woman with a smile, then continued to dance flirta-
tiously with Brielle on one side and the unknown woman on the
other. The girl looked like a beautiful Angie Stone. She was thinner
and prettier but had Angie's style. Brielle sensed that she was a for-
mer lover. *A woman can always tell,* she thought to herself.

Brielle remained observant, yet kept dancing. She started
dancing sexier with Shawn and so did the competition. At one
point, Brielle turned around and Shawn pulled up on Brielle's ass.
No sooner than the Angie Stone look-alike tuned in, she turned
around and danced with her ass against his.

He could see the change in Brielle's behavior so opted to
end the dance. He took Brielle's hand and led her back to their
table where he asked if everything was okay.

"I'm fine," Brielle snapped.

"Sit, while I grab us a few drinks from the bar."

He smiled. Brielle smirked mockingly.

Like clockwork as soon as he moved toward the bar,
"Angie Stone" followed. Fuming in the seat, Brielle sat and
watched.

Shawn ordered the drinks and turned around to see the girl
approaching him. He looked at Brielle and their eyes met. The girl
started talking and you could tell that she was beefing with him.
He was agitated but he stood there listening. The girl walked away.
He turned around, picked up their drinks and sat back at their table.
The other couple was still on the dance floor.

"Wow, you have a fatal attraction?" she asked. He didn't
find the joke funny.

"Brielle, that was Audrey. She was the girl I was telling you
about." He took a sip of his drink and put it back down.

"Oh yeah, are you still seeing her?" She sipped hers.

"No, I told you that I stopped seeing her."

"Well, that's what you told me, but…" He cut her off.
"Brielle, that's all I have to say."

"What? What do you mean?" Her eyes widened.

"I said what I mean," he answered.

"What's all that for?" she asked.

"Brielle, I said what I meant."

She was quiet. They started sipping on their drinks and were silent.

Another woman came up and Shawn stood up and gave her a hug. She pulled him onto the dance floor and he went along. They were dancing in front of Brielle in a respectable manner. Brielle didn't want to act out of control, so she sat patiently and just watched. The girl, Audrey, walked over and started dancing behind Shawn. He ignored her for a few minutes and then she tapped his shoulder. He turned around and danced with her unenthused. He did not dance close and neither did she but she just kept looking into his eyes.

Shawn said something in her ear and she walked away calmly. He then turned around and continued to dance with the new girl for one more song. He said something in her ear and then walked back over to rejoin Brielle at their table. Brielle didn't look at Shawn when he sat down. She continued to watch the other people dance. He leaned over and asked Brielle if she wanted to dance and she shook her head no. She excused herself from the table and Shawn gently grabbed her arm and asked her where she was going.

"To the bathroom," she replied, with an attitude.

She went to the bathroom, but instead of going back to Shawn when she came out, she walked around to see what was going on in other parts of the of the boat. She figured he had a lot going on so maybe she would find something to get into, fuck it.

Brielle was walking down the stairs to the lower part of the yacht when someone reached for her hand and stopped her. She looked into the green eyes of a very good looking man. He was tall and light skinned, with a low cut of sandy brown colored hair. He looked like Rick Fox.

"Hello Gorgeous, what's your name?" He kept holding her hand.

"Brielle."

"Brielle, I'm Jason. And I want to buy you a drink."

"Okay."

"There's a bar down here, follow me." They walked over to the bar. She ordered her usual vodka with pineapple juice. They took a seat at a table. She hoped that Shawn didn't decide to come looking for her. She knew she was just being spiteful.

"Who are you here with?" He looked her up and down for the second time.

"I'm on a date." He stepped back.

"I'm scared of you, girl. What's his name, cause if he's my boy I'll have to send you with a drink and a great regret that we couldn't get better acquainted?"

"If I tell you his name you might tell him that I was on our date checkin' for you. I'm just giving him a minute because he has a few women trying to get his attention and they seem to be people from his past. I don't want to be a ball and chain."

He shook his head in disagreement. "Is it that, or did you catch an attitude, like most women do?"

She laughed. "It might be a little bit of both. But why is it that you men can dish it but you can't take it. If I had been dancing on the floor with two of my exes in his face he probably would have been ready to fight."

"Well, is he your man?"

"No." She looked behind the guy's shoulder hoping Shawn didn't come.

"So, what you mad for? That's another thing you woman do too early. You start acting like you own us the minute we take you out."

"Look, I just took a walk and you stopped me. If you want me to leave, I can get up and go." She wanted to leave before she got caught.

"Nah, I really want your number and for you to leave with me. Now, is that possible?" He flashed a fake pimp smile.

"Damn, just like a man," Brielle said and then noticed Shawn coming in their direction. Her face must've shown fear because the guy looked in that direction, too.

Shawn walked up and looked at Brielle disgustedly. He reached his hand out and shook Rick Fox's hand.

"Peace man, I see my lady found someone else to spend the party with." The guy shook Shawn's hand and they let each other's hands go.

"Oh, nah man, we were just talking. She's all yours." The guy got up and walked behind Shawn, looking at Brielle, and then winked at her. He grabbed the hand of another girl who was walking past him. They said a few words and walked to the bar together.

"Brielle, what's up?" He asked agitated.

"That's what I was asking you, but I see what's up with you so I don't have to ask anymore." She tried to keep the focus on him.

"Oh yeah? So, I bring you to a boat ride and you go on the prowl?" He had a disappointed look on his face.

"At least you don't have to be on the prowl, you got prospects already lined up," she retorted.

"I'm gonna ask you again. This is how you do when somebody takes you somewhere? You disrespect them by being up in another man's face?"

"Weren't you up in two bitches' faces?"

"Do you realize that you keep answering my questions with a question, instead of making it clear to me what you thought you were doing? You standing your ground? You consider yourself being a strong woman right now?"

She didn't know how to answer his question. She was apprehensive because he seemed to be really getting mad in a calm way.

"Shawn, I asked you about the girl and you acted like you didn't want to answer me, why? That makes it seem like there's something up."

"It does?" He shook his head again. "Now *I'm* going to the bathroom." He got up and walked away.

Brielle sat there wondering if she'd done something wrong. She couldn't deny that she had gotten a little attitude and acted immature about the situation. She was trying to show her ass, but the effect that she wanted wasn't what she got. Now Brielle was feeling like she had messed up instead of him. She waited for a few minutes for Shawn to come back but he didn't. She then went back up to the upper level and back to their table. She didn't see Shawn. She walked outside on the deck and he was talking to the second girl who had taken him out on the floor to dance with her.

Brielle walked up to them and just stood there. The girl didn't even acknowledge Brielle's presence.

"Brielle, wait for me inside please?" Shawn didn't turn to look at her.

"Shawn, I need to talk to you right now?"

"Brielle, wait for me at the table."

Brielle couldn't believe Shawn was being so short with her. She didn't know whether she should stay there or do what he said. She decided to go back to the table. While she was sitting down a guy came and took her hand for her to dance. Not wanting to sit alone any longer, she got up and started dancing with him. Brielle was just trying to save face because Shawn was on the deck with another woman. She wasn't dancing in a provocative manner, she was just dancing. When Shawn came to the table he sat and watched her. She felt uncomfortable and told the guy she was going to sit down.

When she sat next to Shawn, he didn't say anything. She just sat there with him silently. He talked to the other couple and acted like she wasn't even there.

"Can you dance with me Shawn?" she asked and grabbed his hand.

He got up and followed her to the dance floor but even though his body was there his mind wasn't. The spark that they had earlier was dead. There was no intensity, no attraction coming from him to her. Brielle got scared. She figured that he wanted to be with one of the other two women instead of her. She walked away and sat down. He kept dancing and another woman who seemed more like a stranger to him started dancing in front of him. He danced and smiled and talked to her, right in front of Brielle's face.

After about two songs Shawn finally walked off the floor and sat next to Brielle, but he still had no words for her. At that moment, the yacht was pulling in to dock. They walked from the boat to the car in silence.

When they got to the car he passed Brielle her keys. He looked at her and said, "Goodnight."

"Shawn, what's the deal with you?" she pleaded, knowing

he wasn't trying to hear anything she had to say.

"I'm trying to figure out the same thing about you," he replied.

"Well, let me just ask you, if the things that occurred were the other way around, would you have felt disrespected?"

"I would've given you the benefit of the doubt."

"Shawn you had two women pursuing you, you danced with both, had private conversations with both, danced with a third. If you were going there to be single, you shouldn't have taken me." She tried to use reverse psychology.

"Brielle, first of all, I'm single. But where you were wrong was to continue to question me from the beginning. I didn't want to elaborate because I wanted to enjoy the time with you. I handled myself properly; you on the other hand wanted to be vindictive and vengeful. I would've talked to you about it later, but you just started tripping and acting like you weren't. I'm not a little boy or a toy and if you can't respect me when I tell you something, that's going to be a problem. We're adults. I wasn't in a bathroom stall with either of those women and for your information the one I was on the deck with was my deceased wife's sister. I didn't like how you came by us and just stood there. She's having marital problems and she was discussing it with me. I would have explained all of that to you but your actions showed me that you didn't deserve that much respect. Now, goodnight."

Brielle was too stunned to move. She couldn't believe that their night had ended like that. She decided not to try and get him to come back. It was very clear that he wasn't interested in being around her. She wondered if that was going to be the end of her and Shawn that fast. She thought about Darren and how he may have been good for her.

Brielle shook her head. "Damn, I know how to pick the wrong ones."

❦ Chapter 23 ❦

Brielle awakened Sunday morning, close to ten o'clock to the sound of Channel 12 news. The verbal announcement and yellow police tape in the background caused Brielle's jaw to drop at the sounding of the reporter's voice.

"Fort Lee Detective found dead in his condo, foul play suspected."

Brielle gasped. *They suspect foul play? Why?*

The story continued with the reporter stating that Detective Darren Lewis had been found by the superintendent of his building. He was supposed to have had some work done in his apartment and when the super let himself in he found Detective Lewis in his bedroom, dead on the floor. They said his apartment had been ransacked, but not broken into.

"Ransacked?" Brielle asked herself in awe. "I left his apartment in perfectly good shape. Maybe his soon-to-be-ex-wife went in there, found him, and tried to take whatever valuables she could find."

Within minutes, hundreds of alibi's crept into her mind. One excuse, she would say that she'd taken Darren some soup, and that he was alive when she left. Another was to say that they'd been dating for a couple of weeks, and Darren decided he needed some time alone. Another excuse- she hadn't seen him in weeks.

Brielle's cell phone rang, causing her to jump and look toward her bedroom door. Everything seemed to cause nervousness; even the fact that the number couldn't be recognized. She let it go to voicemail, then listened to the message from the unknown caller.

"This is Sergeant Petersen from the Fort Lee Police Depart-

ment. I have a few questions to ask about Officer Darren Lewis.
Please return the call immediately."

Brielle swallowed. Hard. Followed by a lump forming in
her throat. She didn't know what to do. Her first thought was to
call Janay. Then she considered calling her Aunt Janelle, then her
thoughts switched back to Detective Peterson. The thought of
inviting him over to see what he knew crossed her mind. But she
knew how the meeting would end.

Frantically, she hopped out of bed, pacing the floor and
scratching her arms neurotically. Then out of the blue, her doorbell
rang. Brielle rushed toward the door, barefoot, wearing a white,
cotton one-piece. Taking two steps at a time, she tiptoed toward the
front as if she knew someone was there for a not so friendly visit.
When Brielle finally peeped through the hole suspiciously, she noticed two plain clothes officers with badges pushed toward the
peephole.

Within seconds, Brielle lost all self control. With her hands
held frantically in the air, she hugged herself like a child needing a
hug in a horrific moment.

"Shit, shit, shit," she mumbled, as she did an about face and
pressed her back quietly against the door.

Her next move was to figure out if the officers would try to
get in. Then what? Thought after thought bounced around in her
head as she stayed low, and away from the windows. Suddenly, her
cell rang again from her bedroom. Brielle got in gear in a hurry,
and jetted back up the steps to the bedroom.

Janay always had bad timing, she thought.

"What Janay?" Brielle whispered.

"Guess what?"

Brielle heard her doorbell ring again, but sat on the floor,
ignoring it. "What?" she whispered, while perspiring like crazy.

"Darren is dead."

"I know already."

"Girl, I heard it on the news last night. And hell, after Peyton's mysterious death, and now Darren's, I figured you needed a
call."

"Janay, I'm not sure what that means… but is that it?"

"No, Bitch that's not it. Don't you want to know how my situation is going?"

"Wait. Hold on," Brielle said abruptly, then waited quietly for any more sounds coming from the front door. Seconds went by… nothing. "So, what's going on Janay?" Brielle asked, holding the phone receiver half-way to her ear.

"Well, the Russian fuck was a diplomat, so the Feds are on the case, that's what's up. I'm not a suspect yet but they did come and interview everyone at my office. I told them that I didn't know anything. I've been going to work and my boss has been filling me in on the developments of the case. The police know that he was with a call girl so they think that maybe she tried to set him up with someone else, and the person robbed him and killed him by accident, and then killed her so that she wouldn't be a witness."

"Damn," Brielle mentioned casually. The intent was to act interested. But it didn't go off too well.

"I did retain a high powered Russian attorney just in case. I gave him five thousand dollars as a retainer…*just in case.*"

"That's good, so you straight then. Well listen, I gotta go," Brielle stated, lifting herself from the floor. She crept toward the window to peep outside.

"Yeah, I'm straight for now, but I will need a few thousand if anything pops off."

"Look, I'll be honest," Brielle started while she slipped on some jeans. "I really don't have it."

"Find it," Janay barked. Or, I'll make that call to Fort Lee Police. Know what I'm saying?" she asked grimly.

Brielle didn't feel like playing games. "Janay, let's get off the phone. I've got enough problems.

"Here me out Brielle, Crazy Lady Prescott! I know about Dante…and Peyton…neither were a mistake. Oh, and the baller in Houston…I know too dear. And let's not even discuss Darren. All I gotta say is have that money when I need it."

Click.

Chapter 24

Hours passed as Brielle remained glued to her living room floor, with a bottle of Vodka in hand, and her hair spread across her head wildly. The weather had begun to change as the clouds put a gloom over the city. Brielle sat on the floor clipping her nails so far down into the nail-bed that they began to bleed. But for Brielle, it didn't matter. Nothing mattered. She felt like everyone had turned against her; all the men in her life, her parents, and now even Janay.

Her only hope; was Shawn. She hadn't had time to really think about the boat ride, or why she behaved the way she did. It had started out so good, almost picture perfect, of course ending like a nightmare. She'd finally felt like his woman, but wasn't sure where things had gone wrong. Shit, she had acted like Glen Close in the movie, Fatal Attraction.

Without delay, Brielle dialed his phone hoping to apologize, but it went straight to voice mail. "Hi Shawn, I'd like to talk to you, call me back when you get a chance, please." She hung up.

Brielle thought about her depression, and tried to think of something that would cheer her up. Then it clicked, the insurance check. She desperately needed money to finance her blues away. Brielle jumped up, slipped on some blue Crocs, and rushed outside toward the mailbox.

Just as she stepped across the threshold, the phone rang again. Brielle checked the caller ID and answered the cordless with speed.

"Shawn," she called out, putting the phone to her right ear. "I'm so glad you called me back."

"Yeah. I decided to give you another chance. But don't mess up again."

"Look Shawn. I'm human."

"Brielle, I'm here for you. But you can't expect me to overlook whatever you do because you're hurting."

Just as he said his last word, two plain clothes officers approached Brielle just yards away from the mailbox.

"Mrs. Prescott?"

"Yes, that's me."

"I'm Detective Stanford and this is Detective Arthur. We're from the Hackensack Police Department."

Badges flashed as sweat quickly covered Brielle's body. "What is this about?" she asked frantically.

Shawn listened on the other end as a voice said, "We need to take you down to the station. You're being charged for the murder of Darren Lewis."

Shawn speedily began coaching from the phone. "Don't say anything. Go down to the station. But don't protest. I'm on my way and bringing you a lawyer!"

"But I didn't do anything, Shawn." Her voice trembled as the officers read her the Miranda rights.

"I'll come straight there baby, okay? I know where the police department is. Stay calm, and don't do anymore talking. My lawyer will be on it. Do you hear me?"

"I hear you. I hear you," she sobbed, as the shorter officer removed the phone from her ear, ending the call.

Brielle was cuffed, hands behind her back, looking a mess. She cried out, "Can I at least lock my door?"

"I'll take care of that," Detective Stanford announced.

He was an older gentleman, near retirement who'd heard and seen it all. Brielle's constant sobbing wasn't fooling him one bit. Her file had been pulled, and he knew she was trouble. "Watch your head," he told her as his partner placed her into the squad car.

On the short ride to the station, Brielle held her head low, contemplating her responses to any questions that would come her way. After going over her story a thousand times, Brielle knew that after she came back from Atlanta, Darren had confessed to her that he was a police officer, and that she wasn't offended. Also that they'd spoken on the phone only about five times, which was actually true.

She would also say that she went to his house when he told her he was sick and took him some soup, and that she left when he fell asleep about eight o'clock.

The most important thing that she needed to get across was the fact that Darren was alive when she left. As long as they weren't going to check him for poison she would be fine. If the autopsy revealed that he had died from a heart attack then she would really be fine. As far as Brielle was concerned, she was straight. Or so she hoped.

When the car pulled up to the station, Brielle felt relieved to see Shawn waiting outside the police parking lot gates. He would have to use the Civilian entrance, on the opposite side of the building but she was glad to see him there. As she got out, hands still behind her back, Shawn shouted out, "I'm here baby. Mr. Rabassi is on the way!"

As the two officers walked her into the station, they pushed Brielle along as if she had already been convicted. Once inside, the detectives talked in codes to a young guy in his late twenties, who Brielle believed was a Muslim. He had hair everywhere, from the top of his head to well below his chin. When he spoke and flipped through her file, she knew he was in charge.

"I'm Sergeant Maddix. You've been charged with Darren Lewis' murder. So you'll be transferred to county for now."

"What!" she shouted, ready to win an academy award for her performance.

"That's what happens when you commit murder. You wanna let my guys ask you a couple of questions?"

Brielle couldn't believe her ears. She was about to black out but she thought about Shawn. "No," she shot back as if the light bulb went off.

"No problem," he said, after signaling the officers to escort her to a back room where four people where sitting on several benches.

"Shawn came blaring through the front just as Brielle was almost to the back of the station near the detainee area. Officers watched him from the over-sized front desk wondering what he thought he could do.

"My lawyer is on the way, Brielle!" he shouted. "Don't worry; you still don't have to answer any questions without a lawyer. You're good, I got you."

Brielle's body was pushed through the back door, and disappeared when the door was closed. She felt helpless without Shawn and vulnerable to the two ladies sitting on the bench beside her. They talked about celebrities and every bit of gossip that hit the streets, as Brielle cried faintly.

They sat for over an hour until a uniformed, white officer came and told them they were all being transported to the county jail. Brielle was pissed. She knew that the ride to County was just the beginning of her problems. She needed money for a lawyer, a good story to stick to, and a hell of a lawyer.

By the time she'd gotten into the van and drove the first ten minutes toward the jail, she felt like a juvenile on the way to Juvee hall. The group that she was traveling with made crazy jokes, and asked Brielle how long she'd been killing people. They thought it was funny as they shared the various reasons they were there; weed, stealing, car theft, and ironically, murder.

Once the van arrived, Brielle and her fellow inmates were all processed and logged in with a number. Brielle knew things were official, but hoped that Shawn's lawyer was going to be able to make it soon. The thought of spending the night would surely send her into a tragic mental state. Between the reoccurring dreams and the thought of someone touching her in jail caused her to pull at the strands of her hair, deep down in the root. She vowed not to do anything stupid, hoping that her situation was temporary.

Soon, Brielle had been taken to her cell where she studied the metal sink and bland concrete walls. Her heart plummeted as the doors slammed, and an officer told her, "You may as well get comfortable."

Brielle wanted to cry but before a tear could fall, she was told that a lawyer was there to see her. Her heart raced as she stood by the black bars waiting for the door to reopen. Brielle knew that whatever she told Shawn's lawyer would be heard by Shawn later, so she had to keep that in mind.

When she entered the small interview room, the lawyer was

a well-dressed Italian in his late forties. He extended his hand and introduced himself. "Mrs. Prescott, my name is Paulo Rabassi. I'm Mr. Shawn Ellison's attorney." He took a seat at the small table, and nodded for Brielle to do the same. "He asked me to represent you. So I have acquainted myself with the information about the death of the Detective Lewis and I need to know why you believe you are a suspect."

"I believe that my phone number was in the officer's phone and they want to know how I know him."

"I think it's more than that."

"Well, I shouldn't be a suspect, I hardly knew him."

Mr. Rabassi shook his head. "I understand, but my sources tell me they have a woman saying she saw you with him."

Immediately, Brielle's mind switched to Monique. *Only she would do some shit like that,* she told herself. "That's not true," she belted.

"Is there anything that I need to know about your relationship with Mr. Lewis?"

"No, I met him in Aruba, where he had me under investigation. When I came home, he told me he was a cop, and that the case was closed. He wanted to date me, but we never dated." She sighed and kept her eyes lowered. "I only spoke to him on the phone a couple of times," Brielle ended by shifting in her seat.

"So, you never saw him. You never went on a date?" He wrote some notes down and looked up and into her eyes.

"No, we never went on a date." Brielle didn't consider being at someone's house a date; so she felt that wasn't a lie.

"When was the last time you saw Detective Lewis, Mrs. Prescott?" Mr. Rabassi tapped his pen on the table.

"Last Tuesday," she said sternly.

Mr. Rabassi spoke quickly, in his northern accent. "Oh, where did you see him Tuesday?"

"At his place. He wasn't feeling well, so I offered to take him some soup."

"Did you stay long?" he shot back.

"I stayed maybe three hours and when he fell asleep, I left," Brielle said confidently. She hoped that the lawyer didn't share everything word for word with Shawn.

"Okay, first of all, you're going to help the state convict you with your twisted stories. First you told me you only talked to him on the phone. Then in the next breath you tell me you've been to his house. Let me say this Ms. Prescott... there were cameras outside his building, so the police know exactly when you were there."

"For now, they're trying to figure out when he died. But they think you were the last to see him. I believe I can fight this enough for now saying that there were other people coming and going into the building on that tape." He paused... "But I need for you to work with me. Can you tell me anything else?"

Brielle slumped down in the chair, resting her elbows on the table. "No," she said quietly.

"Okay, so I'm going to go out and call the detective on the case. I think they might be stalling to see if they can get the results of when and how he died. I'm going to see if I can get you out of here first thing in the morning."

"Morning?" Brielle jumped from her seat.

"Yes. There's a bond hearing in the morning. You do realize you've been charged, right?"

"I do," Brielle said innocently.

"There's money that will need to be put up. And then I'll have to be paid."

"I'll take care of it," Brielle announced in an antsy tone.

"Nooo, hold off worrying for now. I believe Mr. Ellison will cover my visit today. But then there's the trial, or if you plead guilty it will cost less money."

"Guilty?" she questioned as if she was offended. "I'm innocent."

"Yes, I know," Mr. Rabassi said sarcastically. "So sit tight tonight. Pray, and think about all the things you've told me. I'll have you out in the morning."

Mr. Rabassi got up and walked out leaving her alone in the private interview room, watching as the correction officers rushed back inside to give Brielle the bad news. Dinner would be served soon, and the expression on her face showed she would enjoy it.

⤍ Chapter 25 ⤌

Two days later, Brielle was released on a $50,000 bond along with a mandate not to leave the state. Even though the bond was paid for by Shawn, when she walked out the front door, he was waiting with a disapproving frown.

"How do you mange to always get yourself involved with murder?" Shawn asked.

Brielle shook her head like a five year old. "I don't know. I just spoke to him the other day so my number was probably still in his cell when they found his body."

"So, were you seeing him?" Shawn questioned.

"No."

"Brielle, you're a liar, and you're too jealous by the way."

"Don't say that Shawn," she trailed along his side in a panic.

Shawn burst through the final set of double doors to leave the facility. "A friend of mine told me you called her last week after seeing her number on my phone. I don't like that shit, Brielle," he ranted. "I told you. I don't need another fatal attraction and I don't need you being immature and playing kid games. Okay?"

"Okay. I do get jealous sometimes. It's just that I've been hurt so many times. But believe me, I am innocent."

Shawn snatched the driver's side door open with an attitude, and never considered opening the door for Brielle. "Brielle, I'm just telling you. My patience is short. I get fed up easily so you can start the bullshit if you want. I'm telling you I'm not gonna be down for it."

"Alright already, damn. Let's not spoil this day, too. I just need to get home and get cleaned up. I swear I'll make it up to you."

The ride home seemed just as lame as Brielle's story. Shawn wasn't buying it, but agreed to spend the day with her regardless. Later in the evening, they were both relaxed and eating Chinese food, mostly talking about what happened with the detectives questioning session, and how Shawn was able to act so smooth in chaotic situations. Time flew as they continued to talk, questioning one another about their past.

Shawn finished his food and took his plate into the kitchen. Brielle secretly hoped that he wasn't ready to start making sexual advances. She wasn't in the mood, considering she had a thousand and one lies swirling through her head about her murder defense. Sadly, she didn't get her wish.

When Shawn walked back into the living room he took her plate and set it on the coffee table. He then got on his knees slipping his body in between her legs.

"You're not even eating. Do you want to talk?" he asked.

She shook her head. "I can already tell what you wanna do, Shawn."

"Oh, you do, huh? I just think you need some TLC."

He grinned just before his first kiss, sticking his tongue deep in her mouth, and hoping to get as much tongue in return. But Brielle barely kissed him back. Shawn moved toward her neck and started kissing from her chin down to her chest aggressively. Yet, Brielle still didn't respond. Shawn wouldn't give up though, his next move was to remove her shirt slowly, seductively revealing her bare breast. He kissed both of her nipples hungrily, hoping to get a rise from Brielle. Still nothing.

Brielle laid back and tried to allow herself to feel the affection she was getting. She let him make love to her breast with his tongue and caress the crevasses of her stomach while she remained still. She seemed to be in another world until she began to feel nauseous. Suddenly, she pushed him off of her and ran to the bathroom by the kitchen.

"Are you okay?" Shawn called from behind.

She rushed inside the bathroom and spoke with the door closed. "I'm okay. I'll be out in a sec."

"I'm staying right here until you come out."

Brielle swung the door open. "That wasn't the right time Shawn." She rushed toward the couch, laid down and curled up.

"What are you doing, Brielle? You don't want me kissing on you?"

"Can you just lay with me and watch a movie?" she whined, showcasing her puppy dog face. "I'm worried about the case that's all."

"I told you my lawyer will take care of it. You didn't do anything. And he'll prove it."

He pulled her so that they could sit up on the end of the couch which was like a chaise lounge. They sat there next to each other while they pretended to watch T.V.

"Brielle, do you have anything to tell me?" Shawn asked.

Brielle didn't want to answer any questions about the case so she tried to distract him by rolling over on top of Shawn, kissing him energetically. He kissed her back yet with not as much vigor as she all of a sudden obtained. Brielle moved her upper body downward as if she was going to give Shawn head, but Shawn lifted her up to stop her.

Shawn sighed. "You know what? We're rushing. Let's go outside and get in the hot tub for a while. You need to relax."

Brielle was offended, but glad Shawn stopped her. When he pulled her to stand up, Brielle simply nodded when he told her to go change into something to swim in. After going upstairs to her bedroom and putting on a sexy bikini, she came back down to see Shawn in a pair of Polo swimming trunks and nothing else. They were plain, but his body looked like a prize boxer's body. The daily work-outs were paying off.

She started letting the stress go after seeing him with his shirt off. Shawn's body was incredible, and Brielle seemed to be in awe every time she saw his muscular frame. She told herself not to ruin their evening. They walked down the steps of the deck and onto the grass. After turning on the motor in the whirlpool, they both got inside and Shawn immediately pulled her close. Moments later, they started singing old school R&B songs that were coming out of the outdoor speakers and enjoyed each other's company.

It wasn't long before Shawn's manhood rose. It was thick, hard and pulsated to a speedy tune as he pulled her bikini bottoms off along with his own trunks. Brielle looked into the water to see what he was working with but before she could see it, she felt it plunging deep inside of her moist walls. They grinded up and down, back and forth, as the bubbles continued to emerge. Brielle took every long, hard stroke like a pro. With her legs opening wider and wider, she absorbed him into her, hoping he would never leave her.

As the water began to splash, she took in each of Shawn's quickening strokes. "Oh Shawn," she moaned, realizing he had her on cloud nine. She wanted to shout for all her neighbors to hear, instead she released, clutching his back with her sweaty arms. Shawn wasted no time, he dug deep and followed suit, moving faster and faster just before pulling himself out, climaxing into the water.

With sweat dripping from his forehead, he kissed at Brielle, "Soon, I'll be cumming inside of you so we can make some babies."

Brielle smiled, however, when his comments sank in, Brielle burst into tears.

"Brielle. What the fuck is it?"

"It's Summer. I'm just thinking about the daughter I just lost."

Shawn reached for his trunks floating in the water, and located Brielle's bikini. He helped her get her swim gear back on, then reached for Brielle's arm, pulling her from the water.

"Baby, come on over to the lounge chair," he coaxed, after wrapping her with a huge towel. "Brielle, maybe it's too soon for you to be involved with someone," he said, looking into her eyes.

"Oh my God, are you telling me that you don't want to see me anymore?" She continued to weep softly then wiped her eyes. "Of course after you get the ass you want out!"

"Brielle, don't worry about me right now. I'm telling you that you need some help. I could've kept it moving after your stunt on the boat. And I could leave right now. But I have to be honest, for a man to just meet a woman who has so much on her plate, most wouldn't even deal with it. Most men would just use your vulnerability to get in your pants and then leave you without caring if the situation wrecked you mentally."

"Shawn, I am ready for a relationship. I'm ready for you," she pleaded.

"You don't know me like that Brielle. I'm a good guy but what lets me know that you're hurt is that you can say that you're ready for a relationship with me. You don't even know me. Let's just take it one day at a time. In the meantime, you've got to go and talk to someone professionally."

"I'm ready to move on. I have moved on. That doesn't mean that I'm not going to think about my daughter sometimes."

"I don't think it's about your daughter."

Brielle was becoming angrier by the minute. "Listen, you're no damn psychiatrist. You wanna be a shrink, obviously. How can you say that it's not about my daughter? Fuck her father. But it ain't fuck my daughter!"

Shawn was pissed. "Hey, hold up. First of all, lower your voice. I'm not with that making a scene shit. There are people in their backyards. Are you trying to give a matinee show?" She looked at him and listened. "Maybe I should've said it this way then; I think it's more than your daughter. Do you want me to leave now, Brielle?"

"I know you wanna leave, Shawn. You don't have to play that reverse psychology bullshit with me," she sobbed quietly.

"Yeah I'm beginning to want to leave. Hell, I wanted to enjoy you, Brielle. I wanted you to enjoy me. But you can't seem to clear your head. Don't sabotage this. I thought I was coming here to be with you all day. But, don't worry, there's always later."

"No Shawn, stay," she said, giving him a hug.

"What do you want to do now?" he asked.

Brielle displayed her school girl smile. "I'm ready for round two."

❦ Chapter 26 ❧

One week later, Brielle found herself on 139th Street where Shawn's brownstone was located. The outside of his house had nice stone statues at the foot of the stairs and the lawn was well manicured. Brielle rang the doorbell with a smile, and was greeted with a strong kiss when the man of the house answered.

"There's my lady," Shawn chanted, pulling her inside.

Once inside Brielle immediately fell in love with his place. The faux painting on the walls and the expensive tiles held her captive. Brielle could tell that a woman had been at his house considering it was spotless. She wanted to say something, but tried her best to hold off on any smart remarks. The past week had been rough enough with her constantly worrying about her case. Then something hit her inside. An urge she couldn't resist.

"I see your place has a woman's touch to it. Is that Audrey's touch?"

"No. It's actually my momma's touch. She comes over every Sunday and brings me dinner, then cleans my crib."

"Uh oh, a true momma's boy, huh?"

"I'm a woman's man. If I got a woman, she gotta do what my momma does and better."

"So, it's Sunday. Is your mother coming?"

"Yup. She should be here any minute."

Brielle was shocked. "You knew that she was coming all along, didn't you?"

"I figured what better time for the two of you to meet than now. Don't you want to meet her before our wedding?"

He laughed. Brielle didn't.

Brielle felt uncomfortable. She wasn't ready to meet Shawn's mother. She figured his mother would just use her female intuition to know that Brielle wasn't right for her son.

"I hope your mother likes me."

"She will. Don't worry, just don't let that other personality of yours come out. You know she's a shrink. She'll be able to read you like a book." Shawn laughed again, while pulling Brielle by the arm up the stair case. "Come up here to my room."

"I'm not afraid to meet her."

"Yes, you are. It's written all over your face. You wanna give me a quickie before she gets here?" he asked, walking into his bedroom.

"No Shawn, I don't. Come on. You're starting to make me feel like this is just about sex."

"Brielle, your mood sucks. Damn are you ever happy?"

"Yes, sometimes."

"Well, try to be happy more. You have your whole life ahead of you. Whatever doesn't kill you makes you stronger."

"Or sends you to the death chamber," Brielle commented under her breath.

"What did you say?"

"I said, thank you Dr. Ellison."

"I'm going to the bathroom. When I come back, have a better attitude," he instructed sarcastically.

As soon as Shawn rushed off to use the bathroom, Brielle started rambling through his drawers in search of anything that belonged to a woman. At first, nothing. Then her eyes focused on the items in the second drawer. Surprisingly, she found two drawers full of women's underwear and clothes. Brielle held a pair of huge bloomers in the air to examine briefly before getting caught.

"Brielle, what the fuck are you doing?" he yelled just as his doorbell rang. "Come on downstairs, that's probably my mother.

Shawn rushed downstairs, opened the door with a fake grin, and let his mother in. He was agitated but of course didn't want her to pick up on it. "Hey, Ma," he said, looking over his shoulder to watch Brielle prance down the steps. He reached over giving his mother a hug and a kiss. "This is Brielle."

"Hi, Brielle."

"Hi, Mrs… I mean Dr. Ellison."

They shook hands.

"Oh no honey, call me Dorothy." Shawn's mother's name reminded Brielle of the Dorothy whom her dad used to cheat with so she instantly developed a sick feeling.

"Uhm, okay, Dorothy."

"So, my son has told me about you. It's good to finally meet you."

"You, too," Brielle said dryly. She instantly thought of her father's wife Dorothy. *What a difference between a doctor named Dorothy and a whore named Dorothy,* she thought, and missed Shawn's mother's comment in the process.

"Huh, Brielle?" his mother asked.

"I'm sorry, did you ask me something? I was thinking of a lady that I knew when I was younger named Dorothy."

"I said how do you like my son?" Dorothy asked.

Brielle looked at Shawn and laughed. "Oh, you don't waste any time. I like your son. He's been a great help to me over the last few days. Showing me that the world doesn't revolve around me." When his mother seemed confused Brielle continued, "What I mean is I've realized now that I've let a lot of things burden me and he's helping me to put things into perspective." She cleaned up her statement.

His mother smiled. "Yes, Shawn has always been a very caring and loyal person. He has empathy for others. I'd like to think that I instilled that in him from an early age."

Shawn blushed when his mother squeezed his cheeks.

Brielle smiled. "Well, that's good of you. I guess that's why so many women want him."

"Huh?" his mother said, looking at Shawn and giving off a nervous chuckle.

"Brielle, don't start," Shawn said sternly.

"I'm not starting. I'm sure your mother knows that you have women chasing after you." She smiled and winked at Dorothy.

Dorothy smiled back at Brielle. "Yes, he does. And for

good reason. He's a good catch and that's why I always have to re-mind him to leave his options open. He falls in love too fast and with the wrong women sometimes. He likes needy women."

Brielle smiled. She knew as a woman that his mother was making a statement to Brielle. She wanted to let her know not to hurt Shawn.

"Okay ladies, before this turns into a debate, instead of the intended greeting that it was supposed to be, let's get ready to eat."

"I have to heat up the food. Unless your friend would like to do it," his mother said, looking into Brielle's eyes. The intent was to study Brielle. She was trying to see if Brielle was trying to play house with Shawn already by pretending to be the lady of the house.

"No, that's okay. This is my first time here, so I'm at least a guest for today," Brielle replied.

"Well, I'm glad you know that. Next time you come, I'm putting you to work," Shawn stated.

"No, come with me in the kitchen Brielle, and let's talk. You know men are primitive, they don't like too much conversa-tion."

Brielle followed Dorothy into the kitchen while Shawn re-laxed on the couch.

Brielle assisted with warming the food and preparing the plates.

"Dorothy, Shawn talks very highly of you and his dad. I think that's great that you and his father made sure he had a posi-tive upbringing."

Dorothy stopped what she was doing to ponder what Brielle just told her. She smiled. "Well, thank you for telling me that. It wasn't easy but we had a common goal."

Brielle looked sad. "I hope you don't mind me asking but did you ever think about leaving your husband?" she asked inno-cently.

"You know honestly, I never did." Dorothy paused to think, "I can say maybe once or twice, but it was just a thought. I was blessed to have a good husband. A lot of women aren't so lucky so I can understand how hard it is for some women to have to give up their hopes of keeping their family complete and have to be single mothers in order to be happy or safe. Have you ever been married?"

Brielle shrieked at what the next question would be.

"Yes, I was married once. Some say that it's not good to feel incomplete if you don't have a man, but I just feel it's supposed to be man, woman, and child."

"And you're right. That is the way God meant for it to be." Brielle felt at peace about Dorothy. A peace she wished that she had. She liked Shawn's mother a lot. She wished that she had been given a mother like her, not like Rochelle. Brielle felt envious that Shawn had been brought up by such a strong woman. They continued to talk as Brielle drew closer.

Twenty minutes later, they were in Shawn's dining room on his huge glass dining room table. It was Roman inspired with white columns holding up the glass. When they finished eating his mother started cleaning the house, which made Brielle feel a little uncomfortable. She wanted to know whose clothes were in his drawers. She knew not to ask though because he wasn't happy when he caught her snooping earlier.

She was ready for his mother to leave so they could play the sex game that they'd bought and so she could pry about the underclothes in the drawer. About an hour later his mother got ready to leave. She hugged and kissed Shawn, then hugged Brielle.

"It was very nice meeting you, Brielle. Take care of my baby, okay?" Dorothy winked at Brielle.

Brielle smiled. "Okay. It was equally nice meeting you, too."

"We'll talk again. And if you have any problems out of him, just let me know and I'll straighten him out." Dorothy put a fist up and waved it toward Shawn.

When Dorothy finally left, Brielle was more than excited.

"What's up? You ready to play that game?" She noticed an instant change in Shawn's attitude as soon as his mother left.

"Nah. I don't want to play that." He sat on the couch like he was exhausted from dealing with Brielle.

"Why not?" She jumped on his lap only to be pushed off.

"Brielle, you just don't seem to get it do you?" He glared at her.

"Get what?" She became serious.

"You were looking in my damn drawers earlier. What's next, my cell phone? And you're not even my woman yet. I'm feeling like it's going to be a whole lot of drama with you. You seem different from when we first met. You've now shown me a very insecure and conniving side of you. I don't like it."

"Shawn, I just have trust issues. I don't trust men."

"Brielle, it's not a man or woman thing. It's people. You have to get to know the people you're dealing with before you can expect certain things from them. I don't have to be trustworthy right now. I just have to treat you with respect. I'm not obligated to you." He flipped through the channels on the television that no one had been watching the entire evening.

"I know. But I don't want to get involved and get my feelings all wrapped up and then you turn out to be a dog."

"Did you know that you could turn me into a dog? I don't know why women don't see that the biggest turnoff to make a man cheat, is a snooping woman." He took a deep breath and sighed.

"So, whose clothes are they?"

"What?" Shawn decided against blacking out on her. It didn't matter; it wasn't like he was still sleeping with Audrey so why hide something that wasn't a big deal? "The clothes are Audrey's."

Brielle stared at him. "Why are they still here?" she questioned in between clinched teeth.

"Because she didn't take them the last time she was here and I don't want her to come and get them. You want them out, you go get them and take them to the garbage outside." He said that as a test to see if Brielle was really going to do it.

At that moment, she got up, walked up the stairs emptied both drawers and walked down with both hands full. When she stood at the door, he opened it for her and watched her walk outside and dump everything in the garbage. Shawn was turned off by her actions again. She just didn't know what her erratic behavior was doing to him.

Brielle came back in and he said, "Now, are you ready to

play the game?"

He laughed. "No, are you ready to go home?"

"No, I want to stay." Brielle realized that she'd messed up again. She started blaming her actions on the fact that she was worried about her upcoming case. "It's this whole Darren thing that has me all messed up," she pleaded.

"I have to get up early for work tomorrow," Shawn countered with half a frown. He stretched.

"So what, you work in Jersey. You can drop me off on your way to work."

"Brielle, I don't want to talk anymore. I want to take you home."

"Because of that girl's clothes? You told me to throw them away."

"Brielle, because of you. I'm not going to explain it to you again."

"I'm sorry. I'll start trusting you. I promise." She grabbed his hand.

"We haven't even gotten to that point yet. I don't even want you to trust me. I'm allowed to do what I want Brielle and I really want to be with you, but you have a whole other agenda going on in your head."

"Okay. I'll stop."

Shawn moved toward the door. "No, how about we stop. Let's take a break from the relationship."

Brielle's mouth fell open. "Shawn, nooooooo," she cried, as he opened the front door for her to leave.

ᥫ᭄**Chapter 27**ᥫ᭄

Only two days passed and it seemed as if Brielle had called Shawn a thousand times. With each dial she became angrier, wondering why this was all happening to her. It was clear that the world had a vendetta against her; her parents, Janay, strangers, and any man she ever met. She contemplated doing something dreadful to herself as Shawn's voice blared through the phone.

"What do you want, Brielle?"

She crossed her arms and patted her foot. "I want you, Shawn."

His voice showed his anger, "I want a sane woman. Are you a sane woman?"

"Yes Shawn, I am. But I called to tell you that I'm going to go to counseling. I just need your help." He smiled. "I just ask that you bear with me."

"And what's the incentive?" he asked in a lighter tone.

"We could possibly end up in a great loving relationship and get married and have some babies. I can be the woman that you want and need."

"Okay. I'll be there in fifteen minutes. I'm not far away."

She grinned, hung up, and flew into the bathroom to freshen up. In fifteen minutes flat, Shawn was walking through the door, ready to please his woman. While Shawn kissed her all over, Brielle was busy removing her sexy terry cloth jumper. However, suddenly she stopped.

"What about the sex game we keep saying we're going to play?" she asked.

"The game already started," he answered and continued kissing her neck as she started sucking on his ear. He picked her up and carried her to her bedroom hoping for some good make-up sex.

As soon as they entered the room, Shawn threw her on the bed and took his clothes off. Her eyes widened when she saw the dick that had become her best friend. She was about to grab his big tool and put it in her mouth when he pushed her down and grabbed her legs. He threw her ankles up to her ears and entered her without warning.

After thrusting his dick in and out for several minutes, he then flipped Brielle onto her stomach and pulled her to the edge of the bed, attacking his pussy from the back. As soon as she began to moan, he was ready to cum.

"Don't- don't –do –it yet baby, I-I-I-I'm cumming," she groaned in delight.

"Where should I put this baby?" Shawn grunted.

"Put it on my breasts!"

Brielle showed that she was still horny as Shawn maneuvered her body and quickly pulled out, squirting all of his creamy liquid onto her skin.

"Yeah. Right on those pretty titties," he said still erect. "Now ride me," he commanded.

When he laid on his back, Brielle got on his piece and rode it like a pony. She looked in the mirror that was on the wall and looked at them together. She liked how they looked, a couple, and in love. He lifted his head up and looked in the mirror, too.

"That looks good don't it?" She nodded her head yes. "Ride that dick! Yes!" he chanted. Brielle kept riding him until they both climaxed. Afterwards, she climbed down then laid down next to him.

He kissed her lips. "You lucky you got some good pussy. I'll give you one more chance just because of that. But you ain't gonna drive me crazy."

"I just want you to be crazy for this pussy, that's all." She cupped her pussy like a male cuffs his nuts.

"I can do that," he said. Within minutes they were both asleep.

At about 2:00 a.m. Brielle woke up screaming. Shawn jumped up startled. "What the fuck. What's wrong?" he screamed.

"I'm sorry. I had a bad dream, that's all."

"Listen, you better do what you promised me and go and see someone."

"I will."

He pulled her into his arms and tried to rock her back to sleep. "Shawn, why are you going through this with me?" she asked.

"Because I want to, that's why. I see who you are on the inside and it's not who you may be right now. I see you in my future, so I'm gonna try to make the fantasy a reality."

They slept in each other's arms and for the first time in days she was not afraid. She had a peaceful sleep. She felt protected and secure.

They woke up the next morning, still intertwined. After getting up and making a big breakfast for her, Shawn grabbed a New Jersey phone book and placed it in front of Brielle while she sat up in bed.

"What's this for?" she asked.

"Start looking for a therapist," he instructed.

Brielle flipped through the pages to the physician's section and looked at the names. "Who do I look for?"

"You have health insurance, right? I know you're on a leave of absence from your job, so I'm asking."

"If they haven't fired me by now," Brielle mumbled under her breath. "I've always had insurance through Dante's company, but now that he's gone I guess it's still active."

She turned on the television and began flipping through channels showing Shawn that he didn't have her undivided attention.

"Sweetheart," he said, grabbing her chin gently, "find out if you still have insurance and if you do...pick out a few doctors. Even if you don't I'll pay for it. Hell, I'll have my administrative assistant at the office help you call around if you want. We'll go from there, okay?"

"Yes, I'll do it. I'll call, I promise. Let's not talk about that anymore. Okay, baby?" She leaned over and gave him a subtle kiss, then turned her attention back toward the television.

"Okay, for right now. Remember, I'm calling the shots cause you ain't got it all upstairs right now," he joked.

Brielle was noticeably offended. "That wasn't funny, Shawn. Don't make fun of me like that. I'm not crazy, damn it. I just have anger issues."

"I'm sorry. That wasn't right. I was just playing. Come on, if you're crazy then I would be crazy for dealing with you so...I didn't mean it."

They laughed a few seconds until a breaking news tag, popped up on the screen. The reporter announced, "The death of Officer Lewis, the New Jersey detective who was found dead in his home, has been solved. It appears two robbers were caught on tape leaving the vicinity of his building. The most bazaar part of it all is that authorities say it was his estranged wife who was also arrested and charged with conspiracy in his death. And would you believe this," the reporter added, "they were caught on surveillance tapes leaving the building. Details shortly."

The announcement sounded what seemed like four times for Brielle. As soon as the broadcast switched to a commercial, Shawn peered into her face with a joyful smirk. Brielle gave no reaction, just words. "See, I told you so."

"Well, I guess we need to talk to our lawyer as soon as possible. No trial, baby!" He leaned to kiss her on the cheek.

"Yeah thank God."

"Yes, you should thank Him. Maybe we can thank Him together this evening. What you got planned for the day?"

"I don't know. After I call the list of therapists then I'll probably call Talia to see if she wants to go to lunch or something. None of my other friends from the past know how to deal with me, so I really haven't spoken to anyone. Plus, I have been avoiding people and being standoffish too. I haven't really called anybody or taken anybody's calls."

"Hey, just take it one day at a time. Don't jumble all your thoughts at once. You asked me why I was willing to go through this with you, especially since I don't know you from Adam. But, I went through a torturous period in my mind at a time in my life so I know you can come out of it. And I don't have to know you from before. I know you now…enough to see you. I see you on the inside and you are beautiful."

"Thank you baby, give me a kiss for that. I see your beauty, too. I like the outside a lot!" She wrapped her arms around him and kissed him.

"You my little devil, you know that?" He kissed her all over her face about five times.

"Damn, I thought you were gonna say angel," she said, hitting him in the stomach.

"How would I say that? You're far from being an angel."

"I never said I was."

She began blowing kisses at Shawn while flipping through the pages with more interest. She started making the list of doctors that she considered seeing. She picked them for various reasons since she knew nothing about them; names that she felt comfortable with, locations, or gender. She didn't want to give her list to Shawn for his administrative assistant to call. She wanted to feel worthy and decided to pick up the phone to call on her own.

She made an appointment with a white woman with a plain, American name, Dr. Crawford. She knew not to rely on a white male to have any concept of her pain. She would have loved to have a black man or woman but none of the names on the list seemed to be of either. Her time was set for Friday, and she hoped that Shawn would go with her.

As soon as she hung up, Brielle was shocked at the ringing of the phone. The name on the caller I.D. read *Marilyn Porter*. She hadn't spoken to her father or his wife Marilyn for about five years; for something else foul that Marilyn had done to her that her father stood by Marilyn. Brielle knew that he was always going to take Marilyn's side because Marilyn took care of him.

"Hello," Brielle answered with an irritated tone.

"Brielle, your father is dying," she announced abruptly.

"He wants you to come and see him as soon as possible."

Brielle stared blankly and imagined the sight of her elderly father.

"Ahhhhhhh…." She hesitated then spoke. "Okay, I'll come down tomorrow or Wednesday. See you then, she said before hanging up.

She didn't want to see her father or Marilyn, but she sure wouldn't disrespect her father's wish before he died. She would go, see him, and leave with a new attitude. He had been out of her life for so long, off and on, that it was like he didn't even exist. To her, he was already dead anyway.

Suddenly, Shawn appeared at the opening between the bathroom and the bedroom, with a towel wrapped around his waist. "You ready to get your pipes burst?"

"It would be nice but I just got a call about my father. He's dying and I have to go see him. His wife Marilyn called and said he wants to see me."

Shawn looked confused, and rushed over toward the bed to sit next to her. "I don't know why I was under the impression that your father had already passed. I know you said your mother died when you were young, but I thought your father had died, too."

"He's already dead to me, but I'm going to respect his last wish."

"Okay, well, be strong. You may feel better after going. Remember, you have to deal with your past and leave it be."

"I hate my past."

"Say, 'I'm going to let the past go so I can enjoy my present and build a future. Say it." Brielle felt funny but she repeated what he said.

"Shawn, what was it that you had to go to counseling for? It must have really worked for you because you remember the slogans and shit. You kill me when you start reciting things that you've learned, like it's your own idea."

"No, I continue to practice certain ways to deal with stress. One day I will tell you what I was going through then, but now is not the time." He tapped her lightly on the thigh like a trainer would a horse. "Get dressed, and let's go to the mall."

"I wanna drive the CLS. I almost love it like my GT."

"Oh you do? Then let's trade. You can have the Benz and I'll take the Bentley," he joked.

"No, that's okay," she replied. They both laughed.

Within the hour, they'd hopped in Shawn's car with Brielle behind the wheel, adjusting the seat. Before they knew it, she'd gotten on the highway and started driving toward the mall. Ten minutes later, they were parking in one of the indoor garages ready to do some damage to Shawn's credit cards.

Walking through the mall hand in hand, they were laughing, joking and having a good time. They went in and out of all different types of specialty, electronic, and department stores. Shawn bought a pillow for Brielle that had, "Daddy Loves You" written on it and told her to sleep with it the nights that they slept apart from each other. He wasn't sure whether he loved her for sure yet, but he wanted her to think of him whenever she looked at the pillow. He was intent on being there for her through this rough time, whether the relationship would grow into something or not. He knew that she needed a companion. He was trying not to get his feelings too involved until he could get her the help that she needed. They were walking into Macy's when they heard someone yelling at them. Brielle knew the voice.

"Sir, you better watch out. She'll end up killing you. She killed her husband and my unborn child's father. Shit, I know she killed the cop I reported her to. You better watch your back. She's crazy. She's evil!"

They turned around and Monique Troy was standing behind them shouting at them. Brielle remained calm. She knew she couldn't lose it in front of Shawn.

Brielle calmly placed her hands on her hips. "Shawn, allow me to introduce the bitch that caused me to lose my daughter. The whore that slept with my husband for years. The trick who is about to have my no good son of a bitch, husband's baby. Bitch, what are you stalking me for? Haven't you done enough?"

"Haven't you gotten away with murder, twice? I know you had something to do with that cop's death," Monique replied.

Shawn pulled Brielle away as she lifted her right hand,

ready to punch Monique in the face. He held her back in an attempt to silence the women.

"You've been warned, handsome. If I wasn't pregnant, I'd take you off her hands, too," Monique continued.

Brielle broke from Shawn's grip and ran up to Monique and punched her right in her left eye. Monique was immediately knocked to the floor, pregnant and all. When Shawn ran to see if she was okay, Brielle began to scream at the top of her lungs.

"Fuck that bitch, leave her there!"

"Nothing seems to break you!" Monique looked at Brielle as if she were the anti-christ. "I know that Darren followed you to Aruba. You were there...it's when you first met him. I know in my heart...," her voice rose in ager. "I kept calling your phone. You never knew it was me, bitch!" Monique continued to rant. "Oh, but you're gonna pay! You're gonna pay!" As someone rushed to help her up, Monique's last words stung Brielle. "I've got proof!"

ꙮ Chapter 28 ꙮ

Midnight approached way too soon, and Shawn and Brielle finally got a chance to play the sex game Brielle had wanted to play so badly for days. Shawn took out the board game while Brielle made Tequila shots, potent Tequila shots. Once the game started, Brielle became overly excited. She wanted to do something wild and crazy reminding her of her college days.

The object of the game was to roll the dice, and the loser of the shoot had to move the amount of spaces of the winning number and take a shot. Luckily for Shawn, he landed on the space that said he had to let Brielle do whatever she wanted to do to him for five minutes. Seductively, she took out the chocolate syrup from her goodie bag and squirted it all over him. He had a statue of his own, standing straight up in the air with chocolate syrup all over it. Brielle wasted no time polishing all of the syrup off the tip of his dick, and left a spit shine to showcase her work. Excitedly, Shawn hopped off of his back, threw the board game to the side and walked butt-naked into the kitchen. She watched his fine ass, built body, come back holding the stool from the kitchen.

Brielle was confused until Shawn put the stool down in the middle of the floor and asked her to sit, front and center. As soon as she obliged, Shawn pulled her shirt up over her head admiring her beautiful frame. He started nibbling on her nipples through her bra, causing her to squirm in the seat. Then he reached back and took her bra off with his teeth, and threw it on the couch.

With gentle strokes, he cupped her breasts gently and moved his tongue from side to side. She locked her fingers together and threw her arms around his neck while he slid his tongue down to her belly button. Brielle could feel herself getting wetter by the second so she leaned back, pulling him closer. Shawn lifted his head up, still locked by her arms and crossed fingers. He untied the belt that was around the embroidered cotton skirt she had on and threatened to tie her to the stool.

She lifted herself up boldly, unafraid as he slid the skirt down her legs and off of her body. He gently bit her clit through her panties then placed her feet on the edge of the stool and opened her legs widely. He moved her panties over to the side and started sucking on her juices like a hungry scavenger. He sucked and licked for a few minutes, but she didn't want much more of that. Brielle wanted that stiff statue. She closed his head in between her legs until he released himself and stood up.

"I want you now, Shawn," Brielle begged as he slid inside her gently, followed by a slow stroke that made her ooze within. With each thrust Brielle creamed inside. One orgasm after another, she wanted more. So much more that she sat up on the stool with her knees by her chest asking Shawn to make love to her all night. He felt so good; she could do nothing but melt.

Their love making session went on for hours until Shawn carried her upstairs and they laid in each other's arms throughout the night. Shawn was finally getting used to his woman, and she finally felt at peace with him.

The next morning arrived way too fast. Shawn woke up and saw that it was 8:00 a.m. He jumped up, which immediately startled Brielle.

"Baby, you've been getting me off my schedule. I'm supposed to be up at six and working out at seven."

She sat up, stretched and yawned. "Baby, you have been working out. You had a good workout last night didn't you?"

"As a matter of fact, I did. I can work out right now, too," he remarked.

"Let's go, you want to do sit ups or push ups?" Brielle

asked with a wide grin.

"I want to do sit ups. Come on. Get on top and give me some breakfast." He grabbed Brielle, then rolled her over on top of him.

She rode him for a few minutes feeling his morning hardness deep inside. For Brielle she'd had enough orgasms to last for the week, but Shawn needed more. It didn't take him long though; he just wanted that morning shot. Within minutes he was moaning, and relieved himself, ready to start the day. He threw her off of him after being satisfied, and stood up and stretched.

"Damn, babe, you just throwing me around like that," Brielle said.

"You know you like it. You make me want to throw you up and let you land on my dick. You can be my rag doll. I can't be gentle to you all the time; you might take me for being soft and try to walk all over me."

"I promise I won't. Stay with me today, okay?"

"I gotta go to work."

"No...please..."

"We'll see, let me jump in the shower."

At that moment, her phone rang. It was Janay. Brielle didn't want to let Janay spoil her mood, so she waited for the call to go into voice mail then listened to the message as Shawn rushed off into the shower.

"Brielle, it's an emergency, call me," Janay stated. "I'll call her later," she told herself but Janay called again. Brielle wasn't in the mood to duck her cousin the rest of the day so she boldly answered.

"Yeah, Janay. What's up?"

"You got my money," she asked Brielle like a school-house bully. "Girl, they got me, so this is getting serious," Janay blurted. "They locked me up for conspiracy and for second degree murder. My bail was a million dollars. So I had to come out of my pocket with a hundred thousand. I'm almost broke....so come through, cuz."

"Girl..."

Janay cut Brielle off. "Look Brielle, I didn't want to say

anything to you because everybody's been tiptoeing around it for years. We think you killed our cousin Tony when you were like ten. I know you killed Dante. And I'm sure you killed Peyton and the cop. Now I don't want this to get ugly."

Brielle took the phone away from her ear again and looked at it and put it back to her ear. "Janay, are you threatening me again?"

"Take it how you want to. If you think you're gonna get away with four murders and I can't get away with one then your ass is wrong. We either both get over or we both go down."

"Bitch, do what you gotta do then. But just to let you know, Darren's wife and the guys that robbed him are responsible for his heart attack."

Brielle hung up the phone. Janay had done some hurtful things to her in the past but that was the last straw.

"She needs to be deleted," she told herself.

Trying not to let her cousin fuck up the rest of her day, Brielle started making plans to visit her father the next day. She and Shawn spent the day together like the happy couple avoiding Janay's repeated calls.

"Shawn, go with me tomorrow?"

"I will, especially since you're willing to bury that hatchet. There's no reason for you to still let your past negatively affect your life."

"Oh my God!" Brielle called out. "You preach way too much for me."

The next day they woke up early and got on the road by eleven. Shawn drove so that Brielle could relax. They listened to old school hip hop from a CD that Shawn had made allowing Brielle to remember some fun moments in her life. He had a vast collection of all types of music. They were rapping along with each other the whole way to Philly.

Shawn had suggested that Brielle write some things down

that she either wanted to say to her father or that she wanted to ask him. She was jotting some things down into a planner that she had in her purse.

An hour later, they pulled up to a red row house. It was dilapidated. They got out and stretched. Brielle felt a funny feeling come over her. She felt frightened. She felt anxious and she felt angry. She stood still looking at the door and realized that she felt the way she used to feel when her father would make her go with him to Dorothy's house. She had a flashback of a time when he kissed Dorothy goodbye in front of Brielle and told her he loved her. In the beginning, he had been secretive and wouldn't show any type of indication that Dorothy was more than a friend. That's what the closed room was for. But after a while he didn't seem to care anymore and Brielle had to see how he would treat Dorothy with so much kindness and her mother with so much hate. At that moment, her blood started to boil.

Shawn noticed that Brielle was already getting upset. He put his arm around her and started moving her toward the door, but she was hesitant. "Come on baby, let's get this over with. It's gonna be okay."

Brielle felt the tears streaming down her face and got mad at herself. "I didn't want to do this. I didn't want to get upset. I wanted to be strong," she replied.

Shawn rubbed her back and stood still while she got herself together. "There's nothing wrong with tears, they wash the dirt away. You're cleansing, that's all. It's a good thing. You've been holding so much in and now you're finally starting to get rid of it. It has to come out in some way."

Suddenly, they heard a door open and an older woman who Brielle recognized as Marilyn stood there. She didn't say a word. She just stood there until Brielle started walking up the small steps to the door. As they finally walked in, Marilyn walked Brielle into a back room. Her father was frail and wrinkled. He was only fifty something years old, but the liquor had taken a toll on him. He looked up at Brielle and Shawn as a tear rolled down his cheek.

"Hello, father," Brielle said. She began to squeeze Shawn's hand for strength.

"Hello, daughter. How long has it been?" her father asked. He tried to sit up but couldn't lift himself up. Shawn pulled him up and put a pillow behind his back.

Brielle tried to smile. "Father, this is Shawn, my man." She finally smiled. "It's been four years since I last spoke to you and five since I saw you. I saw you once after me and Dante's wedding."

"Oh yeah, that sounds about right. Well, how come it's been so long?"

Brielle took a deep breath and prepared herself to answer. "Because I had to keep you out of my life. You have brought me a lot of pain, father. You have impacted my life in a negative way. I have suffered a lot because of my childhood." She held back the tears.

"Brielle, a lot of people suffer. I was suffering when I was raising you. I was suffering because of how I was raised. At least you had a father."

"A father to put me down and mistreat the woman who birthed me? You hated us. You blamed us for everything in your life that was wrong. Because you didn't give me the love that a daughter needs from a father, I married a man who didn't love me right."

Her father looked down. "Brielle, I didn't love your mother. I stayed with her because of you. I sacrificed my happiness to do the right thing but it ate me up inside. It only made me resentful. It's important to be happy yourself so that you can make someone else happy."

"Well, then you should've left. I would've been better off. Why did you make me go and see you with another woman? Why did you force me to see you loving someone else besides my mother?" Tears began to well up in her eyes.

"I wanted you to see me happy so you could see that I wasn't just an evil man. I wished that Dorothy was your mother. It was wrong, but I wanted you to see what you should be getting from a man. Not what I was giving your mother but the glow that Dorothy gave to me. Then when Dorothy died, I met Marilyn."

"So, why didn't you just leave and not kill my mother? You

killed my mother! She died because of you! She couldn't be a loving mother to me because of you! Because of the pain and anger,
I've killed people!" As soon as that came out of her mouth, she
looked at Shawn. He had a calm expression as if he wasn't at all
surprised.

He kissed her forehead and said, "We'll talk in the car."

Her father lit a cigarette. "What do you mean you killed
people?"

"I killed Dante in self-defense. I killed my cousin Tony
when I was ten. I've had a rage in my mind for years. I've tried to
have peace and I never can. Everyone that comes into my life hurts
me. All because I didn't know what to look for when it came to
love. Because the people who were supposed to show me love and
teach me how to love didn't." She turned away, wiped her tears,
and turned back around.

"Brielle, my life has been meaningless. I haven't prospered.
I didn't accomplish anything great. I only had you. That's the only
good thing that I ever made." He pulled on his cigarette and
coughed.

Brielle continued to sob like a baby. "I'm not good. I'm
emotionally damaged. I'm a prisoner of my own mind. When I
think I'm good and I deserve something good, bad comes to me to
show me that's what I really deserve."

"Brielle, just move on with your life. I called you here to
tell you to move on. I know I was a horrible father and I paid for it.
Nothing good came out of my life. You reap what you sow. If you
want good Brielle, you have to stop blaming and make good. I'm
making good right now, but I'm on my death bed. Don't do the
same thing. Don't wait until it's over to have a few moments of
peace when you should have peace and happiness while you are
living." He got choked up, but quickly got himself together. "I
probably never talked to you like this one day of your life, but I've
thought about it. I didn't try to make up for it because I knew I
couldn't. I knew that you hated me, so I decided to leave you alone
and hope that you could come out of the hurt. I just want what I'm
saying to you to make it right for you now. I have drunk myself to
death over my guilt. It's over for me; it doesn't have to be over for

you. You're young. Make a change. I don't know if I ever told you but I love you."

At that moment, Brielle's sobbing was out of control. When Shawn consoled her, her father finally began to cry himself. "Brielle, I just want a hug from my baby girl. I've thought about you everyday, but I was a coward. I was too scared to try to apologize. I was too scared to be a real man and cry. Now I'm crying because I lost all this time. We could've made amends and had a relationship. Now, I'm almost gone." He put out the cigarette that he had smoked half of.

Brielle wanted to hug her father and didn't want to at the same time. She wanted to kill him and love him at the same time.

"Brielle, you only get one dad. I'm not the best but I'm here to tell you I'm sorry."

She walked over to his bed and leaned over. She then put her arms around his neck and laid her head on his chest. Her father began to pat her back as the tears streamed down both of their faces. Finally, Brielle felt a feeling of love. She felt the protection.

"I'm sorry Brielle," he said again.

She lifted her head up. "I love you, dad."

"I love you too."

A tremendous weight had been lifted off of her.

"Heal Brielle. Heal."

Marilyn came into the doorway. "He talks about you all the time. He missed you so much. This has burdened him for years."

Brielle turned around and looked at Marilyn. She wanted to get over the hate she had for her, too. She always resented Dorothy and Marilyn for being able to get love out of her father. She walked over to Marilyn and hugged her.

"Can I talk to you in private?" Brielle asked Marilyn. When Marilyn nodded and walked back to the living room, Brielle turned to Shawn. "Please keep my father company for a minute." He nodded as well.

Brielle and Marilyn sat on the couch. "So, how long does he have?" Brielle looked around the almost empty room. They hardly had any furniture or decorations or pictures.

"Well, he's only got a few months if he can't get a liver

transplant. He's been like this for the last year."

"Why didn't you call me, Marilyn?"

"He said that he'd done enough damage to you and that he didn't want to ruin your life any more than he already had."

"I missed out on having a relationship with my father. I wish he would've talked to me like that years ago."

"Baby, he was torturing himself with the liquor. He was drowning his sorrows away. Brielle I want to apologize to you, too. I never could have children so when I met your father I made him my world. I didn't want anything to interfere with me and him. I resented you. I was jealous of you because even though he never knew how to express his love to you, you were all he talked about. I tried to buy his love away from you. I know I did vindictive things to make him turn against you. Because of that, he resented me when he realized that he had put me in front of you. I paid for it. He began being abusive to me, too."

"So, why did you stay?" Brielle asked, knowing the answer was probably the same as why she had stayed with Dante.

"Because he was all I had. I didn't have the confidence to leave him. Although I knew I deserved better I didn't know how to get better. I settled for a man who mistreated me and now almost twenty years later what do I have? I wasted my life on an unappreciative man. I have nothing because of him." She paused. "I know that you're here to rectify your problem with your father, so I'm not here to turn you further against him. I'm just trying to tell you Brielle, that we all get what we have given. You will have to be responsible for your actions in life and they will come back to you. Don't use your parents' hang-ups as an excuse to do wrong to others because God only holds you responsible for what you do. You cannot do harm to someone because someone has done harm to you. You will pay just like they will."

Brielle was shocked by her step-mother's words but showed no emotion. Shawn had appeared near the doorway out of the blue signaling her to return to spend time with her father before they left. Brielle was scared that Shawn was going to break it off after hearing her confess to murdering her own cousin. She couldn't believe that she had let her emotions take over that much to tell something that she was supposed to take to her grave. However, at least she hadn't told about Peyton, the man in Houston, or Darren. She wondered what he meant when he said that they would talk about it in the car.

Brielle enjoyed her father a little while longer. They stayed until about 8:00 p.m. She wanted him to give her his last will and testimony before they left. Shawn helped him get comfortable in the bed and left of the room to give them privacy.

"Dad, I really am glad that I came. For the first time in my life, I saw you as a human being and not an adversary."

"I'm glad you came, too. Now, I will be able to rest in peace." He re-lit his cigarette.

"What would you have done differently if you could change something in your life?"

"I would have been a better father to you. That was the one important job that I had and I messed it up. If I could tell every man who has fathered a child to be a father and not just a donor, I would."

"I forgive you, Daddy. And you should stop smoking," she said and hugged him again.

"Brielle, I'm dying. It doesn't matter." Although the matter wasn't funny, they both laughed at the way he said it. When Brielle stood up, he pulled her back. "That's a nice man you have there. I hope everything works out for you two."

"I do, too, dad. He's been through so much with me already. I don't even know why he hasn't left yet."

"He will tell you in the car," her father answered. She was shocked that they had bonded so fast.

She gave him one last hug and kiss and did the same to Marilyn and left. She didn't shed a tear; she cracked a smile and walked to the car.

Shawn got behind the wheel again and they got on the expressway. She was instantly nervous.

"Your dad has a lot of remorse," he said.

"Yeah, he does. I feel good about the visit," she replied.

Shawn then got straight to the point. "Brielle, how do you feel about me?" he asked looking over at her.

"I feel like I can be good with you. That I would love to not have to look for love anymore."

"Well, you are good. We are meant to be, I know it."

"Why do you say that?"

"Brielle when I was twenty-two, I was a hit man. I killed five men. I was supposed to go out one night and do a job and I had a big argument with my father and he said I couldn't go anywhere. Although I was considered a man, the look in his eye told me not to challenge him. He stood at the front door and said that he was saving my life by not letting me go. That night my boys got caught red-handed right after killing somebody. I was supposed to be with them. They are doing life in prison." Brielle looked stunned. "I owe that to my father. And not only that. He paid Mr. Zannelli a visit and spoke to him and got me the job I've worked at for the last twelve years."

"Wow. So, the man who left you the company was who was hiring you to do the jobs?"

"Yeah. That's how I met him. I was a young knucklehead from the Bronx and his nephew and I had gone to school together. He came up to me and said his uncle had some good paying work. When I found out what it was, I had to keep that macho bravado bullshit going. I was scared at first but then it became nothing. I had no remorse. It started taking over me, the feeling that I had the power of life and death in my hands. It tormented me though at the same time. My father knew something was really going on with me. He knew something was wrong. When my friends got arrested, he asked Mr. Zannelli to give me a chance at an honest life, not at prison." He reached over and rubbed her shoulder. "You can get past this Brielle. I knew there was something that you weren't telling me and I knew it was something that I would understand. It's like we have the same demons in common. I was able to conquer mine, and you're gonna conquer yours as well."

"I feel better. Not about what you did but knowing that you did not decide to judge me or run away."

"Everybody needs someone and I need someone like myself. I didn't have a poor family life, but I had a poor sense of myself. We all have struggles that we go through whether our life seems to be good or not. It is the inner conflict that we all face."

"So, you don't see me as a problem that you want to get rid of?"

"No. I see you as my soul mate. Both of our spouses died young. We both had a problem with being violent. And you see I said had, not have. Do you want me to go with you to counseling on Friday?"

"I don't know yet. I might want to just go the first time alone. I want to get everything off of my chest that I need to get off."

"What happened with your cousin?"

"Well, he was always fresh and all of the little girl cousins liked him. But he was always trying to touch me, or force me to touch him in places that wasn't right. That day we were out in the rowboats and he tried to put his penis in my mouth, I pushed him. He fell back and just went under. I stuck to my story that he was playing around and fell, but I guess I was never the same because my cousin said my family suspected something else but never brought it up. I was always the one going through some type of changes and having anger fits and rages. So they swept it under the rug because it couldn't be proven. I guess they knew how bad he was too and figured he must've done something to me. "Is there anything else that you want to tell me about?"

Brielle took a deep breath. "Well, Dante really did beat me for years and emotionally battered me but the night that he was trying to explain about Monique sending the pictures, I lost it. And I killed him. It happened so fast," she said getting choked up. "I just stabbed him right in the chest."

Tears began to flow from her eyes as Shawn looked on in awe. His expression showed uncertainty. Doubt about his woman's ability to repeat her past crimes overwhelmed him.

"Did you kill that cop, too?" he asked suspiciously.

Brielle knew she couldn't tell him everything at once. She felt safe with the confessions about Tony and Dante because it was really so long ago with Tony and she had her domestic violence cases to back her up with Dante. She wasn't ready to trust Shawn just yet with the information about the other three murders, yet.

"No," she answered with a straight face. "Why would I do that?"

Shawn looked over at her and left the issue alone. He figured that she would tell the truth later. He knew that she was apprehensive about opening up, and understood completely.

"I'm going to leave it alone. I'm just glad that you are on the road to recovery."

"Yes, I am. Thanks to you."

"Well, it's thanks to God, but I'll take the credit for now. I'm the one he's using to do it. You just gotta come clean with everything at some point."

Brielle's eyebrows rose high above her eyelids. "Do you mind if I take a nap?"

"No baby, rest your brain. You need it."

❧ Chapter 29 ❧

The next day, Brielle woke up and threw on a white sun-dress, and tons of new jewelry. She then got the Bentley washed, stopped past the florist and bought a bouquet of flowers. It seemed like a breath of fresh air invaded her soul as she pulled into the graveyard. Strangely, she blocked all memories of going there just a month before and tearing her mother's grave apart with a shovel.

Brielle parked along the grass and walked until she found her mother's tombstone near the top of the hill near the back fence. She was pleased to see that all the dirt had been replaced and the grave appeared to be in well kept condition. As soon as she stopped, and gazed at her mother's name, the tears started to fall. Brielle put the flowers down, cleared the dust off of her tomb, and she sat down on the grass in Indian style position. She just stared, reading the dates over and over. Her mother had only lived to see the age of thirty-six. She had Brielle when she was twenty and lived a miserable sixteen years with her father until her death. What a waste of a life; all for a man.

Brielle thought about her own life, and how attached she was to Shawn already. She had let her guards down from the mo-ment he gave her his number. She really liked him, but she vowed never again to get caught up in love the way her mother had with her father, and the way she had with Dante.

She didn't care how much she wanted to be with Shawn, if he ended up mistreating her, she would choose to leave. Murder was not an option. She had gotten away with killing five people, and didn't want to take that chance again. Brielle struggled to push Shawn out of her mind and focused back on her mother.

"Mommy, I'm sorry," she said. "I'm sorry that you didn't know how to love. I'm sorry that you had to be punished for trying to love. I'm sorry that you had to die not feeling loved." Brielle wiped her tears away, unable to speak clearly. Her next few words seemed jumbled as she spoke. "I hated you for being weak. I hated you for not teaching me what to do with a man, how to love a man. I hated you for not knowing how to love me. I know now that you only did what you knew. I want to get better so that I can love right. Then maybe God will give me a child." She was surprised that she referred to God.

Brielle started getting angry. "Why me? Why do other people get blessed with children, and not me!" She tried not to think about Monique, but she couldn't stop. She just sat in silence looking at her mother's grave hoping that an answer would fall from the sky. "Mommy, I just needed you so much. I needed you to tell me I was somebody. That I was beautiful. That you loved me. I don't ever remember hearing you say it. I needed that from you. Wasn't I enough to make you feel loved?" Brielle stood up, wiping her tears away. She sniffled, "And lastly mom, the voices will cease. You have no control over me anymore, so don't try."

Brielle hadn't heard her mother's voice in weeks, but wanted to make it official.

She stood in silence for nearly twenty minutes, then said a prayer. The first in years, "God please let her rest in peace."

After that Brielle found herself slowly walking back to her car. Even though she loved the Bentley, it didn't make her feel better at this particular time. Brielle thought that she was going to feel better after leaving the gravesite the way she felt after leaving her father, but she didn't. She felt depressed. It was like the visit to her mother wiped out the peace that she had gotten the day before.

Brielle left the cemetery and stopped at the grocery store. As she was shopping she ran into an old friend from high school.

"Hey Brielle, how you doing girl?" the woman said.

"Hey Shanta, long time no see. What's been going on with you?"

"Oh, I just moved back here from Chicago. I've haven't been here since college. But my cousin who I haven't connected with in a while needed a place to stay so I've got a roommate."

"Oh, really."

"Yeah, she's having a baby, and her baby's father died so she wanted to move back to be close to our family. Girl, she's been going through it but I just went through a divorce so it all works out."

"How did your cousin's husband die?" Brielle asked, getting an eerie feeling.

"Oh, his wife killed him."

Brielle looked stunned and asked herself, "Could Shanta be talking about Monique?"

"I don't know the whole story. Monique is very distraught over it, so I don't pry. She just said that she knows in her heart the wife killed him, and she's running her own campaign to have her charged." Shanta stopped to chuckle, and waved the situation off with her hand. "I don't really want to know any details because as far as I'm concerned she shouldn't have been messing with a damn married man anyway. I'm stuck with two kids now because my husband fell in love with his mistress. So, she doesn't really talk to me about it. She's only staying with me for a little while. She's about to sue the woman for child support."

Brielle was pissed as she took out a piece of paper from her purse. "Girl, we gotta keep in touch, so where do you live?" she tried to ask calmly.

"Right on Tenafly Road. It's a big yellow house about two houses down from the corner of Ivy Lane. You can't miss it. Come by anytime. If you see a Black Volvo in the driveway that means I'm home. I gotta run, gotta go get the kids, hope to see you soon."

"Okay. See you soon."

As Brielle continued shopping, all types of thoughts were going through her head. She tried to ignore them. She finished her shopping and went home to cook dinner. She called Shawn but he didn't answer his phone. She waited ten minutes and called again, but still got no answer. So she decided to leave a hostile message, "I wonder why you can't answer your phone. I guess now that I told you the truth you're going to try and distance yourself from me."

When she hung up, Brielle thought about it and wished that she hadn't left that type of message. Her anger and mistrust was showing again. Shawn called back just ten minutes after that.

"Baby girl, what's the matter? You sound like something is bothering you. Please don't start that mess again."

"I'm just frustrated. I'm sorry about the message."

"Okay. Well, I'm not going to be able to make it tonight. I'm at the hospital with my mother. She fell down the stairs."

"Is she okay? Do you want me to come there?"

"No, baby, that's okay. I'll call you back in a little while."

"Why, do you have another girl there with you?"

"Brielle, I just said don't start." Without warning he hung up.

She didn't like being home alone now that Shawn had started staying there frequently, she felt dependent again. She vowed to learn how to control her emotions.

Brielle fell asleep and slept until 10:00 a.m. the next morning. After realizing she hadn't heard back from Shawn, she picked up the phone to call him. Her counseling appointment was at one and she had decided that she did want him to go with her.

"Hey, baby," he answered.

"Baby? Why didn't you call me back last night?" she asked with an attitude.

"Shouldn't you be asking me how my mother is doing?"

"Oh, how's your mother?" she asked uninterested.

"She broke her hip so I stayed with her last night. I don't like when you start accusing me of shit. I'm gonna tell you right now. I don't like that!"

"I'm sorry, I'm gonna work on it, okay?"

"You better. I'm not trying to have a bunch of drama in my life, Brielle. I want to be happy and it's really simple to be happy. You just make yourself happy."

She sighed. "That's easier said than done."

"Only when you want to be miserable, it is."

"I said I'm gonna work on it. Are you gonna go with me to counseling?"

"No, I can't. I have to go back to the hospital. Don't start buggin. Just go in there and be open and honest. Well, you know what you can't say but say everything else."

"Okay, well can I see you after that?"

"You sure can, since you asked like that. See baby, it pays to be sweet sometimes. Be strong. Call me when you're done."

Brielle said okay and hung up. Afterwards, she took a long bath and got dressed in a business skirt that she used to wear to work. She wanted to look professional so that the therapist would think she had it all together.

At one o'clock sharp, Brielle was in the office of Carol Crawford. She waited patiently in the reception area for about fifteen minutes. Then a white, forty something looking, sharply dressed woman came out and introduced herself. She extended her hand.

"Brielle? I'm Doctor Crawford. Come on inside."

Brielle got up and followed the psychiatrist into her back office. It was very cozy and well designed. Brielle always admired nicely decorated places. That was her passion. A passion she hoped to get back to soon.

"So, what brings you here today, Mrs. Prescott?"

"Well, I'm at a point in my life where I need to change a few things about myself. So, I came here to get a clear understanding on how some things have affected me in my past."

Dr. Crawford nodded in agreement as Brielle spoke.

"Well, that's good. Most people think that there is something wrong with getting therapy, but it's like tending to your insides. We get colds and the flu, and sometimes we get some sickness in our minds based on our emotions, which can be fixed, too. It's not something that is always irreversible and the earlier you tend to it, the better the outcome can be. People spend years agonizing over things and eventually it destroys them."

Dr. Crawford paused to analyze Brielle's emotions. For the

most part it seemed as though she was still in tune with the doctor.

"So, can you give me some background on your upbringing? Start telling me from as far back as you can remember up until now. Anything memorable that comes to your mind about your life," she added.

"I was born a mistake, raped at nine, and never loved."

"Whoaaaaaa," Doctor Crawford emitted. "I guess we do need to talk."

Brielle began to talk about how she grew up in Paterson, NJ and how she always felt inadequate. She talked about the things that she had been dealing with pertaining to her parents, how her mother hated her and allowed her cousin Tony to molest and rape her as a child. That went on for nearly thirty minutes, then she talked about Dante, giving Dr. Crawford plenty to think and write about. She didn't get to finish because her hour was just about up.

Doctor Crawford was still taking notes as Brielle finished up with a humiliating story of abuse by Dante. "Listen Brielle, for the first two sessions you will spill your guts just as you did today, then by the third session, I'll have some feedback. But it's safe to say young lady, you have some deep issues." She patted Brielle on the back. "I'm glad you're here."

Brielle left and drove home wondering what she could do nice for Shawn. She wanted to get something nice for him for being so good to her. She remembered that she had the watch that she had given Peyton. She decided to find a box to put it in and give it to Shawn as a gift. She stopped off at the jeweler, picked up a box from the jewelry store and went home. When she got there, she took the mail out of the mailbox of course on the look-out for the insurance check. Surprisingly, there was a notice for her to appear in court. It was papers from Monique, a civil suit.

Brielle picked up the phone and dialed Janay's number.

"Hello. You must have reconsidered," Janay said sarcastically followed by a loud laugh.

"No. But I do have a proposition for you. I have fifty thousand for you but you have to do something for me."

"What I gotta do?"

"I can't talk over the phone. How soon can you come up

here?"

"Soon enough. I lost my job so I can come tomorrow."

When Brielle said okay and got off the phone, she read over the papers. Monique was trying to get half of Brielle's assets; which included Dante's pension, retirement, and anything related to him. She had to do something and she had to do it fast.

The next morning, Shawn rang the doorbell early after spending the night at the hospital with his mother. He told Brielle that his mother was in so much pain that they had her heavily sedated. He seemed very worried and upset.

"I just need a shower," he said sadly.

"Go on upstairs, I'll fix you something to eat." She patted him on the ass.

"No need. I can't eat at a time like this.

No sooner than Shawn got to the top of the stairs the doorbell rang. Brielle knew it was Janay so she took her time getting to the door, making sure Shawn was no where in sight.

She opened reluctantly, "Come in and be quiet, my man is in the shower."

"Oh yeah, that's the new man that you don't want me to see? I can't wait to see him."

Brielle grabbed Janay by the throat. It was the first time she'd ever taken such a strong stand with Janay. "Bitch, let me tell you something. You better not even look at Shawn for more than two seconds at a time. Do you hear me?"

Janay was strong but she couldn't pull away from Brielle's grip. She started gagging for seconds until Brielle let her neck go.

"Damn, Brielle, is the dick like that? Shit you making me want to see him even more," Janay said attempting to laugh.

"Janay, I'm not playing with you. I'm telling you right now. Don't play with me on this one."

"Okay, okay. Now what is it that you want me to do for fifty g's?"

Brielle listened to make sure she didn't hear Shawn moving around upstairs. She then motioned for Janay to follow her into the living room where she turned the T.V. on. "I need for you to kill Monique."

Janay stepped back and shook her head. "That's a no no."

"Look, this bitch is trying to take me for half of Dante's money. She's trying to get one lump sum in child support. It ain't gonna happen if I have anything to do with it."

Janay shook her head in agreement. "Damn. Okay, I'll do it but you gonna have to give me seventy-five."

"I'll give you fifty before and twenty-five after everything is cleared up. If you mess up and get caught I'll give you another fifty not to speak my name. Shit, it's up to you not to get caught."

"Well, how do you want me to do it?"

Just as Janay asked that question, Shawn walked into the living room wearing a wife beater and some black basketball shorts. By the way Janay was looking at him, Brielle knew she would have to keep a close eye on her cousin.

"Shawn, this is my cousin Janay, Janay, Shawn. Shawn you're not allowed to talk to Janay unless I'm around. Better yet, you're not going to be around Janay when I'm not around."

Shawn looked at Brielle with despair, but when he waved and saw how Janay was looking at him, he understood why. He could tell that this cousin of Brielle's had just as much if not more drama than Brielle did. He wasn't trying to do anything grimy like mess with her cousin, but he could tell that Brielle wasn't acting that way for no reason.

"Damn, where do you workout?" Janay asked like a man hunting scavenger.

"Don't worry about it," Brielle interjected.

"What's on the agenda today?" Shawn asked.

"I say let's go out to eat," Janay suggested while sizing Shawn up with her seductive eyes.

"Honey, Janay was just leaving," Brielle said, ushering Janay toward the front door. "I'll pick you up tomorrow," she whispered to Janay, "we'll finalize our plan then."

"See you soon, Shawn," Janay waved, just as Brielle closed the front door in her face.

Brielle asked Shawn to take a seat while she rushed off to get the present she had for him. She went and got the Rolex watch, sat beside him, and handed him the box. "I just thought I would give this to you as a token of my appreciation for you being by my side through this rough time in my life."

Shawn opened the box and smiled from ear to ear when he saw it. "You know what Brielle? It may seem like I'm just here holding you down, but believe me you are holding me down, too. Your strength is amazing. I don't even care about the things I had been doing before I met you. I was just living my life waiting for you. There was no one exciting in my life; there was nothing that I cared about besides my son."

Brielle kissed him long and hard. She wrapped her arms around his neck and just sat there holding him for a long time. "Baby, I just need you to do one thing for me."

"What is that?" she asked curiously.

"I want you to promise me that you will not let your anger lead you to murder again."

Brielle wanted to agree, but knew that she had one more score to settle. She didn't want to lie. He looked at her unresponsive look and said, "Brielle, promise me. I don't want to lose you to no bullshit. Handle your anger. As a matter of fact, is there anything that you're dealing with that you feel will cause you to react that way again?"

She didn't know whether to tell him that she was planning to have Monique killed or not. Of course he would talk her out of it. She just had to promise and mean that after Monique she wouldn't do it again. "I'm waiting for you. What do I have to do to convince you that I mean what I am saying? Don't be scared that I'm going to leave you. I'm here."

"I promise." She crossed her fingers behind her back, then kissed him passionately on the lips.

"Do you mean it, Brielle?" he asked, looking intently in her eyes. He then asked her again, "Do you mean it?"

"Yes, I mean it."

Both of their cell phones rang at the same time. When they each answered their phones, both had different reactions.

Shawn screamed, "What?" while Brielle said, "Okay, I'll call you later on."

After hanging up, Shawn rose from the couch, crying and

yelling, "No!"

Brielle knew that it was his mother. She had just gotten the call that her father had just passed. "What's the matter, Shawn?" She jumped up trying to get the news.

"My mother took a turn for the worse. Some type of infection; she just died. I have to go to the hospital. Can you come with me baby?"

"Yes, I will. My father just died, too."

❦ Chapter 30 ❧

Less than six hours later, Brielle pulled up outside of Corey's building in Brooklyn and blew the horn loudly. As soon as Janay hopped in, Brielle started with her needs and requirements to fulfill the job.

"Listen, I know where Monique is staying. All you gotta do is go ring the doorbell and shoot her point blank in the face, then bounce and take your ass straight back to Atlanta. It's simple. Do it at night," she added, turning the corner with speed.

Janay just turned and looked at Brielle in amazement. "Anything else?"

"Just make sure that her cousin's Volvo is not in the drive-way and that you shoot to kill, not injure. We'll have to go by the house and see what it looks like."

"Sure, boss lady."

They drove back across the bridge, and headed toward the yellow house where Monique was staying. She showed Janay Monique's Infiniti and her cousin Shanta's Volvo. It was dark so Janay decided to get out and walk around the outside to study the house while Brielle parked up the street inconspicuously.

Janay ran back to the car suddenly saying that she thought someone had seen her, but she had seen enough to know how to handle Monique. Brielle took off, headed home. The drive was mostly silent; especially considering how Brielle no longer trusted Janay. It was clear that Janay knew all the men she'd killed, and was willing to tell the authorities if it ever became necessary, so for

Brielle the bond was broken. Brielle didn't want to entertain Janay's questions about anything so she told her that she was tired and was going to bed.

Brielle called Shawn to see how he was doing. He and his sisters had decided to stay together at his mother's place so they talked briefly until he said he would call her in the morning. The funeral was set for Tuesday night, after the wake. That's when Brielle decided she would have Janay kill Monique. Brielle sat around for a few more minutes planning how to take care of Janay after she killed Monique. It was something she needed to think deeply about so she decided to call Marilyn for the moment.

When Brielle got Marilyn on the line, Marilyn told her that the funeral was going to be Thursday morning. She was glad that it wasn't going to conflict with Shawn's mother's service because she probably wouldn't have gone to her father's funeral. She had indeed forgiven her father but Shawn had made such a positive impact on her life that she had to be there in his time of need. Her father had years to need her and be a part of her life. He chose otherwise.

Brielle asked Marilyn if she needed anything. Marilyn said that she didn't. "Just bring yourself, honey," she answered sympathetically. "You've had a rough life. Find happiness and bring it with you to the funeral."

Brielle got off the phone and cried herself to sleep.

❦ Chapter 31 ❦

Two days later, Brielle accompanied Shawn to the funeral home to finalize the arrangements, and to drop off his mother's dress. He cried off and on the whole time using Brielle for support. "You'll be okay, honey," she coaxed.

From the funeral home to the florist, Brielle chauffeured Shawn around as a good woman would. When they got back to his house there was a house full of people. She met a lot of his family, mingled, and got acquainted with them in a warm way. They accepted her right away on the strength of Shawn.

Although he was really upset, he proudly introduced Brielle as his woman. Brielle in turn stuck to him like glue, rubbing his arm, and telling him that it was going to be okay.

"So, you're the one who has my brother falling in love again finally," a chubby woman in her late thirties commented.

"So good to meet you," Brielle said after realizing it was Shawn's sister.

"I'm Sheila. I wish we could've met on better circumstances, but it's nice to meet you."

As Brielle got to know Sheila and Shawn's other siblings, she held Shawn the whole time. As big as he was, he was like a little baby. She thought about her father dying and she smiled. She wasn't happy that he was gone, just happy that she'd gotten to talk to him before he died. She knew that Shawn's grief was going to be a whole lot different. He'd had a lifetime of good times with his mother. He had every right to cry.

Most of the people had left by nine so Brielle and Shawn

got in the car and drove back to Jersey. As she was driving, Shawn started asking her questions.

"Did you cheat?"

"What?"

"Did you ever cheat on Dante?" he asked with no remorse.

"No, I didn't. Why?" She was curious as to where the conversation was headed.

"I want to know. As much as he did to you, you never thought to cheat?"

"I thought to cheat, but I didn't want to shit on my vows. I figured me cheating wouldn't do anything but make matters worse. Besides, I'd probably be the one dead right now."

"So, why didn't you leave him?"

"Because I took vows. That meant a lot to me."

Shawn listened intently. "Do you ever want to get married again?"

"Of course, just with a better man. I still want to have children, Shawn." She rubbed his knee gently.

"I know you do."

Shawn had a weird look in his eyes, but made sure to change the subject. Not only did he switch the subject, but he also refrained from talking until they made it back into the house. As soon as they got inside, Shawn brushed up against Brielle and began taking her clothes off. She wasn't in the mood, but she knew that he needed some sexual healing. She was honored to be able to be the one to give it to him.

They made love, fast and hard, and were fast asleep shortly thereafter. The next morning he got up and said he had a few things to do. She offered to go with him and he said that he wanted to go alone. She decided not to take it personal for once.

Brielle decided to go to the mall to pick up something classy and elegant to wear to the funeral the next day. She also wanted to pick up something to wear to her father's funeral as well. She shopped at Saks Fifth Avenue and found an off white cocktail dress and jacket with pearls around the collars and lapels, by St. John. She then found a cream colored pair of snakeskin sling back shoes to go with the suit and a nice Christian Dior clutch to match. She decided to wear that to her father's funeral, too. She wasn't going to be dumb with her money and just splurge it all away anymore, and she surely wasn't going to give it away to Monique either.

After remembering that she had another counseling session with Doctor Crawford, Brielle went straight there from the mall. As soon as she sat down with the doctor, she asked Brielle to start talking about Dante and how they met and how things had drastically changed by the end of the second year of their relationship. She described in detail some of the instances when he had really been evil to her. She ended by saying that she killed him in self-defense. The doctor who had otherwise not really been moved by the rest of Brielle's story seemed startled when she heard Brielle say that part.

"How do you feel about committing murder?"

"I just want to feel normal. I just want to stop being haunted by my past."

She became increasingly upset, but the doctor kept digging.

"Well, how do you feel that these killings have affected your life so far?" The doctor put her pen down and folded her hands on her desk.

"I've been angry. I've been violent. I have never looked for positive love, but have always felt comfortable in the worst kind of relationships."

"Well, you probably felt that was all you deserved, but now you know better, correct?"

"Yes, I know that I am a good person deep down inside and I deserve to be treated that way." Brielle took out a tissue and wiped her tearing eyes.

"You've told me you have a good man now, correct?"

Brielle not only told her about her good man, but devoted twenty minutes to telling the doc how he made her feel. Eventually her time was up.

"I wish that we could continue. I'll want to hear more about your history. I'll have some observations for you when you come for the next visit. Are you feeling okay to leave? You seem more upset than normal," Dr. Crawford commented.

"I've just got a lot on my mind, that's all."

Tuesday morning came quicker than Brielle expected. She woke up bright and early, preparing for murder. Janay was to be there at 10:00 a.m. so that she could give her the key to the Tahoe to drive to Monique's while Brielle was at the funeral. She was already ten minutes late which frustrated Brielle. When Janay finally pulled up, Brielle had the door wide open.

"Are you going to do it right?" she asked Janay with her arms folded.

"Of course I'm gonna do it right. Bitch, you think I want to go to prison or have two murder trials going on at the same time? I got this. Now go tend to your man before I do."

Brielle shot Janay a glaring look even though Janay told her that she was only kidding.

"Remember to take the truck to Brooklyn. Wipe down the steering wheel and the door handle. I'll report it stolen when I get back late tonight. Mail the keys right back to me so that if the insurance company asks to see the keys, I have them."

"Okay. Where's the gun?" Janay asked.

Brielle got an unregistered gun from the basement. She handled it with a wash cloth. "Remember to dump it in a dumpster somewhere in New York. And remember do not leave this house until it is dark. Make sure none of the neighbors see you get in the truck."

"Where's my money? I'm going to take a train back down to Atlanta tomorrow morning. I'm leaving from Brooklyn."

Brielle got the bundle of money that she'd taken out over the course of the last three days. She didn't want to have a record of taking it out all at once. She gave it to Janay.

"Is this fifty?" Janay asked looking at the stack.

"No, it's twenty-five, you ain't skipping town on me without doing what you gotta do. You think I don't know who I'm dealing with? There's more where that came from if you handle this right. All you have to do is make sure that you're not seen. Park on a back street and go through backyards to get to her back yard. Make sure that it's not attempted murder but the real thing. Make sure you have the mask on that I gave you so she can't identify you if she doesn't die."

"I got this!" Janay shouted, slipping the money into her bag.

Brielle put her stockings and her thousand dollar suit on with all of her bling. She wanted to make an even better impression on Shawn's family than she already had. She drove the Bentley to his house. As she was pulling up, Audrey was leaving. Brielle watched her walk down the street. She got out of the car and rang Shawn's doorbell. He came to the door and had a nervous look on his face.

"Did your company spend the night last night?" she asked without even saying 'hi' to him.

"No, she just came by because she heard about my mother."

"And you let her in?" She told herself to remain calm.

"What was I supposed to do, talk to her through the glass door? Come on Brielle don't start."

"But how do I know that she didn't spend the night?"

"Because I just told you. Now, are you going to start because my mother is being laid to rest today and I have a lot of other things on my mind?"

"Okay. I'm sorry."

"I'm for real Brielle, this is a serious day for me. Are you with me or against me?"

"I'm with you," she ended, slipping her arms around his waist.

As they moved in unison toward the couch, Shawn seemed overly nervous. Brielle knew he would be sad but she couldn't understand why he seemed so nervous. She wondered if Audrey had really spent the night. Her mind began to spin uncontrollably. Images of Audrey, naked in Shawn's bed infiltrated her mind. Then thoughts switched to Audrey brushing her teeth in the bathroom mirror, with Shawn just inches behind, nibbling on her neck.

Brielle was pissed, but she knew better than to ask him about Audrey again.

"Shawn, I have a confession to make."

Brielle was going to tell him about Darren. She felt that she should come clean so there weren't a lot of secrets between them. It would make them closer. She would never tell about Peyton or the Houston guy because to her that was just what they had deserved. But for Darren there was guilt.

"Brielle, not right now. Whatever it is can wait. Just sit here quietly with me until the limo comes."

Brielle did just that. She sat quietly as her mind wondered, both about Audrey and Janay. She knew the night would be long, and filled with anticipation.

❦ Chapter 32 ❦

Funerals were always treacherous days for Brielle; reminding her of her mother's. When the limo pulled up she gave Shawn a kiss and said, "Okay, I'll follow the limo."

"No, you're coming in the limo. I need you right by my side. You're my strength right now." Shawn grabbed her hand without taking no for an answer.

She was really happy that she and Shawn had grown so close the way they had. Maybe he was right that there was a God because Shawn sure seemed to be sent from him. There were two limos and she and Shawn had their own. She thought it was very strange that his brothers and sister and their kids were all riding in one and they were alone in the other.

"Why do we have our own limo?" she asked. "You're gonna make them not like me. They might think that I asked for us to have our own…"

Shawn put his finger over her lips. He reached over to the bar and took out a bottle of champagne. He popped it, poured them two glasses and toasted, "To us."

At that moment, she figured that he ordered his own limo to show her his appreciation and that they were probably going to go somewhere after the funeral. Maybe he was taking her to Atlantic City. She couldn't think of anywhere else that they might go by car. She decided to stop asking questions and just enjoy her man. She liked how that thought sounded, "her man".

She lifted her glass. "To us."

When they pulled up at the church, it was beyond packed.

His mother must have been a well-loved woman. They walked up to the first row and sat. His mother looked so beautiful and peaceful in her casket. Brielle had helped Shawn pick out her dress. She had on a light gold African inspired dress that had shells and other adornments. When Brielle picked it out of her closet and asked if he wanted her to wear it, he said that it was one of her favorite dresses. She looked like a queen. She looked like a matriarch of a whole country and by the turnout she was obviously a matriarch to half of New York. The church was Ebenezer Baptist Church in Harlem, a historical site where the Reverend Calvin Butts was the pastor. Many black leaders and dignitaries had been eulogized there. It was a staple of the black community. It was a huge building and it was filled to capacity.

The family took their seats in the first few pews. Shawn's brothers, his sister, their spouses and children were in the first row, of course. The procession of people walking up to view Mrs. Ellison began and as the people passed, they kissed and hugged Shawn and the family. Because Brielle was sitting next to him, she received some customary hugs and kisses as well. Depending on who approached, Shawn got emotional. Some of the faces he saw led him to reminisce and he shed a number of tears. Brielle held his arm and was his rock. She patted him, rubbed him, and comforted him. He fell for her even more that day.

When the viewing was over and the funeral was about to begin, Shawn regained his composure. The funeral director walked up to the casket and was about to close when Shawn stood up. He walked up to the casket and put his hand on the man's shoulder and asked him to wait before closing it. His brothers and sister looked at each other, confused.

Shawn turned around to the congregation and motioned for the microphone from the podium. It was handed down to him. He took it and turned back around.

"Pardon me, ladies and gentleman. I have something that I must do before my mother's casket is closed. Doesn't my mother just look beautiful?" The crowd said their "Yes", "Yes she does", and their "Halleluja's. Shawn cleared his throat and continued. "You know before my mother died she talked to me. She was in so much pain and she must have felt ready to go. She told me a few things. She said for me not to mourn her but to rejoice that I had had such a great mom. I said "Mom be quiet you're not going any- where." She said "Son; I wouldn't mind seeing your father." He wiped a tear and continued. "So, I just listened. I thought she was talking crazy because they had her so drugged up. She said, 'Son, you're my favorite'." He looked at his brothers and his sister and stuck his tongue out, "I'm only kidding." Everyone started laugh- ing. "But seriously, my mother told me to always look forward. She knew that I have been pretty lonely since my wife Sharay died. She said, "Live your life and marry that girl." Everyone looked at Brielle. Brielle was confused.

"My mother only met my girl one time and my mother told me that she was the one for me. My mother will not be here to see me get married. But while she is here right now, for the last time, in my presence I must do this. I will never see my mother again but I want her body here while I prepare to 'marry that girl'." He pointed at Brielle and a tear rolled down her cheek. "Brielle, come here."

Brielle got up and made her way next to her man and his mom. He put his hand out and she took it. He turned them around to face each other and the audience had a side view. He held her one hand and put his other hand in his pocket. Brielle put her other hand over her mouth. He moved her hand away from her mouth. He took out a pretty yellow box. He handed her the mic and pulled the pretty ribbon to open the box. He took out a beautiful canary yellow marquis cut, five carat diamond ring. Her eyes widened. He took the mic back.

"Brielle, in the presence of my mother, I want to know if you will marry me and be my loving, lovely, to have a lot of love- making..." Everyone laughed. "Will you be my lawfully wedded wife?" She was stunned. As she was opening her mouth to answer, he cut her off and said, "Now, don't make my mom come back from the crossover to beat you. You better say the right thing." The people cracked up laughing.

She held her hand out for the mic, "Shawn, emphatically yes I will be your wife!" she said loudly and then gave him a juicy kiss on his lips. He slipped the ring on her finger and kissed her again. Everybody clapped and stood up.

She turned to his mother and said, "Thank you Mom, for the short cut. It probably would've taken him a couple of years had you not said what you did." She leaned into the casket and kissed his mother's cheek.

Shawn took the mic back and said, "I'm sorry but all of y'all ain't invited to the wedding. But we'll send pictures. We're going to Hawaii to do it."

Everyone stood up again and clapped. Brielle hugged him and buried her head in his chest. He passed the mic back to the minister and motioned for the casket to be closed. The man stepped up and closed the casket while Shawn and Brielle, arm in arm, returned to the first row and sat. His brothers shook his hand as he passed them. His sister stood up and hugged them each one at a time. It dawned on Brielle that the questions Shawn had asked her about whether she'd cheated on Dante or not, the other day, were because he was contemplating the proposal. When they sat, she smiled and kissed his cheek. He told her that he had gone to buy her ring the other day when he told her that she couldn't come out with him. The funeral began.

The program was filled with people singing and many different people speaking about Shawn's mother. There was even a group of children who did a praise dance. Brielle liked that. She was in awe as to how kids so young could worship God and not be embarrassed. They were sincere and enthusiastic. Brielle wished that she had been brought up to believe in God. Maybe if she had, she would have been able to deal with things better and not try to handle them in her own twisted way. She looked at the Rolex on Shawn's wrist and it read 8:30. It would be completely dark soon and Janay would be putting the plan into action.

The praise dance was the last performance before the sermon. The Reverend stood up and approached the podium.

He looked at Shawn and smiled. "Well, well, well, Shawn. I've known you from a tot and boy did I teach you well. What a way to win with a lady." Everyone laughed. "You know, I've known this family for...ever. It's too many years to count. I love this family. And I love this woman." He pointed at Mrs. Ellison's casket. "She is an example of what is good. When I learned of her passing I said, 'Now, how can you preach at an angel's funeral?' But we know that funerals are for the people who are left here. The word is for those who must continue life's journey. Mrs. Ellison completed her journey and I can tell you that she did mighty good works. Look at all of these people. She helped many. She knew, though. I said she knew. She knew that her condition of being alive was not an everlasting one. She knew that her 'Condition was not her conclusion'." A few people clapped. Brielle didn't know what they were clapping about.

"Did everyone hear me? I said her 'Condition was not her conclusion' so she prepared for her conclusion. She knew that she wanted to conclude in Heaven. She knew that the condition that she put herself in would determine where her soul would end up." He cleared his throat and took the mic out of its stand. He began walking around and looking intently at people in the crowd. "Now, I know that some of you just don't understand. I know that some of you feel like a preacher is just doing a job; that I am just a paid public speaker. Well, I'm here to tell you that I'm more than that. I have a greater job than that. I have to be the tool that the Lord can use to save a soul." He went back to the podium and took a sip of his orange juice and put it back down.

"You don't have to hate and be jealous. You don't have to. I hope we don't have any of these in here but I'm here to tell some-body, you don't have to be a murderer either." Brielle felt a jilt to her stomach. Shawn squeezed her hand. "You just don't have to. You can live a different life. One that is blessed. One full of joy. Now, let me start from the beginning."

Across town, Janay looked out of Brielle's kitchen window with the lights off in the house. She scanned the houses to see if anyone watched from afar. With her gloves, mask, and her gun in tow, she was ready to handle Monique once and for all.

Janay opened the sliding door of Brielle's living room and walked out onto the deck. She kept telling herself, "You can do this. You must do this. You have to do this."

She walked down the deck stairs and around the side of the house, unlocking the door to Dante's Tahoe, backing it out of the driveway. Slowly, she drove down the street with the lights off, and her covered hands gripping the wheel. Janay turned the corner with her headlights on, checking her rear view mirror to see if any cars, especially police cars were behind her. She drove the speed limit and was very cautious just as Brielle had instructed.

Her first step once in the neighborhood, was to drive past Monique's house to see if the Infiniti was there. It was, and so was the Volvo. Janay was supposed to wait until the Volvo left, but she felt antsy and didn't want to wait around. There was no guarantee that Shanta was going anywhere.

Janay wanted to get the murder over with so she drove two blocks away from Monique's street. She planned on walking through four sets of backyards, but there were people out on that block. Quickly, she changed up her game plan, drove up the next street behind Monique's where the block was clear. Janay shut off the lights and pulled over in front of a house that was pitch black. She then reached into her bag, slipped the mask on, and pulled the gun out ready for action.

Janay inched across the street and into the backyard behind Monique's house like an armed army on attack. Clearly, she could see Monique, Shanta, and two young girls all eating dinner. Janay stayed low in the bushes and watched and waited. She came up with a few options. She could ring the doorbell and push through the door when it was opened and run into the kitchen, shoot Monique point blank in the face and then run out the kitchen's back door. The problem with that would be them not opening the door but looking through the peephole and she would not be able to stand there with her mask on or off, for obvious reasons.

A second thought she had was to break Shanta's car window, which would make the alarm sound and then when they came outside she could shoot Monique point blank in the head and run. The problem was that the alarm would alert the neighbors and

Monique may not come outside. She really didn't want to have to kill Monique in front of the girls, but she didn't seem to have any other options.

The third scenario would be to shoot through the window, but she could've missed Monique and shot one of the girls or their mother. As the group continued to talk, Janay kept coming up with different ideas. Shanta and the girls got up from the table and started scraping their plates. All of a sudden, the kitchen back door opened and Shanta came out with a garbage bag.

Without a second thought, Janay jumped up and started running toward the open door. She skipped the stairs and jumped onto the porch like Rambo on a mission. She ran into the house, and pointed the gun directly at Monique. Without hesitation, she shot four times right into her face, just as she was sticking the fork back into her mouth. Janay grinned as she watched Monique fall back in her wooden chair; then within seconds darted back out knocking Shanta down on her way out. All she could hear were screams behind her. Janay darted back through both backyards and was at the truck within about thirty seconds. She unlocked the Tahoe, jumped in, started it, and took off down the street.

Janay huffed and puffed crazily, attempting to catch her breath. She pulled the mask off, keeping her foot pressed forcefully on the pedal, and sighed while looking in the rearview mirror. She saw nothing and no one. By the time she reached Harlem, her breathing started to calm down and the adrenaline rush slowly started to go away. She looked over to the seat next to her to make sure the gloves, mask, and gun were still there. They were. She knew the gun could not be stashed with the gloves and mask because her DNA would be on them. Her intent was to wipe down the gun, throw it in the Harlem River, and then throw the mask and gloves away in Brooklyn. She pulled off of the Harlem River Drive and onto the boat basin. She put the gloves on, wiped down the gun, and put it in her bag. She took off the gloves and put them on the floor. She got out of the truck and started walking. There were people sitting on benches by the water. She walked along the path until she got to a place where there was no one. She pulled the gun out of her bag and threw it over the guardrail and into the water. It made a light splash, but it felt good knowing the evidence was gone.

Janay turned around and walked back to the Tahoe and drove back onto Harlem River Drive on her way to Brooklyn. She crossed the Brooklyn Bridge feeling relieved that she'd gotten away with murder and would be getting $25,000 from Brielle soon. Her instructions were to call the truck in stolen, but she had never considered doing that. It was all a part of *her* plan. As she drove along Fulton Street, she decided to pull over at Junior's Cheese-cake Restaurant. She got out and bought a box of strawberry topped cheesecake, and called Corey on his cell and told him that she'd taken the train to Prospect Park and for him to pick her up there.

Janay drove the Tahoe to a parking lot of a church in walk-ing distance from the park, and left it. She then parked the car and wiped it down, removing her fingerprints completely. She then walked to the park and waited for Corey.

When they got to his building and on his floor she let him walk ahead. She pretended that she was looking for something in her bag. He opened the door to his apartment and walked in. She took the gloves, mask, and screwdriver out of her bag and threw them down the incinerator. She went inside with Corey and made sweet love, the kind she wasn't used to having with men.

Chapter 33

The pastor said, "Now, somebody who doesn't want to raise their hand, wants to ask 'What do you mean her Condition was not her Conclusion? Well, I'm glad you asked."

Everyone laughed including Brielle.

"Life is a journey. It's a learning experience. If we knew everything we needed to know when we came into the world, we'd be ready to die when we are first born. The challenges and ups and downs are pruning you. They are building you, making you. Who you were ten years ago is not who you are today, I hope. Some people are the same though because they are not trying to grow or learn. What does God have to do with this, you ask? Why do we need God if we are going to learn along the way? Well, because we need to learn and grow and start to go in a direction that will make you be a better person. To be 'like him'. Because it's easy to go from being a liar, and grow into a robber. Growth in Christ means growth towards inner good which will manifest into outer good. When you don't have Him, you feel alone through all of your trials and conflicts. When you start to let him in to your life, it's like when you open a shade in a room, it lets the sunshine in!"

"Amen," people from the congregation bellowed.

The pastor continued, "Whatever you are feeding, it will grow. If you are feeding the evil in your life, you will always have drama. If you live by the light, your life will have the truth and the truth is Jesus saves! No one person can save you. God will save each of you so that you can be a better partner for each other. Remember people, God has something else in store. Dr. Mrs. Dorothy Ellison lived her life with God and now she is with Him. Grab on to God, change your condition. Amen."

Most of the congregation stood up and cheered, including Shawn and Brielle. She liked the way the pastor explained why people choose God. It sounded like it made a lot of sense. Why not? She never tried but she figured her turmoil was a result of turmoil so if she started surrounding herself with good, she would probably be able to have a good life. She wanted a good life. She didn't want the trials and tribulations of trying to figure things out on her own; she wanted something that she could lean on. She decided that she would start going to church to learn about God. It's hard to judge something if you know nothing about it. She wanted to know about the good thing that so many people acknowledge. It must be something for so many people to be involved in it."
The people started going downstairs to have the repass. They had the famous Sylvia's Harlem restaurant cater the food. Brielle checked her voicemail on her phone and got the "It's a wrap" message from Janay.

She felt relieved. She didn't feel bad because she felt that Monique had caused her to resort to those measures. She was harassing her and then trying to take her money. Janay's last comment on the message caused a lump to form in her throat. "And Brielle...just one more thing, that situation in Houston was totally my fault. I was sick of you trying to be a goodie-two shoes. My bad, but don't worry, I've been raped before, too."

Brielle took seconds, while staring into space before pressing end on the cell. She thought about what the pastor had said and hoped to heal and change over time.

Shawn and Brielle were the focus of everyone's attention. She met so many people. When it was time to leave, Shawn wanted to show her a romantic time so they took the limo to Central Park and rode a horse and carriage through the park. He asked her if she liked her canary yellow diamond. She looked at it and told him that she loved it but not as much as she loved him.

They stayed at the W Hotel that night. By the time they got to the room, it was already past midnight. The room was decorated with yellow roses. He had ordered five dozen roses to adorn the room and it looked beautiful. On the bed was a yellow negligee and a bottle of Cristal. Everything was yellow to match her ring. They drank and made love like it was the first time.

The next morning they drove straight from the burial to Brielle's house. When they pulled in the driveway Brielle said, "Oh my God, the truck is gone!"

"Oh shit!" Shawn said.

Quickly, she called the police to report the theft. An officer arrived on the scene within fifteen minutes to take the routine report. Shawn didn't think anything was too out of the ordinary; stolen cars were not a rarity in Jersey.

Besides, their focus was getting to bed at a decent hour so they could get up and drive to Brielle's father's funeral the next morning.

His service was at a funeral home and there was not a large turnout. He was in a casket that looked like it didn't cost more than a few hundred dollars. It was a modest service lacking the life and energy of Mrs. Ellison's. It spoke to the different ways the two had lived their lives and it confirmed what the pastor had preached at her funeral. Brielle saw and met some long lost relatives. The communication was cordial, but not warm.

Her father had lived an unproductive and miserable life and had a funeral to match. The whole program consisted of about three old songs sang out of a hymnal book and three speakers who read poems by poets who knew nothing of her father. These people did not pour love out over his casket with the reading of the poems; they just read the poems and sat down. The pastor read the eulogy and said a few kind words and that was it. Brielle was more upset over the difference between her father and Shawn's mother, more than the fact that he was gone. Shawn stood by her side, and the highlight of the day was being able to introduce him as her fiancé and being able to flash that ring to whoever would look.

Her father was being cremated and Marilyn had something small at their house afterwards. Both Brielle and Shawn joined the mourners at her father's house after the funeral and were en route home within an hour. When she walked out of her father's house, she left the pain of him right there. Everything in Brielle's life had begun to change.

Shawn and Brielle started planning their wedding on the way home. She didn't have a great deal of family and those who were still living probably wouldn't be able to afford to go to Hawaii anyway. She would pay for Aunt Janelle and Janay too, if she was not incarcerated by then. Shawn's family was larger and Brielle was looking forward to becoming a part of them. She always wanted a big family and she felt that this would be the family she had always longed for. The more they drove the more they talked, and both knew it was rather soon to be getting married so they decided to wait a year. It was more Shawn's decision to wait but Brielle understood. They agreed that she would continue going to counseling and he would join her. The wedding was set for June of 2010.

By the time they got back home, Shawn and Brielle had planned out a large portion of their upcoming life. When Shawn pulled into the driveway, Brielle asked him if she could hop out to check the mailbox and put something in the box to be delivered to Janay. Little did he know, she had an envelope addressed to Janay with a check enclosed in the amount of $25,000.

As soon as Brielle opened the mailbox to stick Janay's envelope inside for the mailman, she smiled. An envelope for Brielle from The Great American Life Insurance Company caught her attention. Her life was finally changing for the better. She'd gotten her insurance check, and found true love. She hoped that she would be blessed with children. Many children. She desperately wanted to put the past behind her and she was off to a good start.

She turned around to tell Shawn about the check when she was met by two plain clothes officers standing before her with stern faces.

"Brielle Prescott?" one of the white men asked.

"Yes?" she asked nervously, feeling a jilt in her gut.

"You are under arrest for the murder of Monique Troy."

"What? Monique Troy? I didn't kill Monique Troy," she said confidently.

"Well Miss, you will have to tell that to the judge. Please put your hands behind your back."

Shawn was shocked. "What is this all about?" he asked a young officer who'd just pulled up on the scene.

He shrugged his shoulders. "A murder charge; all the evidence points to her. Camera's showed her Tahoe leaving the scene. And an unknown witness is willing to testify."

Shawn stood silently in awe. He got ready to say something else to the officer but Brielle stopped him.

"Baby, I'm okay. I haven't done anything, so I'll be fine. Just call your lawyer and have him come to the station."

The officers began reading Brielle her rights when Shawn tried to talk over them. "Baby, this is too much," he commented, agitated with his fiancé and her bullshit.

"Monique Troy was shot and killed on Tuesday," one of the homicide detectives stated. "Your lady allegedly did it." He looked at Shawn with confusion.

"I was actually at a funeral on Tuesday," she uttered with a straight face. "I didn't do anything to anyone. Shawn baby, just relax and come and get me out. Okay?"

Shawn had a strange expression as he spoke, "Just keep your attitude under control, do you hear me?" he scolded.

"Yes, baby. I got you."

The officers finished cuffing Brielle then told Shawn they didn't think she would be getting out anytime soon. The detective ended with, "We've got evidence and witnesses. But of course you should know that Mr. Ellison."

Shawn leaned over attempting to give Brielle a kiss. Instantly, she jerked away. "How do they know your last name?" she asked suspiciously. "You never gave them your name." she added with distrust in her voice.

The officer started moving her away in the cuffs totally disregarding Shawn's beg for mercy in the process.

"I had to do it, baby. But I do love you. Just know that this walked away in shock. "Janay told me everything. And she told the police too." Her mouth hung low as she looked back at Shawn wanting to know why he'd allowed himself to turn on her.

"I love you, baby! You'll get the help you need!" Shawn yelled again as she was put into the squad car. He was sold on what his fiancé had done, and what she had become. He knew that Ms. Brielle Prescott would be going away for a long time.

IN STORES NOW   COMING SOON

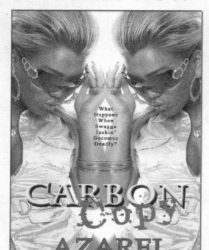
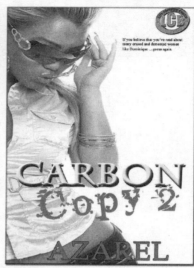

Meet Dominique Lewis, a foul, hard-boiled, go-getter who spends most of her days yearning to be just like her sister, and plotting on taking her man. For her, it's all about money, sex, and power. Although she possesses the perfect physique and sexy features, her life-long dream is to become wealthy and a house-hold name. By any means necessary, she vows to get what she wants.

As Dominique's mission unfolds, she manages to get connected to Yuri, a violent replacement for the man she really sought. After realizing she's partnered with a beast, her world turns upside down. And soon, after the tragic murder of her sister, all hell breaks loose when Dominique's cover is blown.

Armed with revenge on the brain, and a status goal in mind, Dominique soon appoints herself as Rapheal's woman, the most sought after millionaire in Atlanta. Raphael's lavish status in town would put her on a new level, right where she always dreamed...the only problem ...he never said he wanted her. In an effort to hold on to Rapheal, and all the elaborate material possessions, Dominique sets out on a deadly mission to remove anything that stands in her way.

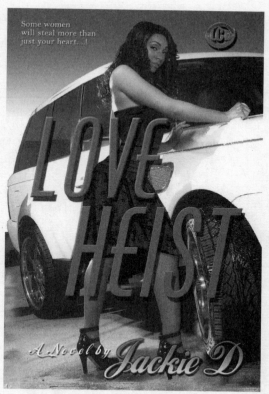

Homeless as a teenager, Lyric Brody soon discovers the finer things in life comes with a high price tag. When she meets a handsome drug dealer name Diesel, she soon gets caught up in his web of deception, lies and sexual escapades. In her quest to exist in a world of opulence, her new found strength helps her to devise a plan that will give her the independence she yearns.

Unfortunately, obtaining her goal will require her to betray the only man she has ever truly loved. So, she uses her beauty and intelligence to mastermind her scheme. The wheels are set in motion when she hooks up with an old friend, Russell King. Unbeknownst to Lyric, Russell is fresh out of a mental hospital and has his own agenda as well as an unhealthy obsession with her. Lyric sets out on a LOVE HEIST, but gets more than she bargained for.

IN STORES JAN 20th

Coming Soon

"A Twisted Tale of
Sex, Lies ... and GREED!"
- Tiphani, (Best Selling Author
of the Mistress Series

MONEY Maker

TONYA RIDLEY

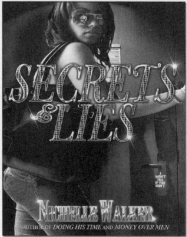

ORDER FORM

MAIL TO:

PO Box 423
Brandywine, MD 20613
301-362-6508

FAX TO:

301-856-4116

| Date: | Phone: |
| Email: | |

Ship to:	
Address:	
City & State:	Zip:

Make all money orders and cashiers checks payable to: **Life Changing Books**

Qty.	ISBN	Title	Release Date	Price
	0-9741394-5-9	Nothin Personal by Tyrone Wallace	Jul-06	$ 15.00
	0-9741394-2-4	Bruised by Azarel	Jul-05	$ 15.00
	0-9741394-7-5	Bruised 2: The Ultimate Revenge by Azarel	Oct-06	$ 15.00
	0-9741394-3-2	Secrets of a Housewife by J. Tremble	Feb-06	$ 15.00
	0-9724003-5-4	I Shoulda Seen It Comin by Danette Majette	Jan-06	$ 15.00
	0-9741394-4-0	The Take Over by Tonya Ridley	Apr-06	$ 15.00
	0-9741394-6-7	The Millionaire Mistress by Tiphani	Nov-06	$ 15.00
	1-934230-99-5	More Secrets More Lies by J. Tremble	Feb-07	$ 15.00
	1-934230-98-7	Young Assassin by Mike G.	Mar-07	$ 15.00
	1-934230-95-2	A Private Affair by Mike Warren	May-07	$ 15.00
	1-934230-94-4	All That Glitters by Ericka M. Williams	Jul-07	$ 15.00
	1-934230-93-6	Deep by Danette Majette	Jul-07	$ 15.00
	1-934230-96-0	Flexin & Sexin by K'wan, Anna J. & Others	Jun-07	$ 15.00
	1-934230-92-8	Talk of the Town by Tonya Ridley	Jul-07	$ 15.00
	1-934230-89-8	Still a Mistress by Tiphani	Nov-07	$ 15.00
	1-934230-91-X	Daddy's House by Azarel	Nov-07	$ 15.00
	1-934230-87-1-	Reign of a Hustler by Nissa A. Showell	Jan-08	$ 15.00
	1-934230-86-3	Something He Can Feel by Marissa Montelih	Feb-08	$ 15.00
	1-934230-88-X	Naughty Little Angel by J. Tremble	Feb-08	$ 15.00
	1-934230847	In Those Jeans by Chantel Jolie	Jun-08	$ 15.00
	1-934230855	Marked by Capone	Jul-08	$ 15.00
	1-934230820	Rich Girls by Kendall Banks	Oct-08	$ 15.00
	1-934230839	Expensive Taste by Tiphani	Nov-08	$ 15.00
	1-934230782	Brooklyn Brothel by C. Stecko	Jan-09	$ 15.00
	1-934230669	Good Girl Gone bad by Danette Majette	Mar-09	$ 15.00
	1-934230804	From Hood to Hollywood by Sasha Raye	Mar-09	$ 15.00
	1-934230707	Sweet Swagger by Mike Warren	Jun-09	$ 15.00
	1-934230677	Carbon Copy by Azarel	Jul-09	$ 15.00
	1-934230723	Millionaire Mistress 3 by Tiphani	Nov-09	$ 15.00
	1-934230715	A Woman Scorned by Ericka Williams	Nov-09	$ 15.00
			Total for Books	$

* Prison Orders- Please allow up to three (3) weeks
for delivery.

Shipping Charges (add $4.25 for 1-4 books*) $

Total Enclosed (add lines) $

For credit card orders and orders over 30 books, please
contact us at orders@lifechaningbooks.net

*Shipping and Handling of 5-10 books is $6.25, please
contact us if your order is more than 10 books.